The
Happy
Hammock

How to Escape the Cold
and Live in Mexico

A Romantic and Hilarious Tale
Based on a True Story

Kathrin Lake

The Happy Hammock

Buddha Press
Copyright © 2017 Kathrin Lake

For information on discounts for bulk purchases please contact info@buddhapress.com
To find other books or follow this author please go to kathrinlake.com or look on vancouverschoolofwriting.com for retreats.

Printed in United States and Canada
ISBN: 978-0-9881041-9-8

Contents

The Start...**5**
Snowbirds 7
Buying Mexican 14
Diego's Blues Bar 25
The Banana Leaf Palm Casa 31
Season 1..**35**
Texas Tommy's Casa 37
One-eyed Barrio Bobby 45
Diego's Cruisers 60
Amigo, Is That You? 65
Los Reptiles.. 70
The Fight 73
La Tortuga 78
Nightmare with No Close 83
The Happy Hammock 92
Season 2 ....**97**
The World.. 99
Siesta Sex 102
My Spiderman 108
El Alacran 113
Se Renta (For Rental)... 117
Guadalajara - Bus Ho! 120
The Squatter Casa... 127
Two Kinds of Football (and a Marching Band) 130
The French Front 140
The CLC 148
Sex Gasoline (rises again) 155
Season 3..**159**
My Clown.. 161
The Dream Casa 170
The Stars... 181
Three Kings and the Clown... 185
The Circus Comes to Town.. 193
The See Sea Casa 198
The Community that Cooks Chili Together.................. 206
Writing with Earnest 211
The Bride 223
Season 4..**235**
The Final Round 237
C is for Caliente 246

Navidad in Libé...251
The Garden 257
The Castle..265
Writers in Mexico 276
La Muerte 285
Post-Mortem...303
The Future..306
The Happy Hammock Builds a House 309
About the Author...310

The town and story in this book are based on real places and events but all the names, identities, dates, some facts and most locations in this book have been changed OR fully created in fiction in order to more freely tell a good story.

Acknowledgements

The author would like to acknowledge all the people who contributed to this book, allowed her to tell the stories, named characters and helped her write and publish this book. A special thank you to experienced readers such as Eileen Cook and Martin Crosbie whose notes were invaluable as well as all other beta readers. Thank you to multiple editors and proof readers including Jacquelyn Johnston and Brenda A, and all others who added their notes and contributions anonymously or otherwise.

The Start

Snowbirds

Both our eyes pop open with the same thought when we wake up in our little Mexican bungalow that morning in November three days after we had arrived. The ceiling fan whirred above us in a tedious rhythm like a scene from a movie. *Did we just buy a house in Mexico?* This was not a case of too much tequila. Our heads were clear and we had no tattoos on our bodies. We did not get roped into a time-share pitch, or any kind of sales pitch. If we were back home, we may have been surer about what we had just done, but we were in Mexico. John rolls over and looks at me.

"I can't believe you pulled the trigger."

Yes, it was me who signed the papers. It was me who said, "Let's go for it." It was me who had fallen in love with a house in a little town in Mexico that I had just seen for the first time a few days before. Let me backtrack a bit and tell it as it happened, from the start.

***

The first time I punched in the word "snowbird" to Facebook, I was rewarded with a number of groups with names such as "I hate snowbirds" and "Snowbirds go home." Obviously these groups are for people who band together in their repulsion of snowbirds. I, myself, remember making similar derisive comments about *those people* a little over a decade earlier. To me, snowbirds were seniors who drove ginormous RVs (that they were incapable of maneuvering), and who insisted on having tacky bumper stickers and kitschy items dangling from their rearview mirrors. They did, however, have a noble objective: get out of the northern winter weather.

To be honest, John and I are not from the area with the bitterest winters in Canada, in fact we are from the mildest city on the "Wet Coast." And, we were in our forties and not our sixties when we started our regular winter sojourns south. One of the things that bonds John and I as a couple is our hatred for inclement weather. One could say that we are wimps. Or as John would say,

"We can take it, we just don't want to."

Up until this point in my romantic partnerships I had never met a man who hated being cold as much as I did. Women seem to be perpetually cold, stowing electric heaters under their desks at the office in winter, and bundling in sweaters at the hint of a breeze. In contrast, Canadian men seem always to be complaining about the heat, demonstrating their discomfort by profuse sweating and by donning khaki shorts whenever there is an absence of snow on the ground.

I remember one of our early dates when John first reached across a café table to romantically take my hand. I could not help but exclaim to him.

"Your hands are as cold as a girl's!"

Okay, maybe not an ego-building comment at the time, but it was the start of a beautiful, mutual hatred... of the cold. We now huddle together under a plethora of blankets, sheets, and comforters, bitterly, bemoaning the temperature, and clinging to each other to generate more heat during every Canadian fall, winter, spring, and occasionally in summer too. One might think that this activity is one of the ways we have managed to stay passionate about one another, but, the truth is, we are more than happy to be in bed with only a thin sheet over us in a warm Mexican casa enjoying what I blatantly call siesta sex. We did not discover the warmth of Mexico in any conventional manner. We did not even find it together.

I had only a brief experience of Mexico twenty years before I met John. At that time I had no intention of traveling to Mexico but was talked into getting an unbelievable bargain basement deal on a trip if I allowed my carpets to be shampooed by a fly-by-night outfit and referred someone else as well. As it turned out, the carpet cleaning company had a deal with an even shadier outfit to sell unwitting tourists time share units.

There I was in Puerto Vallarta with my sister, who also had freshly shampooed rugs, in the midst of a high pressure sales pitch. But we were released quickly and unceremoniously, like two small fish being unhooked and thrown back, when we candidly confessed how little disposable income we had between us.

Other than this experience, and the "don't drink the water" phenomenon, I had absolutely loved Mexico. The eye-popping colors, the easy going, quick to smile people, the heat like childhood summers, the lively village celebrations, the passionate and persistent vendors, the carbohydrate-rich spicy food, and the cheap, cold and plentiful Corona, had all impressed themselves on me indelibly. I felt at home there.

I had wanted to go back, but it never seemed to materialize. There were always other things to do and places to go. Like Arizona and the Grand Canyon for my spiritual desert quest. Like my childhood friend's 150-acre horse ranch snaked along the Slocan River valley. Like Europe, where, six months after we met, John and I ate and drank our way across four countries. And Cuba, because we had to see it before it changed and Castro would either die or step down. But in all these other adventures, my warm and friendly memories of Mexico persisted and I tried to convince John that we must go.

After two years of suggesting, "What about Mexico?" and John adamantly insisting that Mexico was a crime-ridden, dangerous place, and he wouldn't go there in a million years, I had given up trying to convince him.—As an aside, do you ever notice that people who have never been to a country are also the ones who are utterly convinced it is crime ridden and dangerous, but the ones who have been there never are? Hmm.—Anyway, it came as somewhat of a shock when one miserable January afternoon John calmly informed me that he was about to go to Mexico... for six weeks... without me. I'm not sure what most women would have said or done, I, myself, was speechless, and I am not prone to being speechless.

John works outside for half of his workday. He works outside in Canada. He works outside in Canada in winter. John is one of the wonderful self sacrificing men and women in uniform who serve our country day in and day out. John is a letter carrier. For the old school, he is a postman.

This particular January was one of the bleakest kinds, icy rain with the temperature dancing back and forth over the freezing line like a Celtic dancer over a sword. It kept the streets dangerous with black ice. One of John's colleagues would die that year by slipping on the ice and cracking his head only six weeks before his planned retirement.

And still the bleak, wet cold kept coming. It crept into the bones and the sinuses and would lodge there, throbbing, until the spring thaw. The only slight relief John and I found was the commiseration of our miserable, meteorological circumstance.

Unbeknownst to me, this particular winter was driving John crazier than other winters before. Without consulting his loving partner, who could not get away that winter, he started to look for a means of escape. He found it in the pages of a sailing magazine and an ad looking for people to crew on a small sailing vessel. John answered the ad, was briefly interviewed on the phone by the skipper, and was enlisted for a six week crewing arrangement on the Mexican coast which cost him only flight and food. More important than the economics, or the adventure of sailing, the trip blissfully promised to get him out of the Canadian winter for a return when spring would be only a short hop away.

After my shock wore off and my speech returned I started the what ifs:

"But what if this is a scam?"

"What if this is someone luring you to a remote place to do you harm?"

"What if you fall overboard?"

"What if this is a drug dealer or a pirate trying to get unwitting crews?"

"How do you know anything about this guy?"

Our usual roles on the subject of Mexico had seemingly reversed. But once my worries had run their course and John had convinced me he was still going, I admitted that it sounded like an opportunity of a lifetime and I was completely envious. I would be stuck in the cold at my financial sector, administrative, soul-killing but well paying corporate day job that stunted all my creative impulses as a largely unknown writer.

"I am meeting the skipper in a small fishing town he is docked in now. I think it's only a three hour bus ride from the airport," he told me.

"What's it called?"

"Playa de la Libélula… he just called it Libé"

"Never heard of it."

"Me either."

I shrugged. A town was a town.

The fateful day came. I kissed John goodbye and promptly made plans to redecorate the apartment in his absence, including his man cave, the same way your cat digs up your house plants when you go on vacation. It proved to satisfy my envy only a little.

When John returned with enchanting stories of tortoises, dolphins, manta rays, palm trees and stars that seemed to fall into the ocean at night, I was greener still. But I was thrilled that Mexico was the magic that I remembered and John thought so too. He told me he actually felt safer there than he had in our own city.

I was tempted to give him a few fast slaps across the chops to harden him up for the fact that he was back in the cold again, or maybe because I had promised myself I wouldn't say, "I told you Mexico was great," or maybe because the newly decorated apartment including the altered man cave, had pleased him to no end and had a reverse revenge effect. No, it was my own envy that tainted my feelings of happiness for him. I wanted to go!

It was when John casually mentioned that the real estate was cheap in Libé, a plot hatched in my head and took hold. Another trip was planned in the same calendar year, but in early winter, November, for both of us to return and to start our adventure together.

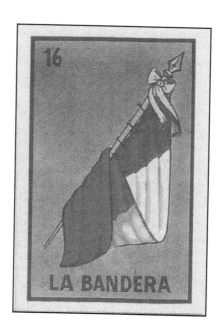

Buying Mexican

It was a long day of travel with two flights before John and I enter Mexico by touching down at a smallish airport. As soon as they open the fore and aft doors we breathe in the fresh warm sea breeze flooding into the cabin. I can feel the heat entering my Canadian winter bones. My sinuses are already sending me thank you notes of sincere gratitude. We step out of the plane, down the stairs to the tarmac and walk into the tiny airport to face the tedium of customs and baggage claim that every airport in the world, small or large, makes you endure. We both push a big button that decides if we will be the random terrorist suspect of the day, and we both get green lights. So far, so good.

We load our luggage into a happy taxi driver's small car and tell him "Playa de la Libélula." He nods and smiles; clearly he knows where this is.

The taxi ride is a whirlwind through the Mexican countryside of coconut groves, banana groves and one rough-looking town that made me wonder what we were getting into. We finally turn back toward the sea, and into Playa de la Libélula, a.k.a. Libé.

Libé is a small, rustic, unabashed tourist town. No stop lights. In addition to a playa (beach), Libé is a system of islands, lagoons and canals that the boaters and fishermen love. It is a town that caters to what are known as the "cruisers." Cruisers are a classier brand of Snowbird. They do not haul RVs, but instead own their own proud floating money pits: yachts.

John tells me that sailing or motor, Libé has been a favorite docking place for flotillas since the Spanish Armada in the 15th century. 20-footers to 200-footers are found cruising into Libé starting in mid November and floating away in April, known to the locals as "the season." Pecking order is measured both in size and where you dock it. And, as John had discovered from his crewing earlier that year, just because the size of the yacht is larger, does not mean the occupants are having more fun.

I already know from John's photos that there is an isolated 5-star marina attached to a 5-star resort across the bay. There are also canal streets where the wealthy have their designer homes with designer yachts in back. And then, he explains, there is the lagoon, where the boat he had crewed on had been anchored.

In the lagoon, boats toss out the anchor and take their zodiac into any number of waterfront restaurants. He tells me that it is because of all the cruisers and sport fisherman that Libé has more restaurants and bars per capita than any other small town along the Costa Allegre.

I am a foodie. To me one of the greatest works of fiction that I revered growing up was *The 21 Balloons* in which author, William Penne Dubois, had created a utopia on a tropical island where the inhabitants all created restaurants and went to each others every night of the week. The thought of a great variety of restaurants at reasonable prices meant that Libé is already sounding like utopia to me.

John is not a foodie. His passion lies in food for his ears, which in turn inspire his toes. John is all about blues, R&B and soul and one of the most knowledgeable people I know about that music. He doesn't play it. He doesn't sing it, but man-o-man can he dance to it. That is how we met, in fact. I am not too shabby on the dance floor either, but after we hooked up John immediately enlisted me in swing dance lessons. He would tell me later his one strict criteria in a mate, "If she can't dance, there is no chance for romance." I guess I passed.

Mexico is a Latin dance zone. The freedom and fun of salsa, the intensity of the meringe, or traditional folk dances and music like danzón. Mexico is *not* known for blues or R&B music. What you hear daily is the loud, combination of oom pa pa, mariachi, Mexican banda brass pop music. By the way, there are only two countries in the world that think the tuba is a sexy musical instrument, Germany and Mexico, I am not sure what this means but there it is. I quickly find out that this music is blaring from the windows of every Mexican home and vehicle, whether from a rusty old pick-up or a brand new Mercedes SUV, whether a youngster or an oldster is behind the wheel. It is uniquely Mexican and I plead the foreigner's lack of ability to discern subtleties when I say that all of it sounded the same to me

So how fluky is it that this little town has the one dedicated blues bar for practically the whole southwest coast of Mexico— Diego's Cruisers Blues Bar. Now I understand why John is enamored with this town.

All we need to do is look at nice places one might occupy if one was going to make a habit of returning. No harm in looking at a few bits of real estate. True, we didn't even own our own place in Canada, but who says there is a law against your first home being your vacation property?

John had pre-arranged a bungalow to stay in that is located in the center of town or *centro*. He had also pre-arranged for us to go out with a recommended real estate agent, Sam. Sam is a fully immigrated gringo[1] real estate agent who had married a local woman with good connections in town. I was told that Sam had lived in Libé for decades and I was happy we could get someone so experienced who was also a native English speaker. We would be getting up and going out with him at 9:30 in the morning after our first evening in Libé.

---

[1] Gringo is a term Mexicans gave to Americans dating from just before the Mexican-American war in 1846. It was a derogatory term directed at Americans. Today it is a term for Canadian and American or Caucasian tourists and most ex-pats have co-opted the term and are not offended by it.

The taxi had dropped us at the bungalow as it was getting near to sunset, so John just had time to show me briefly around the town, including the enormous 100 year old Menefee oak tree, the jardin (town square), the malecón (sea wall walk), and the beach all within easy walking distance. It looked sweet if a little scruffy, but I wasn't a good judge as my eyelids are already drooping and our conversation is punctuated by deep yawns from both of us.

We pick up some milk for a fast cereal breakfast the next morning and then return to the bungalow. We try to stay up as late as we can to reorder our internal clocks before succumbing to the jet lag but we are both succumbing to jet lag and fall asleep easily.

Then we wake up. More correctly, we are woken up.

While it is true that John had been to Libé 8 months ago, crewing on the sailboat, he had slept every night aboard the ship way out in the peaceful lagoon. Waking to the noises of centro Libé was a shock to both our systems. As a city girl, I did not know that roosters love to crack open a full throated cackle at 4 o'clock in the a.m... also 2 a.m...1 a.m. and pretty much any time they feel like it, day or night. So the cock and bull story about crowing at dawn is more bull than cock. So we wake up again and again and again. We are finally sleeping again when at 7 a.m. there is a cry.

"Aaahhh...aaa..aaaa...ahhh!"

"What is that?" We both ask simultaneously, but we have already recognized it as a full throated recording of a Tarzan yell repeating itself as it is wandering through the neighborhood.

Apparently, in small town Mexico there remains a charming disregard for the concept of noise pollution. We discover they have a penchant for mobile advertising. I am not talking mobile phones, I am talking blaring megaphones on cars, trucks and motorbikes. Just as we are drifting off again there comes a blast of a musical jingle, doo, doo, doo, doo (pause) doo, doo, doo, doo (pause), followed by a deep bass voice speaking two words that say… *what are they saying?*

John and I are awake in bed, no opportunity to recover from our jet lag, trying to figure it out.

"He's saying, 'Wake up!'" John is sure.

"I don't think so dear, and if he was saying that, I am pretty sure it would be in Spanish."

It would take us awhile before we would understand that the Tarzan yell was to tell us that the bottled water guy was coming around, and you could flag him down if you needed water, much the way the kids used to run out for the ice cream truck in the suburbs. Likewise, the music jingle followed by the deep voice speaking two words was alerting you the gas guy was coming around if you needed more propane. He was saying, "Global Gaaas," elongating the word gas. Ironically those two words are the same in English as Spanish but you can never quite make it out until you have heard it about four hundred times and seen the truck that says on the side, "Global Gas."

It is in this semi-conscious state that Sam the real estate man picks us up in his air-conditioned SUV. Sam is a little older than I imagined he would be. Okay, he is a lot older. He is thin with white hair, glasses, and is dressed casually in baggy, tan shorts and a light golf shirt with one collar flipped up that I have to stop myself from fixing.

He seems a very genial gentleman, but with a slightly dishevelled absent-minded professor quality. We pile into Sam's SUV and start through the neighbourhoods that Sam thinks we can afford, given our minuscule budget.

A couple of times Sam seems unable to find addresses which we think is odd in a small town. He apologizes profusely, but to be fair the town has few if any street signs and a numbering system which makes my postman shake his head. We are told by Sam that this is normal in most towns in Mexico.

John and I also chalk up our lost detours to Sam getting a little long in the tooth. There are some lost keys, people not being home to let us in, so our list of potential homes to view shrinks to only a few. At least we see the neighbourhoods if we did not always see the homes and they look nice.

In any case, what we have been able to see hasn't bowled either of us over. We thank Sam for the tour and tell him we will drop by his office in a couple of days when he says he will have more homes lined up (including some of the ones missed today).

After our all too hasty breakfast of milk and cereal brought from home I am ravenous. Our first order of business is a proper lunch. John takes me into town telling me there is a casual but nice restaurante he thinks I might like.

Raul's is a local favorite, day or night restaurante. It's easy to spot because it is across the street from one of the major hotels and filled with gringos; a good sign. Raul, a tall guy for a Mexican, is polite and quick with a smile. I notice that in contrast to his patrons in their summer tanks, chino shorts and Birkenstocks, he wears a nice dress shirt, half-sleeved, full length pants and dress shoes in dark colors.

Raul speaks English well and his staff only a little less so, but John and I know that anywhere in the world all people appreciate it when you make the effort to speak in their own language and you make more friends if you try but my Spanish is seriously lacking. John tells me that regardless of time, Raul's is always busy because he and his staff know how to treat the touristas, especially the ones who are down for the entire season. They remember what you like, and how you like it.

John eats the opposite of me, almost as if food were a necessary evil, so he orders a side of guacamole and no entrée, which I think is typically bird-like of him until I see the guacamole. It is enormous, and could hardly be called a side. So naturally, I will have to help him eat it. It makes me wonder how many avocados Raul goes through in a day though.

Perusing the menu I notice something I rarely get on our side of the 49th parallel, tortilla soup.

"Very good," Raul says when I order it, "not enough people order our soup."

John adds, "Because who wants to order soup in a hot country!"

I ignore John's put down of my order and stick with Raul's recommendation, as well as add a fish entrée.

Traditionally, tortilla soups are a sort of thin Mexican stew, packed with loads of ingredients: avocado, tomatoes, corn, onion, beans, peppers, cilantro, hints of cumin, lime all covered with authentic tortilla strips for a taste and texture experience that I love.

Raul's soup has these ingredients and is topped with "queso seco" or dry, white, salty cheese. They bring lime wedges on the side always which John tells me helps with the digestion and "sterilizes things." Translation: the bugs and parasites don't like it.

After the soup, which like the guacamole is a meal in itself, I had almost forgotten I'd ordered an entrée. There is something about lack of sleep that has always made me extra hungry as if needing the extra fuel to keep the eyes open and the body moving. However, perhaps this time my eyes have been bigger than my stomach.

I had ordered their house specialty, fish with garlic. And the smell arrives before the plate. The fish is a white fish, this time marlin Raul tells me but whatever is fresh. I taste. It is cooked to perfection with the garlic and oil, heavenly. I cannot eat all my rice but eat all the garlicky fish and green salad. I have eaten, in effect, three meals, and I am ready to roll away from the table. Except I can't resist one more thing, and ask for something that is met with a snort from John.

"De-caf coffee, por favor." I want to get some sleep tonight but am craving coffee.

"Sanka," Raul answers. I looked confused but nod. I didn't care about the brand of coffee. "Con crema?" he asks, quickly translating for me, "With cream."

"Si, gracias." I congratulate myself on my profuse use of Spanish.

Raul places in front of me a jar of Sanka. Apparently I am going to get freeze-dried crystals, which quickly makes me turn up my nose. *No, no, no.* But, I can't bring myself to cancel the order. A large cup of "coffee" is put in front of me with the cream already added. Gingerly, I sip the creamy hot coffee liquid he has put before me, bracing my coffee-primed taste buds for disappointment. After my first sip I am befuddled. *Why am I not repulsed?* I sip again. It is the cream, thick and sweet, that surprisingly makes the freeze-dried crystals something I could actually crave.

On the table, we see extra condiments of every kind: honey, A-1 sauce, hot sauces, peanut butter, jams, chilli powder, ketchup, mustard, rock salt, and always you are given a plate of fresh cut limes. Again, they appeal to the touristas and I see the place is packed in no time.

I wonder if Raul's should adopt that famous line from the movie *Casablanca* "Everyone goes to Rick's," but make it, "Everyone goes to Raul's." By the way, *Everyone Goes to Rick's,* was the original title of the play that the movie was based on. Only a writer and former playwright would know this. I tell this to John and he, unlike men of my past, *doesn't* roll his eyes. He thinks I'm smart. My know-it-all-ness doesn't faze him, or at least he hides it well, and is another reason why I love him.

What John tells me he loves is the fact that the Mexicans keep their beer ice, ice cold, and Raul is particularly diligent. He tells me that they always have the TV sets on for the big NFL games, or the real football (soccer), for the other fans, and this always draws the handful of European or South American tourists and the good spirits of a sporting match bonds the patrons quickly. But even in non-sporting mode Raul's has a convivial spirit and great food.

After lunch, we go for a blissful stroll and poke around the streets perusing the colourful vendors. We just happen to pass another real estate office that isn't Sam's and automatically start looking at the pictures. We had noticed previously that there is a suspiciously disproportionate number of real estate offices for a small town. But, this office is the only one we have seen with a name we recognize. It is an established international real estate company (with American origins). It doesn't take long before an agent is inviting us in.

Nancy, a delightful brunette from California, shows us some more pictures of the houses we were both looking at and wanting to look at, as well as the handful we had just seen. It is with one of those that Nancy shows us a rather large error Sam has made.

More than just getting addresses confused, he is getting prices wrong. Okay, that isn't reassuring. She also shows us where we can get some bridge financing from a U.S. bank that we would need if we want to buy some of the casas that are much nicer and previously thought were out of our budget. The financing is at a great interest rate (with a few stipulations). We know Sam does not set up financing because we had asked. Perfect. Right there, we decide we need to switch agents. Sam is out and Nancy is in.

Nancy is closer to our own age and when John tells her we will be going to Diego's Blues Bar that evening, she says that it is very likely she will show up too.

Diego's Blues Bar

Diego's Cruisers Blues Bar is not just any blues bar. John explains that Diego would lease a space for only the season so each year you have to ask people where his bar is and if it was open yet. This year Diego has again snagged a premier spot overlooking the beach on the second floor and beside the nearest access to the lagoon. It is the first live music bar that the cruisers will come across. Whether it is the wealthiest cruisers in giant motor yachts with hired skippers, or the dozens of sail boaters who drop anchor in the lagoon, John tells me that they will all climb the stairs up to Diego's sooner or later.

Being upstairs the bar has the perfect sunset view open to the ocean. Diego is a great believer in the myth of the green flash—

the reputed emerald flash that some lucky people see just as the sun is sinking into the ocean horizon—he never fails to look for it at sunset and gets his patrons engaged as well. The bar is under an enormous royal palm palapa that had seen its share of weather and is decorated on the inside with flags of the countries Diego considers representative of his major patrons. There is the American stars and stripes, two Canadian flags, one with a maple leaf and one with a marijuana leaf, the Mexican flag, the Australian flag, the Irish flag, and a Harley Davidson flag. It isn't really a biker bar, although Diego clearly loves Harley hogs—there is part of one hanging over the bar—what he really loves is blues music.

"I am a Mexican who loves the blues," he tells John.

Diego is a small man with a gentle, happy, yet mischievous face. He has a thick Mexican accent when he speaks English that seems to come with its own mythology. People know that Diego had resided in the U.S. for a number of years. He had fathered at least one child there, as Mario, his son, the young man behind the bar, is a grown testament to that child born in the U.S.A. Given that, people wonder why is Diego's English sometimes spotty, and other times excellent? And, what exactly had he been doing in the U.S.?

The myths have as many versions as people and you are not long in the bar before you hear the speculations, rather like a version of *The Great Gatsby*. Some say he had been a smuggler State side, but not illegal drugs, cheap tequila, others said he owned an illegal bar in Texas, others say he was a gigolo, some say he went to a good school in Boston, but you would get none of this from Diego's own lips.

The thing that isn't a mystery is that Diego is more party

animal than business man. John tells me that on his previous stay, everyday, whenever he would meet Diego in town, he would remind Diego to stock up on John's favorite wine. Inevitably, every night John would go to the bar where Diego would greet John as if he was a long lost brother, but he wouldn't have his wine.

John would then walk a few blocks to the store, buy a couple of bottles at full retail price, walk back to the bar, sell the bottles to Diego who would in turn sell it back to John by the glass. Although his grown kids helped Diego in the thriving bar, he is never able to hang on to the money he makes for long, and his women are like his bars, they could change annually and evaporate like the money.

Diego loves John for a few reasons. First, he had established himself as a regular, second, they could both talk about the blues for hours. As we walk into the bar for my first time, Diego gives John a big hug welcoming him back to Libé. I smile to see the short Mexican and the big gringo so different in appearance and yet like a novel pair of "Blues Brothers." John introduces me and Diego immediately turns on the charm and kisses my hand.

"She is beautiful," he tells John and to me, "My place is your place."

"Who is playing tonight, Diego?" John asks.

"Leo will be here soon."

"Excelente."

"You know him?" I ask John, not for the first time since we have been wandering around town. It seems my husband had left quite an impression on several people some eight months previously. We would be walking down the street and someone would say, "Hey John!" and start a conversation with him. I know my John is a charming man but it is never so clear as it is for the past two days that he has been a "man about town" in Mexico.

"Leo is excellent, you'll like him." John assures me of tonight's talent. Not long after a man comes in with his guitar case and starts to plug into the amplifiers, but not before saying, "Hey John! Welcome back, man."

Leo is tall and snowy haired; an attractive "older" man, but it is when Leo sings that I melt. My musician crushes have a panty rating of my desire to throw my panties on the stage. In this case, they don't have a stage just a corner of the floor but nevertheless, Leo is a three panty throw, figuratively speaking.

"He sounds like Eric Clapton," I comment about Leo's gravelly, made for blues voice that also has a sweet top note to it. And the music is old school rock and roll blues, enough that John and I could swing dance to it.

John has already insisted that I take my dance shoes with me whenever we go out and we change into them quickly and hit the floor, small as it is. We dance up a storm for several numbers and show off all our best moves. John is a great lead and a great lead always makes the woman, or follower, look fabulous. He turns me, twirls me and dips me through some snazzy moves. When we get off the floor Diego comes right up to me and makes a declaration.

"You are a professional dancer!"

Even when I tell him that that is flatly untrue he insists.

"You should be on *Dancing with the Stars*."

A day later I happen to be alone at the bar while John is buying his wine, again, and I start to put on my dance shoes. Diego runs up and insists on helping me on with my dance shoes, giving me the "star" treatment which I am sure he would not have done if my tall gringo man had been there.

Later, on the dance floor, he would try to imitate John's dance moves as best he could. Picture a short Mexican man with a goatee and wild hair playing at dance like a child imitating a grown up. He is sweetly naive that you have to practice the techniques to make it look smooth, or perhaps he is just blasted. But, he is cute. Really cute. That, and his natural charm is why the girls went for Diego. But he is also a little bit loco, John warns me.

John tells me that on his first trip he was out for a walk by the lagoon after breakfast and walked by the bar which wouldn't be open for hours. Out from under the sides of Diego's palapa were projectiles sailing through the air and landing in the street. They were CDs. John collected a few of the undamaged ones and went up to see what was going on. Diego was doing his version of winter cleaning, the CDs he no longer wanted, he explained. Plus, he had just subscribed to a satellite radio station.

"All the Blues and R&B music you could want!" he told John with the animation of a child. John took some CDs off Diego's hands and spared the pedestrians.

In addition to the colorful bar owner himself, Diego's bar had its own collection of characters of cruisers, expats, and touristas. Nancy did show up too, so I had a girlfriend to talk to and she seemed to know everyone and made the place seem effortlessly friendly. We dance to my new musician crush, Leo, until his sets are done. Nancy is going home to be in the office early, no rest for the realtors here. She had brought her car and offers us a ride to our bungalow but we want to walk home. You can cross the town in only a few blocks and to us it is a beautiful warm summer's eve, only in November.

We walk in the direction of our bungalow hand in hand just around midnight. The town is still abuzz with activity. Kids are running around playing in the jardin (har-deen or town square), having napped through siesta. Indeed, everyone comes alive at night in Mexico, when it is cooler but still warm.

John takes me on a side trip to a taco stand along the main drag where a small crowd is hanging out. We purchase four authentic tacos between us for the equivalent of two dollars. They are smaller double layered soft tacos with piping hot beef and a series of toppings to choose from. We sit on the edges of the concrete planters at the curb with all the locals having a midnight snack and eat them greedily. They are delicious and well deserved after all our dancing. We return the plastic wrapped plates and walk back to our bungalow gazing at the Mexican moon on our way.

I could barely sleep I am so excited. I, a kid raised in the suburbs, who lived downtown in a big city, is discovering I might be a small town girl. I am also eager because in the morning Nancy is coming around to take us to some of the nicer casas we had only seen in photos. Maybe I am going to be a proud homeowner in a foreign land like *A Year in Provence* or *Under the Tuscan Sun*. I sail off to sleep dreaming of the possibilities.

The Banana Leaf Palm Casa

The first time we step into this house I can feel we are both energized. It is a concrete house, as all the houses here are, painted banana yellow with avocado green trim. Inside the gate is a small entrance garden with a giant banana leaf palm (also called a traveler's palm or paradiso palm), fanned out in its glory and towering over the other bright flowering plants that were a complete delight for us northerners to see in mid November.

The kitchen is modern and roomy, the tiles are glorious and rustic, the walls are painted bright colors: magenta, teal, burnt orange, and look perfectly in harmony with all else, including the furniture, most of which is included in the house price. It is modern furniture, comfortable pieces mixed with the occasional ornate traditional Mexican piece. The artwork is all modern, well balanced abstracts with bold splashes of color. These people have exceptional taste that we haven't seen in other houses we've looked at.

In the back, off the dining room area, is a shaded overhang for outdoor dining that looks out on a nice sized swimming pool. Upstairs, the master bedroom has an enormous terrace overlooking the pool, a walk-in closet and ensuite with a huge shower.

The sinks are all in the brightly colored Talavera porcelain designs and there is a generous, but not too generous, second bedroom with full bath as well. On the terrace, there is a spiral staircase to the roof where Nancy tells us that we can build a palapa—a thatched roof, open air look-out—perfect for hanging a hammock to catch the afternoon breezes.

We are told by Nancy that the Banana Leaf Palm Casa, as we start to call it, is a bank trust house, as are all the houses in the immediate area, which meant they were safe for foreigners to buy. And, better than the house, is that it is a few blocks' walk to the sea and to that cute little town I have now enjoyed a whole two days in.

Back home, real estate prices had gone through the roof so that people were crazily paying 75% of their incomes or more toward mortgages and related costs. Meanwhile, for years we had been becoming debt-free and simultaneously socking money away with our relatively cheap rent, until we were in a healthy financial position. But what held us back from buying on the desirable West Coast of B.C.? Too expensive? Check. Places too small for the money? Check. The affordable and decent-sized places are too far a commute for work? Check. Buying into a high maintenance lifestyle? Check. Worried about buying a faulty "leaky condo" as they were called? Check. We had been down this route before and went so far as to make offers, but something had always stopped us from completing the sale and buying a home in our home city.

For me, hearing my panicked friends say, "We have to buy before we are priced out of the market!" sent a chill down my spine. There was a niggling memory of not so long ago when many of us had lost money on the stock market with the dot com crash. I remember people saying you have to buy while you still can, only to see our stocks and mutual funds plunge to shadows of their former selves. I just had the feeling that as soon as you get on the band wagon and start doing the same thing that everyone else is doing, you are already too late for any possible boon. Whatever my logical or emotional sides had conjured up, I was a property virgin with trepidation, rightly or wrongly.

Yet, here I am after a day or two of visiting real estate in a foreign country (just to look), fully seduced with the lure of a tropical paradise. I sign the offer letter to that two bedroom house with a pool, less than two years old, two blocks from the beach.

Comparatively, it seems like an amazing price. Back home we would not even be able to get a shoebox apartment in a bad part of town for the same price! Sure, the commute is a couple of thousand miles, but you only have to do it twice a year. So that is it. When the offer is accepted, when the American bank has approved the loan, when the deposit and down payment has been put in trust, it will all be done.

Meanwhile, Nancy tells us that everything will take weeks to process and we should come back in the New Year to complete the sale. We can do that. We each had our vacation entitlements renewed with the new calendar year so we can be back in just over a month's time to take possession of our new house. Simple.

John will be down for most of the season (his second season) and I will be down for as long as my conventional employer will allow (my first season). *My Season Under the Mexican Sun.* I am already making up titles of this new, awesome adventure. Nothing can make me believe this isn't the perfect plan.

Season 1

EL GALLO

Texas Tommy's Casa

New Year's arrives and we fly back to Mexico. On our taxi ride in from the tiny airport to Libé we are giddy. Although Nancy told us there were more hoops yet to go through before we move into the Banana Palm Leaf Casa, I had very carefully packed a bottle of champagne for the moment we would take possession. Meanwhile, John had secured some temporary lodging.

Remembering our centro bungalow in November where we heard all the mobile megaphone advertising from fruit sellers to political campaigns, we decided to avoid centro for a place to stay. Instead, John wisely looked for accommodation in the neighborhood where my beloved Banana Leaf Palm Casa resides. It is in the gringo neighborhood that the locals called The Pueblo Blanco. White Town. As segregated as this sounds, it is mostly up-scale homes owned by a mix of people, Mexican and gringo, with a concern for their neighborhood. We just call it the Fraccionamiento (the subdivision).

We had seen the rule book for the Fraccionamiento and it was a formidable document an inch thick at least. Every carefully worded rule (in Spanish) can be completely ignored with the correct greasing of palms (bribe), or, with no greasing of palms but the confidence that no else would be motivated enough to enforce it with more greasing of palms. There is only one rule we care about anyway, and no one, thus far, has violated it. There are **no roosters allowed** and minimal megaphones in the Fraccionamiento, and none early.

John had discovered, via the internet, there was a guest house in the Fraccionamiento called Casa Janine and had booked us a room for our first return trip together. Casa Janine is owned by a Texan named Tommy who greets us with great warmth at the gate.

Tommy seems the nicest and most laid back guy you could ever hope to meet. His eyes twinkle softness from well tanned skin and his Texan twang of a voice is calming and expresses peace and happiness. The fact that he is a surfer dude seems to fit his laidbackness, but the fact that he is a surfer dude in his 50s, and in remarkably great shape with a thriving business back in Texas makes me marvel.

Tommy tells us that he has been coming to the area around Libé for the surf for many, many years before he had decided to buy in. He keeps five guest rooms with private bathrooms downstairs and his apartment upstairs. This pays for the maintenance on his house, and then some. It is a fairly easy venture of taking in vacationing surfers and assorted touristas for the season. The house is just emptying of surfers as we come along. For one week we have the bottom of the house, including the communal kitchen and the garden to ourselves, with only Tommy above for company.

We bounce all our questions off of Tommy for his comments including everything we learn, or think we have learned. I am sure he sees how green we are but never interferes with our illusions. He tells us where to get the best and cheapest tacos in the Barrio (the Mexican suburban neighborhood), where we might find a cappuccino in a town that is void of Starbucks and all other franchises (thank God), and how, when on the road in Mexico, to spot cheap but surprisingly clean motels by their covered car garages designed to hide recognizable cars for the extramarital affairs. We know in short order that Tommy will become a good friend.

After one week to ourselves at Tommy's Casa, another couple comes into one of the guest rooms, but thankfully on the opposite end of the house giving us plenty of privacy. Privacy is what we value and as it turned out they did as well. However, we did start to encounter each other in the common kitchen and finally introduced ourselves.

Jan and Dean are also from Canada and trying their first attempt at retirement. They are not much older than ourselves so we are very jealous of their ability to fully retire. For the first while we all think it is just great that we are mingling with fellow Canadians until Tommy points out to us that the Fraccionamiento is comprised of 30% Canadians, 30% Americans and 40% Mexicans, and the 40% are often renting out to Canadians and Americans during the season. Nevertheless we indulge in what all Canadians use to bond with one another, beer.

The Dos Equis flow with our fellow citizens and the extra intoxication of being void of responsibility have us in a quick bond with our new housemates. John and I have another couple to date.

Being in Libé two weeks longer than Jan and Dean (if you include our time the previous year), and able to tell them nonchalantly how we are closing a sale on a house a couple of blocks away, we are clearly the experts who can impress the newcomers. They marvel at our five minutes worth of knowledge of Mexico, the town, and the half a dozen Spanish phrases we have learned cold.

It does not take them that long to catch up to our "wealth" of knowledge and pretty soon we are sharing any and all tidbits of information we have gleaned, and especially the best places to eat.

We try together an Italian restaurante run by Italians who had immigrated to Mexico two generations before and had a wood burning brick pizza oven with a variety of yummy pizzas and great side salads. We go to the reputed best steak house in town and roll ourselves down the street afterwards weighed down by the beef in our tummies. We try the fanciest seafood restaurant in a fishing town that has the best fresh fish I have ever tasted and prawns that were double the size of what I was used to. But, just like everyone else, we always wind up at Raul's.

At Raul's, John, Jan, Dean and I eat and drink our way into storytelling and laughs about what we discovered since the last times we talked—usually our gaffs at being tourists.

"What did you guys do this week?" Jan prompts us. I perk up.

"We took the funky buses."

"The what?"

John explains that that was my name for the local buses that go between the nearest towns and we launch into our story.

***

We had decided to go to the neighboring town that was reputedly not as quaint as Libé, but larger, better for supplies and has quite a nice beach. So we stand at the side of the road where we have seen others standing, but which has no sign or "stop." We wait for one of the dust covered Mercedes Benz buses we had seen rambling by regularly. We know our bus by a handwritten piece of cardboard in the front window naming the town we want to go to.

As we get on, John asks the driver in Spanish how much it costs. The driver answers in English, "Two fifty." Confused by the English, John converted dollars into pesos and pulled out 25 pesos which is about $2.50, which would be the price of a local bus fare back in Canada for one of us. While he is paying, I turn to sit down but am quickly at a loss for where to sit. All of the seats are ripped to shreds and some of the battered frames that are suppose to hold seats have no seats at all.

While the outside of the buses, albeit dirty, did not look too bad, from the inside you felt as if you were riding in a bunch of loosely welded sheets of metal, barely holding together after having decomposed with the decades, of wear, tear, abuse and graffiti. *How long had these buses been in service?* It is a shock to my first-world sensibilities, but for the benefit of the few locals on board, I try to hide my distress. Meanwhile, as John is trying to give the driver 25 pesos for our ride. I hear the bus driver say to him loudly, in perfect English:

"Buddy, that's a f**k of a lot of money!"

The bus driver is laughing heartily and correcting John that the ride is two and a half pesos (a 2 peso coin and a .50 peso coin), which is around 25 cents... for both of us. John turns and joins me, red-faced, at the back of the bus where I have found some less-crumbling upholstery to perch on. It dawns on him as he looks at the interior of the funky bus that the princely sum of 25 pesos or $2.50—a day's wage in Mexico at that time—would have indeed been a tad overpriced for the rolling junk scraps we are currently aboard. We agree that maybe taxes are not the evil things that we sometimes make them out to be in North America.

We have a nice afternoon of poking around the larger town and then look around for the funky bus that will take us home. We get on one where it seems logical to be going back to Libé. After a short time it seems obvious that it is taking a longer, more scenic route, but I am okay with that.

"Aren't we supposed to be going east?" John states more than asks. I looked out the window and I can see what he means.

"I'm sure we will turn as soon as we hit the edge of the town," I guess.

In fact, that is not what happens. Instead we start going high into the Mexican mountains, the bus's lower gears grinding with mechanical effort, moving us further and further from civilization.

We quickly realize we have screwed up as we gradually become the last people at the back of the bus.

"We'll wait until the next stop and straighten it out," John says to me. I relax a little and realize he is right, except the next stop never seems to come and my growing panic is now transferring to John as well.

Finally, we stop in a remote mountain town, if you can call it that. It is a place with many chickens, a few humble buildings, and a small collection of other funky buses. Before we can get to the front of the bus to ask our driver what to do, he has popped out and is gone. We are not sure if this bus is to go back down the mountain again after a short break and our driver would return, or we need to find another way back which is now a long, long way away. We decide we cannot wait for a maybe returning driver and we exit to hopefully find someone to help us.

Finding someone is not as easy as we thought. No one is in the immediate vicinity. We finally find a small collection of men who seem to be hanging out near the buses. Whether they are drivers or locals we are not sure. It isn't like drivers of the funky buses have uniforms. We attempt to communicate to them in panicked gringo Spanish which I'm sure is quite unintelligible.

After much time of them staring at us like we are aliens trying to communicate with them, because after all, we are, someone finally directs us to another bus and a driver appears shortly. Because there is no cardboard sign at the front of this bus we repeat to him the name of Libé several times to be sure he will be taking us there. He seems to agree and we cross our fingers, board and it turns out to be the correct decision.

***

After having a good laugh at us about the buses Jan admits her own small blunder with the language that day.

"I went to the grilled chicken place on the corner to get an order to go for lunch. I wanted two chicken breasts, so I looked up the words in my electronic translator. I go to the man and very confidently tell him, 'Dos pechos por favor.' He gives me a strange look, so I tap my chest so maybe he will understand what part of the bird I want. He stares at my chest as I say 'pechos de pollos' which I am sure means chicken breasts, but now he is laughing. Turns out I am ordering two women's breasts on chickens. For chicken breasts you have to say pechugas."

Just as the bus driver had delightfully corrected John's gaffe with the fares, so the chicken man had straightened Jan out at the difference between pechos and pechugas. We toast our collective ignorance and the Mexicans' patience with us with another cerveza.

For the rest of the evening and into the next weeks whenever we find it appropriate, it becomes a running gag to repeat our new expression, "Buddy, that's a f**k of a lot of money!"

One-eyed Barrio Bobby

Nancy reports that the real estate closing is going along with just a few more things to attend to that will just take time. There seems to be more hoops to jump through than we imagined, but this is stated as normal by everyone we meet. We just have to wait for an assessment or something, and be on vacation while we wait. That doesn't sound bad at all.

While living cheaply in Tommy's Casa with only Jan and Dean is just perfect, Tommy tells us that three more couples are scheduled to arrive and we all agree our heaven is about to get noisy and crowded, as the communal kitchen, center of the house, also shares walls with nearly all the bedrooms. Jan and Dean made the classic mistake of booking a whole month at Tommy's place. We are only committed to seven days which has already passed. As seasoned travelers, we rarely commit to anywhere for more than we have to because John is one of the best sleuth's I know for finding out where to stay cheap, quiet and clean. Given enough time, and by word of mouth, he will ferret out that which has not been advertised and the person who never answers their phone. He did not disappoint.

Someone had pointed out a little house two blocks away and said it might be up for renting. No sign, no number, just a rumor.

"Who owns it?" John asked.

"Don't know. I think Bobby takes care of it though."

"Where does Bobby live?"

"In the Barrio."

"Do you know his house?"

"No."

"Do you know where he hangs out?"

"The bar."

"Which bar?"

"All of them."

"No favorites?"

"Try the Dolphins, around 4pm?"

"What does he look like?"

"You've seen him before, wears purple shorts a lot, rarely shaves, and sometimes wears an eye patch, or sun glasses." John admits he had seen Bobby before.

"One of the town piss tanks," he tells me before he goes out to track him down. I suspect John's previous sailing visit without me had exposed him to an underbelly of characters that I have not yet seen in our pretty little town. Mexico is an alcoholic's paradise. The drug of choice is cheap and plentiful. John likes to say, "Libé is a drinking town with a fishing problem."

In short order, John has tracked down One-eyed Barrio Bobby. To be fair, I am told that Bobby has both his eyes but one has a deficiency and sensitivity to light so he keeps it mostly closed or covered. John says that Bobby has to check if the house is free and if so, will rent it at the very good price of $500 USD a month. John will be staying for most of that month and I will have to leave early. He gives Bobby our address at Tommy's Casa to find us again.

I hear a buzzer at the gate but am denied my first curious glimpse of One-eyed Barrio Bobby, *El Barracho*. John speaks with him at the door and I only hear his brash American accent, from where specifically I am not sure. Tomorrow we can meet him at the house at 4:30 p.m. with the solicitor that rents the house to see if it is to our liking. I don't know which I am more curious to see, the inside of the house or Bobby.

I am a split introvert-extrovert personality, but decide I am up for some fun and will join John and Nancy for a taste of the night life during the high season. We meet Nancy at Rocko's and start a quest for live music—driven by John—since Diego's is not open tonight. Somewhere between bar one and two John and I notice a man weaving through the street and we both watch, curious at the acrobatic abilities of the truly drunk during the simple act of walking. This man is demonstrating amazing last-second recovery of balance.

Nancy, who catches up to us after chatting with someone else, calls out "Pedro!" to the walking *Weeble* (*Weebles* wobble but they don't fall down), and he starts weaving his way towards us. Nancy, unaware of his state, has unwittingly baited him like a nasty swordfish that you want to throw back but can't. Pedro exults her many charms in an incoherent rash of sounds that seem to pass for words. Diplomatic as always, Nancy treats him respectfully but a glance in my direction and we both exchange the all-knowing womanly look, *we must lose this man.* Another barracho.

However, no matter how hard we try all evening Pedro is either already in the next bar we walk into or follows on our heels looking lecherously at all the ladies and particularly longingly at Nancy.

"Have you noticed he has peed his pants?" she whispers across to me.

I am compelled to surreptitiously glance at the yellow stain at the base of his fly hoping that he does not catch me and mistake this for a come hither look. Fortunately, John is there to look intimidating and manly. He herds his charges like *El Gallo* with his chicks and puts a buzz in the bartender's ears not to serve any more to that customer, which may explain why Pedro kept having to leave the bars when we were leaving.

Besides the Pedro effect the pursuit for music and dancing proves a little challenging too—it is a Monday—but there will be other nights so we decide to pack it in. Nancy takes us home. We sneak into the casa and crawl into our bed for blissful sleep.

The next day, a bike ride in the morning, breakfast, shower, I write, John reads, we siesta, rinse, repeat. During this process, in the back of my mind I am thinking 4:30 p.m., the rental house, One-eyed Barrio Bobby. This should be good. At 4:20 we head around the block and as we approach the house I see a bicycle and a shortish man, tanned leather skin, a shock of red hair, with an extra voltage of red-blonde shadow on his face. John greets Bobby, and as we get nearer, a face smiles up at me with a happy-go-lucky grin and one eye open and the other closed. I can't help staring at the closed eye.

Bobby opens the little house and shows us around. I immediately become the hypercritical little woman. Strange I don't remember ever learning this stereotype so well. The house is small, cute, reasonably clean but very musty. The wet and humid season has not been aired out of its rooms. I sniff disapprovingly as Bobby watches and introduces a few features.

The backyard is very nice. Two small palms and a big tiled bar at the end of the backyard and not one but two outdoor bathrooms. Why, we are not sure since it has no pool. Like I said, Mexico, an alcoholics paradise. But you could not ask for more privacy. An absent neighbor on one side of the high wall and a vacant lot on the other side. It looks good, but I show no signs of approval.

We go back inside when another shadow appears at the front door, the solicitor. His silhouette looks vaguely familiar to me. *Oh my gosh, its Pedro*, last night's Barracho. I keep my mouth from dropping to the floor. I exchange a quick glance with John.

Pedro is casually dressed but looks clean and halfway respectable. Business casual dress back home is super business here. But, it doesn't matter because although it is no longer there, I cannot erase the memory of the pee stain. *This man is the solicitor who also cares for the house?* John and I are confused. Why do they need two people? Pedro comes with contracts but asks me if we like the house. Without having a chance to answer he continues with great animation, similar to Bobby's but more so, professing its terrific attributes, hot water heater, four gas plates, refrigerator, linen, it's got everything.

"Bed bugs?" I ask looking at the mattress and the bed linens sealed in plastic and continuing my criticality.

"Not that I know of. She never said anything," Pedro answers. The previous renter. A woman. I give no hint of either approval or disapproval. However, John has just said,

"We'll take it."

Pedro fills out the contracts in duplicate and I watch him wondering if he possibly remembers us from the night before. Bobby and he go over more details; like who to contact if we need anything—Pedro or Bobby, but Pedro first. The papers are signed, the cash is doled, the keys are exchanged, the hands are shaken. Bobby licks his lips.

"This has cut into my drinking time." He laughs a hearty laugh. I manage a Marge Simpson nervous giggle. Pedro looks directly at me and says,

"I was sober for eight months until last night." *Oh God, he does remember us.* Such are our new landlords for another month.

Before they go, Pedro insists on showing me the fuse box. Why me, I am not sure. But he seems to be leading me outside to the front of the house.

Indeed, on the front of the house is a small open fuse box with one switch. He explains to the "little woman" how to turn it off and on should we blow a fuse, but my mind is not offended at belittling my female intelligence so much as it is asking, *Where are all the other switches? Why is the fuse box on the front of the house? Why has it no cover to it?* It dawns on me that this is not your up-to-code wiring we are used to back home. It also occurs to me that the neighborhood kids could play a lovely little joke by creeping up to our house at night, flicking the switch off, running away giggling like a much better version of *nicky, nicky nine doors* or *knock, knock ginger.* They could hide from a safe distance to hear the ensuing black-out kafuffle inside.

The last thing Pedro says before he and Bobby exit is, "Don't lock yourself in the bedroom." With that cryptic message they are off on their bicycles like a strange version of Batman and Robin, a thin, Columbian solicitor and a short American bar fly, our Barrachos... or would time tell different stories?

***

Back at Tommy's we tell Jan and Dean the good news, but I skip the fuse box story for now, which really has to be seen to be believed, especially to Dean as a recently retired electrical contractor. They are happy for us, but sad to see us go, but we reassure them that we are close by and invite them over tomorrow night after we settle in.

Bumping my rolling luggage along the rock road we do our suburban transfer while I think of all the ways to make our new private love nest even cozier. I notice it needs one more small table and maybe a hammock for the back though it does have loungers. But, it is starting to get late and our first dilemma becomes getting into our love nest. It's dark outside the door. There doesn't seem to be a light outside either, not that we would have thought of leaving one on. John has been given three keys, marked 1, 2 and 3 although it's impossible to tell which is which in the dark. He fumbles through the options and gets us in the door.

Instinctively, we reach around the corner for the light switch to the living room where the front door enters. Pretty soon we are patting down all the walls in the darkened place looking for a light switch. It turns out to be in the middle of one of the side walls, under the sill of the window, exactly in the center. The exact place you would look last.

The bedroom light switch is similarly conveniently placed for people with six foot long arms. No matter. We load all our things in and take inventory and start opening windows to air it out. In the process, we discover that there isn't any *mosquitero* netting on many of the windows. Earlier Nancy had cautioned me about mosquitoes being the cause of what is known as Dengue fever.

Mosquitoes love me in every state, province and nation that I encounter them. My fears of contracting this not so uncommon fever rise. It is dusk and prime *mosquitero* time. I quickly douse myself in eau de *Deep Woods Off* as if I am performing a self-immolation. John doesn't seem to notice as he is fooling with the locks and the keys.

He now knows key one is front door, key two is side door, key three which he thought may be the key to the bedroom is the gate to the garden. There is no key to the bedroom and an extra switch on the lock and that's why you can lock yourself in and imprison yourself in your own home. Many Mexican locks require you to key lock them from the outside and from the inside. Not cool if there is an emergency and you have to get out fast, yet fire is never a concern because the homes are concrete so there is nothing much to burn.

When I rise in the morning John has already left for his morning run and I am looking forward to a nice hot shower of my own before he gets back. One thing I did like about our new little house when I first examined it was the bathroom.

When Bobby and Pedro had been there I had diligently checked out the shower to inspect it for cleanliness and size. The shower was very large, larger than the ones in Tommy's guest house. It was also clean and we had been assured by Pedro and Bobby that the hot water was on.

It passed inspection but I don't usually make a point of noting where the showerhead is located. You assume that a rectangular shaped shower will have the shower head at the short end aiming across the length. That silly assumption is perhaps why I missed it on the long side of the wall when I inspected. If on the outside chance the showerhead is on the long side, the thing you don't expect to see is that it will be aiming out the sliding door of the shower towards the toilet.

When I notice this, I decide to be thankful that the shower has a sliding door that protects the shower from watering the toilet. I get in, close the sliding door and realize that this arrangement makes it a little cramped for showering with the spray hitting the door directly. I can get myself wet, but what I found after a minute or two is the water is piling up against the door because the drain is at the opposite end of the shower—a space which had been rendered useless unless you are in the shower to stay dry, which I'm not. The tiled shower floor seems to have no tilt on the floor down to the drain. Not to worry though, because there is another drain in the center of the bathroom, outside the shower sliding door, and the water ran to that drain… once it had built up a three inch deep puddle around my feet and starts to leak through the door.

Unlike the drain in the shower this drain is properly placed at a downward slope so water can flow towards it. The problem is this drain is not draining. Now a large puddle is forming in the bathroom as a whole. I finish my shower and unplanned foot bath in a hurry and follow the river of water out the bathroom door into the living room.

John is not a handy man, not even generally speaking. Any handyman-ing to be done has always come from my end of the relationship, but my handiness stops at plumbing. So, I sop up the puddle that spans from the bathroom tiles into the living room with a couple of towels and decide to wait for him to return and brainstorm it together. Meanwhile I dress, make my granola and fruit and decide to head out to the backyard where the lounge chairs under the palm tress are waiting for me to eat my breakfast in paradise.

That's when I discover the door is locked and my absent beloved has taken the key.

I try the door to the front. Also locked. I, the claustrophobe, am locked in. Even though we had established the night before that these were Mexican locks that required keys to open them from the inside when they are locked. John, in his fuzzy morning head, ever vigilant about security, has, by habit, locked the doors behind him and taken the keys with him. I am fuming. *What am I? The home slave?*

I am eating my granola inside looking at a puddle of water and wet towels while the Mexican sun shines outside. By the time I hear the lock in the door I am ready to pounce like a panther.

"Did we forget something?" I asked in an unmistakable *you're in trouble* tone.

"Don't think so--hey, what happened here." It's a small house and doesn't take him long to find the water and wet towels.

"We have a problem, that's what happened, and... *And*, you locked me in!"

John has known me long enough to know that that was not a situation I would have taken well. He apologizes profusely but he also has to endure my extra irritation of showing him the results of my shower in dismay.

We had established with Pedro and Bobby that if there was anything wrong with the place, or anything that was needed, we were supposed to contact Pedro at his house a few blocks away. Since we have no phone, John says he will walk over and if he isn't there leave him a note. He leaves to Pedro's only after I have made him give me the keys and have set myself up in the lounger in the back yard—*free at last.*

I am very skeptical about the chance of a speedy correction of our drain situation, but since we have no tools to try to fix the drain ourselves, we are at Pedro and Bobby's mercy. I settle in with a good book and John returns having delivered his note. He is, of course, still sweaty from his run and has to opt for a sponge bath from the kitchen sink, which I consider sufficient pay back for my imprisonment.

Only a couple of hours later I spot an extraordinary sight out our front gate. Pirate eye-patched Barrio Bobby is forcefully pedaling his banana seat bicycle down our street with little Pedro balanced on the back holding a plunger aloft like a royal scepter. The dynamic duo to the rescue! I guess John's brief note had suggested to them an urgent plumbing situation, but when we show them what is happening, it does not faze them. I sense a small disappointment from Pedro, unable to employ his plunger in the toilet, but otherwise they are both keen to help. They get right to it by unscrewing the drain, inspecting, and clearing it, as we remain spectators to our drain fighting super heroes.

Bobby asks Pedro to fill up some water in a container to test if the drain is now draining properly. Pedro brings from the kitchen a small cup of water and dumps it down the drain and smiles triumphantly. But Bobby shakes his head like an Oliver Hardy to Pedro's Laurel.

"Pedro, that's not enough water. A shower produces a lot of water," Bobby instructs his sidekick. Pedro looks confused. The water had disappeared nicely. Bobby tries to explain to his solicitor friend how the small volume of water is not really helping to see if the drain would not back up. Pedro returns, this time with a small bowl of water. Again, dumps it down and grins with a *Voila!* air about him, until he looks at Bobby.

"No, no, Pedro," Bobby says loudly in his frustration, "a shower produces gallons of water. We can't test it with a few tablespoons."

John suggests a bucket in the backyard where the washing sink is. Every Mexican house has a laundry wash basin outside in the backyard. Pedro springs into action to hunt it down. He comes back with a bucket and a big grin. He starts to pour the bucket, but again Bobby looks at him like he is crazy. The bucket is only one fifth full and still produces only one second's worth of discharge. Exasperated, Bobby, tries one more time to explain, as John and I looked on with amusement.

"Pedro. Not. Enough. Water! A full bucket may not even be enough to simulate a shower."

Though Pedro looks incredulous, he runs away with the bucket into the backyard to refill the bucket at the wash basin. Meanwhile, John, who, up to this point had diplomatically decided not to actively intercede, goes into the kitchen and fills the largest pot we have which is smallish at best, and brings it back to the bathroom just as Pedro is walking in with a now full bucket of water.

"Good, good!" Bobby commends the adequate amounts of water surveying it with his good eye. He begins first pouring John's pot and when it quickly starts to empty signals Pedro to continue the pouring with the bucket. Pedro timidly tips a few drops hesitatingly. Bobby, watching his drain test slipping away again, bellows.

"Dump the bucket! Dump the bucket!" But the conservative solicitor was only managing a slightly higher dribble. Finally Bobby gives up, grabs the end of the bucket and gives it a violent upturn.

"There we go, there we go!" he coos, finally satisfied that the drain is working with a proper volume of water. I realize right then that I had misjudged One-eyed Barrio Bobby's character, and am thankful that both he and Pedro took their duty to their new tenants so seriously. That they made such an amusing team was a bonus. We thank them profusely for their promptness and their diligence.

We say goodbye using the phrase, "Hasta luego" (see you later), because in the small town of Libé, you surely would.

***

There is a footnote to the story of Bobby and Pedro. I had to leave to go back to work and John stays and continues to occupy the little house. He had suggested to Jan & Dean to move into the little house on the last week of his stay since his flight home was a week before the end of our Pedro lease.

A week and a half before he would turn it over to Jan & Dean, he was lazing around the backyard of the little house, when a man came through the front door with a key in hand. The man started yelling angrily at

John in Spanish. It became obvious that he was accusing him of trespassing. This, as it seems, was the house's true owner. He did not understand any English.

In what little Spanish John had acquired, he tried to calm the man down and quickly showed him the rental agreement we had signed with Pedro and Bobby, and the keys that he had in his possession to show his legitimacy. The man read the papers, apologized, and quickly stormed off, presumably in search of Pedro. It seems our pair of estate managers had neglected to tell the owner that they had rented the place. We wondered if this had been an intentional oversight so that they could split the money for more tequila without the owner ever knowing he had a tenant. John never saw the owner again, and felt it better to keep the peace by not bringing it up to Bobby or Pedro. We had learned that this was an instance of the haywire negotiations, opportunism and miscommunications that made Mexico Mexico.

Later, when Jan and Dean acquire the house for a week, they report to us that they also had a repeat performance of the owner barging in and them showing him the signed lease and him swearing something in Spanish involving Pedro's name.

From that day forward Pedro would never be seen in town again. Around town, similar stories started to surface of Pedro keeping keys and renting places without permission; a dangerous business in a place where vigilante justice happens. We have no idea what happened to him. However, as far as we know, Bobby was an innocent accomplice and is still seen in his usual haunts to this day.

Diego's Cruisers

We go to Diego's bar pretty regularly. To begin with we are meeting Nancy there often, but as the house closing drags on I notice she is there less and less and I can't help but wonder if it is to avoid our inquiries. But, by now we have made a number of friends who tell us to relax into the Mexican way and find diversions while we wait. So we do.

Diego's is always packed with boat owners and skippers. In fact, it starts to become hard to go into the bar and not get an invitation to go on someone's boat, for fishing, a sail or a cruise. Sooner or later you would have an invite, especially if you were female.

One night, I meet a particularly hard to miss cruiser, who says his name is Vincent.

"But you can call me Vince and save a cent," he tells me with a wink.

Vince is tall, tall enough that he towers over all the gringos let alone the Mexicans. Vince is also fun. There is no other word for it. When he laughs, everyone laughs. He dances, flirts, tells great stories and exudes a love of Mexico. Like that old saying, the women want to be with him, and the men want to be him. Vince also owns a 50 foot sailing yacht that John is salivating over.

In the bar, Vince is telling me some stories about his boat, *The Moon Speaker*, making me laugh. He talks about the bits of racing he does and a few other adventures and misadventures. He tells me how he bought his yacht from a poker game. It was love at first sight. But, she is an expensive mistress he warns, worse than his ex-wife. The acronym for BOAT he tells me is Break Out Another Thousand.

"Nowadays, it's break out another ten thousand," he adds with a shrug, still smiling.

He loves taking *The Moon Speaker* to Mexico the most. He loves Mexico so much he had wanted to change the name of the boat to something in Spanish.

"But, I decided against it," he tells me.

"Why's that?"

"She is known under that name and has such a great reputation on the West Coast," he answers.

"For racing, you mean?"

"No," he says, "for partying," and he bursts into a wide grin, raising his eyebrows and making me laugh again. I believe him.

John could tell Vince liked me, but rather than be jealous, he pimps me out.

"Find out if he'll give me a sail," he whispers to me.

"Vince, did you say you were going up coast tomorrow?" I ask, not so innocently. Before I finish my sentence, Vince replies,

"Wanna come?" That's when I did the nasty switcheroo.

"Well, I'd love to, but I am committed tomorrow to a day trip with friends, but John would love to go." John who has been hovering in the background, magically appears at my arm to seal the deal.

Looking way up at Vince's handsome face I see the disappointment, but John is already accepting, thanking him and talking about the plans. Later Vince would surreptitiously try to make me forget my plans, but I wasn't going for it. He was stuck with the bald guy. But, Vince would get his revenge.

***

John gets up that morning like a kid before Christmas, excited to start his sail with Vince. He is out the door with a quick peck to me while I am getting ready for my own trip with Jan and gal pals. He runs all the way to the lagoon and gets his water taxi to *The Moon Speaker.* Soon, he is getting permission to come aboard Vince's yacht.

His new skipper is nursing his night at Diego's with a cup of coffee but quickly gives John his first task, hoist the main sail. John gets on the winch and starts slowly hoisting the heavy sail up the forty foot plus shaft in the Mexican mid morning sun.

He is perspiring profusely as the skipper watches him sweat. It is not an easy haul. On any boat, no matter the size, when it comes to how people behave, the skipper is God. It is a dictatorship, not a democracy, and probably for very good reasons. That said, we do have a word known as "mutiny," so obviously there have been challenges to the notion, but John had crewed enough to know the rule. When he gets the main sail halfway up, after so much cranking, he is surprised when Vince yells out for John to stop. *Was the skip annoyed at how long it was taking?* You can't sail with the main sail half up.

"I'll take it from here," Vince yells from the helm. John sees him flick a switch on the helm and watches as the main sail motors the rest of the way up as if by magic, or more correctly by electric winch. Vince is laughing.

"Good one," John says, still perspiring. He had to laugh at the skip's joke and Vince had clearly used this prank before. A few moments later the skip had another request.

"John, will you pull up the anchor, please? The electric winch is broken." John wasn't born yesterday. He laughs and shakes his head. Except his skipper is not laughing with him. The winch really is broken. John stops laughing.

If anyone has ever hauled up a 25 pound anchor with several pounds more of chain and the drag of 30 feet of water, you can figure out that this isn't going to be easy. If John was perspiring before he is really sweating now and happy he has spent some time in the gym lifting weights back home. He gets that anchor out of the water to find Vince has cracked him a cold one. He has proved his worth, and maybe it wasn't so bad that he wasn't a chick. They are ready to sail.

John has Dutch heritage and we had been back to Holland to visit his aunts, uncles and cousins. They all had boats. Motor or sail, large or small, floating on the water was considered essential. Whenever I saw John at the helm of a sailboat I was seeing a blissfully happy man. It was in his DNA. But, while John was on his aquatic adventure, I was on a landlubber one.

84

El Cocodrilo

Amigo, Is That You?

I remember seeing a crocodile at the zoo's aquarium when I was little. People were flicking pennies at the great green lizard to try to get a rise out of him, but he seemed unnervingly stoic. You got the feeling that the toothy creature had memorized the faces of everyone who had ever humiliated him in this way for further reference. Yet, those people felt safe. I felt safe.

I had never seen a crocodile in the wild, so it was a little bit exciting that Jan and I were going to the town of San Michele that was famous for its crocodile sanctuary. People told us that there was a particularly large crocodile there that they had nicknamed,

"Amigo" and no one was really sure how old the primordial creature was.

We had been invited by a small group of tourist women who had a car to travel with. The hour long drive without our men gave us time to yack. We start to swap stories we've heard about the town, including crocodile stories. The most famous story is one that each of us have heard before. And, like every good urban myth, each of us added their own details, the combination of which gave us this story:

The crocodiles live in a fresh water lagoon—crocodiles apparently do not enjoy salt water—but there is a surprisingly narrow strip of beautiful beach land separating the freshwater lagoon from the ocean. One year, a big hurricane had the ocean running inland well past the normal tide marks and right into the lagoon. The tidal withdrawal swept several of the crocodiles out to sea. A number of the crocodiles ended up on a sandbar several meters from the shore. Of course, when the storm was over and the sun came out, the tourists returned to the beach, some going in for a dip. Oh, oh, what's that moving in the water? Just like a scene from Jaws, people ran inland screaming. The crocodiles were headed for the touristas! Federales were called in to stand guard and shoot any rogue displaced crocodiles.

Did this really happen? Being a sucker for a good story, I believe it completely, but Jan and another woman are skeptical. In any case, the story primes us for the day's adventure.

On the turn off to this crocodile sanctuary and San Michele is a large albeit somewhat worn out painted sculpture of a crocodile. We are clearly in the right place. We park at the beach area and immediately see the beautiful, flat sandy beach and the stalls selling colorful inflatables to float in and on the water. There are rings of all colors, air mattresses in rainbows, inflatable ducks, frogs, sharks and not surprising the biggest of these inflatables are crocodiles. My mind flashes back to the post-hurricane story and in the movie in my head I imagine people out in the water with inflatable crocodiles while the real crocodiles move in. The irony makes me smile. I am, as John would say, a self-amusing model.

We walk the beach for a time before going back into the town to find the lagoon and crocodile sanctuary. I see the water of the lagoon and a chain link fence with large gaps and gaping holes in it. There are no signs up. *Clearly we are not at the sanctuary yet,* I think, as I lean over the edge beside one of the open spots in the fence to better survey the lagoon. One of my companions puts a hand on my arm and points directly below me. There is a crocodile hidden in the water, just below the gaping hole I am standing at. *Holy shit!* We back away quickly. Then I see another one submerged among the mangrove trees at the waters edge, then another, and another. Their camouflage is impressive. But what about the fence? We all are in a quandary; why are there no warning signs? One of our group finds a small sign a little further along.

There are crocodiles all over. I see one swimming across the lagoon, the bare minimum of its scaly top side showing, but it is gliding smoothly as if motorized. It looks innocent, like a log drifting downstream. I can't believe that under the water there are little legs paddling and a big tail that produces such a fluid motion. This is what makes them dangerous. In the water, when standing still, they are nearly invisible and so slick when they are swimming that you barely register it as a movement and certainly not an animal movement.

Someone asks a local in Spanish why the fences are down. There is a shrug and the answer is they are not fixed yet, no explanation. This town has been living with crocodiles from its inception and from what I heard they have lost dogs, cats and small animals but never humans. The records say no fatalities and few historical attacks on humans but I am surprised that a child or tourist hasn't become crocodile food, yet. It could have been me moments earlier.

We walk a little further beside the lagoon in the direction of the beach. Here there are more warning signs and I can now see the beach from the edge of the lagoon and the whole story of the hurricane taking the freshwater crocodiles out to sea is now very believable. The ocean is a stone's throw away.

We get to a place with a little bridge where a .50 pesos (5 cents) donation is expected to look at the crocodiles that may or may not be in the concrete pens on the other side. We can see there is at least one crocodile there, a big one. *Is this Amigo?* I have a moment in my head of crocodiles that have those stickers stuck to them, "Hi, My Name is…" Self-amusing still.

A couple of tourists start over the bridge, but only Jan and I decide to go from our group paying a peso between us and leaving the others to putter on the beach and wait for us. The other tourists crossing the bridge are some young guys from Australia. They engage us in conversation and start going on about how they are used to "crocs" in Australia. Jan and I have inadvertently started calling the crocodiles "crocs" too which sounds like a new shoe craze to me. The big croc, possibly Amigo, is sunning himself near a concrete barrier that is about a foot and a half high and then there is some plastic coated chain link above that. He is the only one in the pens to look at, so the four of us all lean over to inspect him while the Australians try to impress the Canadian gals with more croc talk. Jan and I are nodding our heads and being polite Canadians.

It is at this moment, with all of us leaning over the big crocodile that he suddenly expands widely and lets out a big sound and a movement. We simultaneously all jump back and scream like little girls, even the Australians. The croc has let out an enormous crocodile sigh and made our hearts leap into our throats. We laugh nervously when we realize we are fine. The Australians look a little sheepish and take off back over the bridge, their croc talk has disappeared. Jan and I look at each other and start laughing. So much for the male ego.

I take a last look at that big crocodile. *Is that you Amigo?* I see that glint in his crocodile eyes and I know what he is thinking, *I still got it.*

30

LA IGUANA

Los Reptiles

In Libé, we are not in danger of a crocodile invasion, but there is one kind of reptile that we notice is very adept at entering homes. They have easily found their way into our little house. Fortunately, they are the beloved *cuizas besuconas*, or kissing geckos. They are small, no longer than a few inches, and harmless. While their presence startled me the first time I saw one at Tommy's, because they can move like lightening, I quickly started to laugh, not scream.

Geckos, I knew, diet on insects, so have everyone's favor. What amazes me about these sweet little creatures, is when they decide to speak up you can't ignore them. Tommy tells me that these particular geckos are called kissing geckos for a reason; the sound they make is like that of a kiss, and not a small quiet peck but a big chirping smooch. When you first hear it in the night, you think it surely must be the sound of a bird except birds generally don't call at night. If you are ever up close to one when it sounds off, it can make you jump out of your skin at the surprising volume. I am told they are using the sound to try and locate a mate. With all of the kissing sounds at night, these little guys are quite the romantic creatures and for me they add to the charm of our little town.

"I jumped over an iguana today!" John tells me, as he comes in from his morning run. John is one of these incredibly healthy people who has to get his daily sweat in. I can only be described as a counterbalance to his exertion.

I look up from my book, "Oh yeah?"

"He was just there in my usual route that I take beside the jungle, so I jumped over him."

"What did it do?"

"I don't know, I kept running."

I don't go running beside any jungles so I am pretty sure I am not going to be seeing an iguana any time soon. Iguanas can be up to six feet long from nose to tail. With the skepticism that only a spouse can have, I wonder if John has really jumped over an iguana or some little lizard that he decided to call an iguana.

The next day, while John is on another quest for sweat, I am sunning myself in the backyard of the little house nose in another book when I get that primordial feeling you get when you know you are being watched. I look up, and a few feet above me on the perimeter wall, looking at me with one red eye at the side of his head, is a huge, huge green lizard…an iguana. My eyes shoot open. Now I understand John's excitement. These are impressive creatures. It was as if a dinosaur had just flopped his head over the fence in a moment that combined Jurassic Park with Sesame Street. His spiky spine was unforgettable and his movement was mechanical and deliberate. He had a motor ability that was beyond my recognition in any other creature. When I drop my book in my excitement, I quickly learn how these large lizards can move exceedingly quickly. He darts away, over the wall, and I wonder how he managed to drop off a ten foot high precipice on the other side so fast.

Later, my excitement at telling John what I had seen is not greeted with an ounce of skepticism from him. Instead he matches my joy and excitement so well that it comes with the bittersweet knowledge and shame that I had been the unbelieving partner. Oh well, these things have a way of going back and forth in a long partnership. Another day I will be the one doubted.

While all the reptilian distraction from our home-buying wait was fun and different, in the evolutionary depths of my own reptilian brain I am registering a deep emotion that is about to surface. Fear.

LOS BOXEADORES

The Fight

They say that couples fight most over only a handful of things. Money, sex, work, domestic habits, relatives, children, or any big decisions. What else is there? John and I never fought over sex or children because we didn't have any (children, not sex), having met later in life. We didn't fight over relatives because they weren't in our face enough to be divisive. We didn't fight over work because even when we each worked overtime we always kept weekends pretty free to catch up, the other categories however are another matter.

Having literally co-written a book on choosing perfect roommates I can tell you that my spouse is definitely a bad choice for a roommate for me. Yet, we duke out our domestic differences and make it work. It's those other two categories, money and big decisions which seem to have us at odds. Mainly this is because our risk tolerances are at different ends of the spectrum. It's not so much than I have a high tolerance for risk as John has a very low tolerance for risk. I asked him once on a scale of 1 to 10 how horrible would it be if he was laid off from his job?

"Twenty," he answered.

I, on the other hand, had maxed out at one employer by staying with them nearly seven years. All employers following I had never made it to the fourth year anniversary without having quit, been laid off or fired. I had always bounced back from any work gaps quickly, partly because along with my day jobs I always had small writing gigs, taught writing at night school and did some contract work that I really couldn't be fired from.

So the realization that we two who had lived together for four years but didn't combine our money, had no joint checking account, had never even bought a piece of furniture together, were now buying our first residence together two thousand miles from where we actually lived, started to sink in and bring out doubts. It started with me, as it usually did.

Low risk John is a laid back, simple guy. Some might even say a little too laid back. "Anything that makes me sweat, makes me happy," he tells people and it's true. He loves to dance, aspires to teach dance, and can dance all night long and still get up and do his physical job. He can cycle for hours in the Mexican sun so few can keep up. He can kick the soccer ball around and keep his woman happy in the bedroom. These are some of the reasons that one of his many nicknames is the "the energizer bunny."

But where there is an up there is a down and when John gets hammock happy there is no budging him. So to my eyes he is having a bit too much fun and loafing a lot afterward. He seems to be putting all his energy into sweating without getting any sweat equity. I start to fret.

"Are you going to figure out how to make more money or just loaf?" He gives me a look over his book. We are on the lounge chairs in the backyard of the little house. I continue.

"Great that you can have fun, dance, bike, sail, drink wine, and lay around and read the rest of the day but we are going to have to pay off this house, and I am not going to maintain it all by myself, you are going to have to help. Are you going to be able to do that?" His answer:

"Sure." This is an answer that seems perfectly reasonable to a man but to a woman is woefully inadequate and examined with suspicion.

"How?"

"What do you mean how?"

"How are you going to have time and energy to do this and still have your fun lifestyle that you manage down here?"

"It will all work out, stop worrying. We can hire Mexicans to do the maintenance. Better them than me." He smiles. He is being cute now and that is another way that men should never answer women when they are being serious.

"It costs money to hire others for everything. You know, sometimes you have to make sacrifices to get what you want John. I mean, what if I got laid off?" I miss saying "again" as it has already happened once since he has known me.

"If that happens," he says, "I'm not taking on all the payments myself. I can't afford to do that."

I couldn't believe what I was hearing. *He would not... he would not...* I can't speak for a second. I feel a well of heat coming up my body. My head feels like it is about to explode.

"What do you mean? You wouldn't take on the payments? Even temporarily, you would not back me up? You would let us lose..." I choke a little, "the house?" *My Banana Palm House!*

"Well, you pulled the trigger on that. What were you thinking? We don't even have a place at home yet." I didn't know whether I wanted to cry or scream. *Hadn't we been through this already? Didn't we agree that this was what we both wanted? Didn't we agree we could manage it financially? Wasn't this our dream?*

When my exploding head is careening inside my skull and I know my frustration level is red-lining there is only one thing to do. Walk out in the most dramatic way possible and slam the nearest door I encounter. Unfortunately, that is a sliding door and is not so easy to slam but I am reasonably sure John gets the message by the absence of dialogue.

Most couples will recognize what comes next. She stews in a separate room. He lets her stew a little too long until she is planning the break-up in detail. But, if he is a good guy, he knows what he has to do, he has to go find her and apologize. And, depending how long he has been in a long term relationship is the measure to what degree he apologizes and how soon.

John finds me in the bedroom ignoring him (and quietly planning our separation). He starts with:

"We need to talk." I note the absence of an apology. It is a frosty start to reconciliation already. We continue talking, sometimes with raised voices and sometimes with calm ones. I have by the end of the evening a somewhat coerced apology from him, but he has levelled his low risk uncertainty on me.

"Maybe we aren't ready for this dream." I didn't like hearing this.

"Do you really think that?"

"Kat, we are fighting. You are getting stressed. Is that worth it?"

"I'm stressed because I'm not sure you are ready, but I am."

"Are you? Aren't you the one who always has buyer's remorse? If you doubt things after the high of doing them has worn off, maybe you are not ready."

Damn we hate it when the men actually say something that makes sense. *Was it me?* I had started the fight. Was I feeling like I bit off more than I could chew? Had I pulled the trigger, as John called it, and shot myself in the foot? Let's hope it was only the foot.

We are not breaking up. But we are not going to bed on a happy note either. I give in and go to my catalogue of Scarlett O'Hara wisdom, *tomorrow is another day.*

71

LA TORTUGA

La Tortuga

The next night we are back at Diego's Cruisers Blues Bar. It is a decent band and we dance but there is now a tension between John and me. We talk and laugh with others in the bar letting their happiness fill in any gaps to our own joy.

When the band is on a break a young man comes into the bar and moves from table to table asking if anyone speaks Spanish. He is a volunteer from the Tortuga Shelter (sea turtle shelter) a short walk away on the beach. Someone translates that if we would like to help release the baby tortugas that were hatched only an hour ago they need more hands. John and I looked at each other.

Coincidentally, John and I had been by the shelter a few days before. We had peeked in at the fenced off section of the beach with the little flags indicating where the tortuga eggs were buried below the sand. We had noticed them before but this time we read the cards on the flags. The cards say "Proximo Nac" and a date. I tell John that this means the next birth time. We look at the dates and John notices that the dates are all this week and over the next few weeks. But we continue on our merry way, not knowing that we will be asked to take part two days later at Diego's bar to release these very babies to the ocean.

We tell the volunteer we want to help and follow him with the other volunteers back to the shelter. The bunch of us gather around a bin of sand with dozens of baby tortugas, only an inch and a half long, all struggling to get out and move forward to the ocean.

The volunteer gives us a little history. The babies are only one hour old and they release them after sunset, about seven p.m., so that the birds won't pick them off. They show us that in the tummy of these little creatures is the area that contains the mysterious locator that will ensure these tortugas will return to this exact spot, fully grown in 15 years, and ready to lay more eggs each season. Over their lifespan, which is up to 150 years, they will hatch 900 eggs of which only a small percentage will survive. They ask us to never take part in, or condone the consumption of sea turtle eggs (a delicacy in Mexico).

They tell us to take off our shoes and socks, and roll up our pant legs as we will be getting wet. Now they prepare the palms of our hands by smoothing a bit of sand across them, so the tortugas are oriented with the sands they will be returning to in 15 years. Then they drop into each of our palms a baby tortuga, so small and new. They try to wriggle up the mini beaches of our sand-laden palms, instinct pulling them to the ocean. We have to keep re-placing them to the bottom of our palms or they will get away on us.

I am amazed to think that this wee creature will one day be as large as a small kitchen table. Out of the bunch of us volunteering John, as the sailor, is the only one who has seen the magnificence of a full grown sea turtle swimming in the ocean alongside his ship.

The volunteers take us down to the ocean and explain that we have to go to the edge of the surf with our wriggling babes, and after a wave the volunteers will tell us when to release our tortugas to their fates. The wave comes crashing in and baptizes our ankles up to our knees.

"Ahora!" the volunteer calls, "Now!"

In we place them, and as the water from the wave withdraws the undertow sucks the babies out into the ocean. The small creatures we let go of are left up to their destinies in the vastness of the Pacific. I am overcome with emotion, and call out "Good luck!" the only thing I can think to wish the small babe that was entrusted to me for mere minutes before I had to release it. My voice is lost in the waves, but I put up a silent prayer as a surrogate mother wishing a long and happy life to this one. And that is all any of us can hope for.

John and I find each other and look out at the ocean, we are both silent as we find each other's sandy hands. We walk hand in hand down the beach quiet with one another, a contrast to how we were in the bar. I reflect how nature has prepared these little turtles to go straight out into the world and handle all that befalls them immediately, unlike us humans. After nearly 50 years I still don't know if I am prepared for all that life may throw at me. John interrupts my reflections.

"Who said making dreams come true is easy?" I nod. He is reading my mind now, but not entirely; there is a confession I need to make.

"Remember when you told me you were leaving to do a sailing trip in Mexico and at first I didn't want you to go?"

"Yes."

"I was envious. You impressed me. I thought I was the one that liked taking risks but you proved to me that wasn't so. You wanted something and you went after it."

"And that's how we found this place."

"That's right and this place feels like home to me."

"Me too."

"Then I guess we are buying a house here."

"If those tiny creatures can face the perils of the Pacific on their own, I think we can make it together."

"It looks like we will be returning to this shore too."

We continue down the beach. Just then a man approaches us selling hammocks. All the other sellers have gone with the sun but he is a die-hard. We look at the hammocks in the twilight and I find a beautiful rainbow-colored one. John and I agree that it will be perfect at the top of the Banana Leaf Casa where we were told a palapa and hammock would be expected, and John can probably rig it up at the little house too.

We buy it from the happy seller and we are happy too, as John says, "Doing our part for the local economy." With the backdrop of a fading sunset we walk down the beach towards the little house and take our cues from the kissing geckos.

Nightmare with No Close

Nancy assures us that while there are a few hoops to jump through, technical details and some assessments to be done for the financing–all perfectly normal–we will be completing the sale soon.

"It just takes longer in Mexico," everyone keeps saying. *That's okay, we couldn't be waiting in a nicer spot,* I keep trying to think. I want to be positive now that John and I are on the same page, yet I still feel that twinge of fear in my inner recesses. And from a practical perspective, after almost three weeks of delays I am getting a little antsy that I am going to have to fly home and go back to work before we close the deal.

Nancy recommends we take a precautionary trip to the nearest town (where we would soon be paying our property taxes), to meet a notario (lawyer) to give John my full power of attorney to make the sale in my absence. We spend the morning in a busy office where we are pre-screened and told to wait and wait and wait until we are allowed to see the lawyer whose secretaries had already collected the information and it felt like we are only there to kiss his ring, or shake his hand, which we did (the hand, not the ring). He is the only man I have ever seen in Mexico wearing a full suit.

When we get back to Libé in the late afternoon John goes off to do some errands and I go into the real estate office to let Nancy know it is done. She seems visibly relieved, yet still not her joyful self. I sense that something else is amiss. I offer to take her out for some margaritas, just us girls, and she happily agrees.

We make our way to the nicest and tallest hotel in town, The Orca, with a rooftop bar and 360 degree views. From atop we can see the whole of town, the sailboats anchored in the lagoon, the five star resort on the other side, the open ocean, the town next door and the distant hills. Everyone who ever comes here for the first time falls in love with the view. Throw in some margaritas and you are pretty convinced you are, in fact, in paradise.

When Nancy and I get there it is happy hour. Nancy is hitting the margaritas harder than I have seen before so I start to gently probe what's wrong. That's when I get her forlorn love story. It turns out she opened the real estate office with her boyfriend at the time, Byron. John and I had only met him once briefly as the office's manager. She tells me the whole sordid story, the last part being that he dumped her and got a new girlfriend but she still has to work with him. Ugh. Not fun. I am sympathetic, but not really our concern as her clients. She starts talking about switching offices to one of their competitors. Understandable.

"I will absolutely finish up your deal before I switch," she reassures me.

"Of course," I say calmly but am truly reassured by this. No more switching real estate agents.

"Even then, I am going to have trouble switching because of him," she continues talking with her margarita loosened lips but I am not really sure what she means. Was she still emotionally hung up on him? Was he making a move difficult?

"Is he trying to convince you to stay after he dumped you for another girl?" I ask with an appropriate note of outrage.

"No, it's not that. I'm over that. It's because I'm not sure he's going to give me my fair share of the business if I leave. I just know it."

"You have a contract with him, right Nancy?" She looks at me with a tell-tale look of embarrassment and admits that all she had was a verbal agreement with him. This was more than just emotions to cry into your margarita about.

"It really burns me up too," she adds, "I'm the one that is a licensed real estate agent back home, not that you need to be in Mexico, but I'm the one with the experience!"

Wait, did I hear that right?

"You don't need to be licensed at all to sell real estate in Mexico?" I ask. "But what about—" I blurt the name of the international company that is on the front door of their offices.

"They don't care, you just need to pay the franchise fee," she reveals looking sadly disgusted while my mind is turning. No licensed agents means no training, no regulations, no associations and no ethical industry standards and practices. Hmm, okay, classic Mexico cowboy differences. I wasn't going to be worried. Until Nancy had another margarita.

Like all accepted offers in real estate you have to put up a deposit in good faith, held in trust, until everything is closed and it will be used towards the sale. We had done so on the Banana Leaf Palm Casa. Even though the conversion to USD hurt a bit, it was done. It was transferred to an account that I was told was the real estate office's trust account.

"I found out Byron's been borrowing money out of the trust accounts." It is margarita number five. My mouth drops. That isn't good.

"Don't worry," she slurs, "now that I confronted him, he won't do it again." *Oh, well, of course because he seems like such a nice fellow. What?!*

"I could send him to prison for that. Mexican prison." She looks away dreamily.

This is turning dark. But just then, in her tequila numbness she seems to remember herself and assures me he has been replacing the funds after "borrowing" them, but I suddenly see our agent as, how shall I say it, a girl who chooses the wrong guys to trust.

***

I report my happy hour Intel back to John. John looks grim. He had also found out some unpleasant news—the real reason we were being delayed in the closing.

Last time we were down we had met the current owners of the Banana Leaf Palm Casa and I had rather liked them, Cheri and Kevin. In fact, Kevin shared a great insight into how I would start to view the rest of my life. He told me that he had always been trying to figure out how to make more money, until he had a conversation on the beach in Libé with a Mexican man. When he started talking business to this fellow, the man had shrugged and said, "Senõr, you can always make more money, but you can't make more time."

Cheri and Kevin were selling the Banana Leaf Palm Casa and moving to a larger house with an artist's studio in back so that Kevin could spend more time doing what he really wanted to do with the rest of his time, paint.

John had run into Kevin and Cheri while I had gone to the multi-margarita happy hour with Nancy—the joys of a small town— and they couldn't help but bring up the delays in closing. They looked surprised that John didn't know why.

"Know what?" John had asked. They launched into the story.

Originally, Byron and Nancy had told them that even though their house had appreciated significantly they would not have to pay capital gains under Mexican laws. That's why it was priced very reasonably. However, the truth was revealed that both Byron and Nancy had not kept up with current laws (because they didn't have to), and that situation had changed with the New Year. Byron had suggested they could get the assessments lowered by "means" (a bribe) and adding a little for himself for the service. But, because of the honest U.S. bank Nancy had gotten involved who had approved our financing, that didn't look like it was going to happen.

"But, they are stalling, trying to get another assessment that will devalue the house." John reports.

"Good lord." This made me very uncomfortable.

Sure enough, a day later Nancy comes to us and tells us that is exactly what is happening.

"Don't worry," she says, "I will get you your house, come hell or high water."

Yes, that is it. We didn't want to lose the house. That's the thing, right? Don't lose the deal. John and I had stretched our resources to the max and we both couldn't and didn't want to pay more money if the assessment was too high or if we were asked to cover Kevin and Cheri's capital gains losses, which was another scenario suggested.

The day comes when I have to get on the plane to go back to Canada. Our casa deal has not been straightened out. The champagne remains unopened, but John is there with my power of attorney and ready to shepherd it through, but neither of us likes the direction it is going in and we especially do not trust Byron. The offer is subject to financing and if the bank is going to demand more down payment money from us, based on their original assessment, then the deal is going to fall through. Byron and Nancy are still trying to find a way to "work it out."

***

A couple of days after I return to Canada, the jet lag not yet out of my system, something is dawning on me. As if going hundreds of miles an hour in the plane has left an unfinished idea behind that is madly trying to catch up to my actual mind. The phone rings. It is a rare call from John who struggles with the phone cards in Mexico. He is calling from an office that has a Vonage account. It is a real estate office, but it isn't Byron and Nancy's office. It is the office of two local Mexican women, making a go of it in real estate. It is at that moment the idea landed.

John tells me that after he had gotten to know these women, Greta and Teresa, and had explained our dilemma and distrust of Byron, they said they were not surprised. He had added the latest rounds of sneaky side deals that were proposed. They told him that they had seen gringo real estate "agents" come looking for quick sales and mucho dinero, before leaving town as fast as they had come. But these women, who lived in the town, had reputations there, they were building a property management business as well as real estate business and could not afford to have a tarnished name. They had kindly let him use their phone to call me privately since they had a long distance plan.

"Why don't we just let it go?" I say to John on the phone. There is a small ache in my heart as I remember Nancy's *hell or high water* remark. "Let's let the deal fall through, no side deals," I repeat.

We both know the deadline to complete for the offer is only a few days away and the bank is going to require more down payment that we would struggle with, based on the legitimate assessment.

"Really?" he asks, "Are you sure?"

"Why don't we buy a lot instead and build later?" My idea was out.

There is silence on the line. Then, he speaks up.

"I like that idea. We could get more rooms."

"Is the power of attorney you have for me good for any sale?"

"I'll find out."

"Good."

"I think I know who our new real estate agents are too," he tells me.

"Okay, go out and see what you can get us in the Fraccionamiento. No roosters."

"No roosters," he agrees.

"What should I do with the table we bought?" he asks.

Ah, the table. When we had moved into the little house which was somewhat spare in furniture, we decided to buy a small table thinking we would just move it into our new casa. Every weekend we saw a man with a truckload of furniture who had lined up pieces to sell at the side of the road. That was our furniture store. We struggled with our Spanish negotiating with him but got our price settled. Now he was asking us something else.

I finally managed to figure out that he was asking us whether we wanted a table that was stained or left unstained. We had been looking at an unstained table so I assumed he had another one in his truck that was fully stained. I said, yes, si, I would like a table stained in the darker color he was pointing out on a stool. I didn't care if I had to pay a little more. But, instead of getting a stained table out for me, the man got out a brush and a can of stain. Right on the side of the road he stained the unstained table in front of us.

It dried quickly in the sun and John and I giggled in fits as we carried it down the middle of the road the three blocks to the little house, our hands a little stained in the process.

"Leave the table in the little house for Jan and Dean and whoever else." Though I was heart broken that the Banana Leaf Palm house was not going to be ours, a weight had also been lifted from my shoulders. It felt like maybe we had gotten out of a deal with the devil. Or, as so many like to say, it was not meant to be. But we still had the rainbow-colored hammock.

"I guess we will hang our hammock somewhere else next year," I sighed, saying goodbye to the Banana Leaf Palm casa.

"Sweetheart, as long as we are together, we will find a place to hang our hammock," John reassured me.

We left the call giggling with purpose; we were on a new adventure, to buy land.

The Happy Hammock

A well known story:

A gringo businessman was at the pier of a small coastal Mexican village when a small boat with just one fisherman docked. Inside the small boat were several large fish. The gringo complimented the Mexican on the quality of his fish and asked how long it took to catch them.

The Mexican replied, "Only a little while." The gringo businessman then asked why didn't he stay out longer and catch more fish? The Mexican said he had enough to support his family's immediate needs.

The man then asked, "But what do you do with the rest of your day?"

The Mexican fisherman said, "I sleep late, fish a little, play with my children, take a siesta in my hammock, make love with my wife, stroll into the village each evening where I sip wine, and play guitar with my amigos."

The gringo shook his head. "I am a Harvard MBA and could help you. You should spend more time fishing and with the proceeds, buy a bigger boat. With the proceeds from the bigger boat, you could buy several boats, eventually you would have a fleet of fishing boats. Instead of selling your catch to a middleman you would sell directly to the processor, eventually opening your own cannery. You would control the product, processing, and distribution. You would need to leave this small coastal fishing village and move to Mexico City where you will run your expanding enterprise."

The Mexican fisherman asked, "But, how long will this all take?"
To which the gringo businessman replied, "15 – 20 years."
"But what then?" Asked the Mexican.
The businessman laughed and said, "That's the best part. When the time is right you would announce an IPO and sell your company stock to the public and become very rich, you would make millions!"
"Millions – then what?"
"Then you would retire. Move to a small coastal fishing village where you would sleep late, fish, play with your grandchildren, take siestas in your hammock, make love with your wife, stroll to the village, drink wine and play guitar with your amigos."

When I left Libé to return to the normal North American life I noticed how pale it was in comparison, physically and emotionally. It wasn't just working or not working, nice weather or not, it was something deeper than that. A sense of true connection. It was a world where the pressure to "succeed" had been put aside enough that I had started to get to know myself.

I felt detached from almost all my possessions which I now viewed as so much crap. As a friend who is part of the simplify movement said, *buy what you need and need what you buy.* But what did we truly need? What kind of "needs" got us into trouble, and what kind of needs got us out? Mexico was starting to change me but we were still buying. I couldn't tell if this wish for sanctuary, for a home, so far away, was going to get us into more trouble or less.

***

We made sure we got our deposit back from Byron and Nancy (minus conversion). A disillusioned Nancy was heading back to the United States and Byron was also packing up with yet another new girlfriend and selling the franchise. I never knew if Nancy got her cut or not. I wished Nancy well, but the whole event had strained my trust and our friendship. Besides, we had our new Mexican real estate agents, Teresa and Greta.

Teresa, John described as the talkative, gregarious charmer, and Greta the happy, sweet and petite Mexican flower who could eat a whole large cheese cake herself yet not gain an ounce. John gave them what we wanted in a piece of property. I weighed in remotely with John giving me reports from their office phone on a regular basis. We knew it might take awhile to find what we wanted and although John had another month in Mexico it was possible it wouldn't happen while he was still there. We agreed not to hold our breath.

Two days later John calls me. Teresa has a hot property. A sale has fallen through and a terrific large corner lot in the Fraccionamiento (no roosters) is available. John is excited. This is a window of opportunity that does seem like it is meant to be. I agree and the next day we are off and running with an accepted offer on a piece of property sin casa (without house) and no financing needed.

It is going through quickly. It seems nothing can go wrong. Or could it? John didn't know it then but someone else had also their eyes on that lot and was very disappointed it had been scooped by him thanks to our new best friends in our southern community.

I am only able to meet Teresa and Greta over the phone lines, but I know I will love them already. I joke with them that we could plant two palm trees on the lot for now and stretch our rainbow-colored, happy hammock across them. Just get John a cooler of beer, a history book, and he would be very happy (for the record, I have never seen a hammock strung between two palm trees anywhere I can recall, although you see that image all over).

In reality, however, I want more than a couple of palm trees. I had had another Scarlett O'Hara moment. Not the one about tomorrow being another day, not fiddle-dee-deeing, not allowing her or any of her folk to go hungry, the one I am talking about is, *Tara, there is nothing more important than land.*

We had the land. Paid outright. Ours. Well sort of, we had a bank trust with a major Mexican bank in which you have to pay an annual fee above paying property taxes except it goes to a bank instead of the community, which annoys me, but it is a small thing. Bank trusts are safe, you can bequeath property to your loved ones, and they had been proven to have no issues for decades in this town. We had been warned not to be tempted by great deals in neighbouring towns where the land is aboriginal and you need a Mexican partner to own it.

There are multiple stories of people who thought they had secured huge acreage with stunning views and had built their dream homes on land they purchased with a Mexican partner. Then their Mexican partner would pass away (of natural causes), and his family would swoop in and take the property including the dream home with more than squatter's rights to it.

But we have a safe bank trust. We are going to be able to build a home in paradise, this place I had only been to twice, but had fallen in love with. I am thoroughly convinced we will be building in the next year or two at the most.

The world thought differently.

The World

The World was in a financial collapse. Most people didn't even really know it yet, but working on the administrative edges of the financial sector I saw it firsthand and it wasn't pretty. It took a lot of financial bailing to get things moving again, and that is the funny thing. Money is abstract, it is a way of accounting for both tangible things (goods) and intangible things (time and labour), but it is a concept, an idea. We have accepted this premise of money and everything that it is built on, which is pretty much everything in our material world and we give no thought to whether the values ascribed to this accounting are correct. In 2009, the emperor of the financial world was wearing no clothes and since I was working in the administration side of finance I was sitting in his court.

I started to understand that today's economy was really built on three abstracts: Will (desire to make something true), Confidence (backing up that will) and Greed (what's in it for me). With this financial collapse, I could see that the world is suffering a reality check from some pretty tricky accounting and often the wrong people are suffering. They say a recession is when your neighbour gets laid off, and a depression is when *you* get laid off. I was laid off.

Thankfully, I have a knack of landing on my feet and thanks to unions and one of those rare, and getting rarer, institutions—the post office—John is not affected. But, the combination of being part of a more balanced way of life in Mexico and seeing what happens when the disease of greed spreads too far, I am being transformed. My heart is no longer interested in operating in the corporate world. I become less and less attached to possessions, and I have been known to be quite attached.

People are feeling a huge pinch in this new world. Their nest eggs and credit lines have disappeared overnight. Many delay their retirement. Jan and Dean, who we once envied for their early retirement, are among those forced to go back to work. I just want to escape it all.

If we want to build a house in Mexico we need financing. That U.S. bank that had financed mortgages for house sales in Mexico is no longer allowed to do that. Unlike everywhere else, financing at banks in Mexico has double digit interest rates (no one can explain to me adequately why poorer peoples get charged more than the rich always). At home, we can't get financing for a foreign property, and even if we could it would be nuts with me out of work. There is no way we are building on our land soon. But what we do have is annual time off and the ability to return. What we do have is a hammock.

John and I start calling Mexico our happy place and decide to manage our spending so that we can rent a casa or two, sequentially, and go to Libé for two to three months of the year in winter. There are advantages to being laid off and also advantages to living in an internet world where you can stay connected if you need to. This will do very nicely for me for my consulting, editing, teaching and coaching contracts I am building up.

We are officially snowbirds in our late 40s. We decide the new plan is to retire in stages, before actual retirement, and unpack the happy hammock annually, hanging it at whatever casa in Libé we would end up at. That is our new world.

LOS AMANTES

Siesta Sex

In our second season John returns to Libé three weeks before me while I finish up some in-person contract work. By the time I am ready to join him, a snowstorm in Canada has threatened to delay many flights. I have been e-mailing John my concerns that my flight may be delayed, but on the day of travel I am happy to arrive in Mexico as originally planned, late in the afternoon.

I take a cab into Libé as a necessary expense. I know the area now, so upon approach can direct the driver in Spanish with *izquirda* (left) and *dereche* (right), and the ever confusing *derecho* (straight ahead), but occasionally my high school French—the minimum that every Anglo Canadian learns—gets mixed up with my newly acquired Spanish. My "stop" and "here" which should have been "alto"[2] and "aquí" comes out "arrêt" and "ici." So it is several feet past the correct address that I belatedly got the cabdriver to come to a screeching halt and then reverse to the gate.

The gate is locked, so I yell out John's name, and the helpful driver honks his horn for me. From a balcony upstairs, I spot a vision that raises my eyebrows. A fully naked John has emerged on an upstairs balcony, the balcony railing strategically placed for our eyes, but otherwise leaving little to the imagination of the cabbie. It is nothing I have not seen before, but am a little befuddled to see it on public display.

John, seeing me, raises his arms in half greeting, half shrug. Having misinterpreted my last e-mail message it seems he was not expecting me until much later. This is my first clue as I walk into the rental casa that in three weeks, John has reverted back to pre-civilization.

I move into his bachelor pad with two bedrooms upstairs, one for sleeping the other for dumping stuff. The kitchen downstairs is a mis-construction marvel, not helped by John's bachelor ways. The cabinets in the kitchen are mounted on the wall on such an obvious slant that it has the look of a fun house. At least this crazy house has WiFi and I write an e-mail to friends in Canada:

---

[2] By the way, that word "ALTO" that appears on every red hexagonal Mexican stop sign may confuse some people as alto means "high" in Spanish not "stop." I was informed that "alto" was used because the first traffic signs were introduced when there were still horses and you pulled up high on the reigns to bring your horse to a halt. Notice also the similarity between the words "alto" and "halt." Although "halt" has German origins, there was a strong presence of German immigrants in Texas when it was still considered part of Mexico and the combination of these two facts was likely why alto means stop when it comes to traffic in Mexico - it may also explain their mutual love of the tuba as a musical instrument.

John has turned native on me and gone back to all his bachelor domestic housekeeping ways (how fast civilization falls away). I feel like Katherine Hepburn in the movie The African Queen *trying to impress upon Humphrey Bogart the importance of keeping up our civilized ways, "Nature, Mr. Allnutt, is what we were put in this world to rise above."*

I have come to terms with the fact that this will be home for another week (when we are to move to another supposedly better casa), but after a day of travel I am happy to have a bed. I have no knowledge yet how this nature boy introduction will set a tone for the season.

***

The day after my arrival, by siesta time I am in bed listless from the combination of jet lag and heat. John goes out to scavenge the only store open in the late afternoon and lets me nap. Our two-floor casa is attached to two other casas, like townhouses, all three meant for rentals. I have not seen the occupants of the other casas yet, but as I lay dozing I hear some familiar sort of cries, albeit louder than I would normally hear such things. Someone is having sex. Siesta sex.

Another perk of Mexico, things shut down from 2 p.m. to 5 p.m. in the hottest hours and you can go home to your spouse, partner or lover, crawl into bed for a snooze and wake with a bang. This is clearly what is happening next door and the woman's cries are so fervent and prolonged, I have to say I am quite envious.

By the time John comes back I am ready to show him how happy I am to see him, jet lag be damned. I mention to him that I heard our randy neighbours and they are unabashedly loud. He admits that this is a regular occurrence every siesta.

"Didn't you notice anything about it?" he asks me.

"Other than it was loud and intense?" I respond tentatively, not sure where this is going.

"It took me awhile to figure it out," he says. I am still mystified.

"Figure what out?"

"I couldn't figure out why she was having two climaxes so close together." I am casting my mind back to what I heard and thinking of the joys of female multiple orgasms, when John tells me the truth.

"They are lesbians," he says. "Our neighbours who have sex every afternoon, are lesbians. Two orgasms, one for each."
Oh. After a moment of silent thought I make a pronouncement.

"We can't let it be known that lesbians are the only ones that have fun." My competitive streak has come out, and for once John does not try to quell it. It is our turn to have raucous, loud, siesta sex. *Take that, lesbians!*

For the next week in this casa every siesta we find ourselves having loud, competitive sex with the lesbians, well, not *with* the lesbians, against the lesbians... not against the lesbians, oh, you know what I mean. It is the first time that I remember thinking of sex in competitive terms, but I don't mind it. John and I could still rock it.

***

Everyone knows that Mexico is a Catholic country, and they love their children, so of course they love the act of conception, at least it seems to literally follow. Mexico is muya romantico. The popular romantic song, Bésame Mucho (Kiss me a lot), was penned by a Mexican woman, Consuelo Velázquez. It is one of the three Mexican popular songs gringos know, the other two being Feliz Navidad (Jose Feliciano version) and the third being, La Bamba (Richie Valens slowed down version—the guy who died in the plane with Buddy Holly and changed his name from Ricardo Esteban Valenzuela Reyes). But I digress, my point is Mexico is romantic, sexy and macho.

Whenever John and I are late for something, by way of excuse, I say we are on Mexico time but John prefers to say we had a Cialis moment (whether we did or not). Such is the male ego around virility. So, it puts a smirk on my face when I find something at the local corner store in Mexico. I grab a can of pop out of the store refrigerator that has inadvertently caught my eye. It is called Sex Gasoline. I study the label in Spanish and notice a very suggestive phallic icon that says under it, "with Erectus." I look at the Spanish list of ingredients which does nothing to enlighten me, but I buy it if for no other reason than the joke value.

I show the Sex Gasoline can to John and mischievously suggest he should give it a try. He is not amused. The male ego does not take to joking about such things, and I think the pressure from the lesbians is getting to him. But, he takes the tack that the best defense is a good offense.

"Why don't you try it?" he suggests. And I think about it for a few moments. *Didn't I read somewhere that women took Viagra too?* For all I knew the lesbians *were* taking it. But I am no way going to risk Mexico's lax consumer product protection laws on my body. However, it gives me an idea for a scene I am writing.

In the historical novel I am writing my turn of the century heroine will take a shocking substance believed to enhance male virility. Myself, I take the Sex Gasoline can and push it to the back of the fridge and forget about it.

After that first day back, I have nicknamed John "nature boy," but I start to notice other occurrences of nature in our new casa that are not so fun for me.

My Spiderman

Mexican houses, built for Mexicans, frequently have features that Northerners don't appreciate. One such feature is the placement of a bed is usually predetermined by having a solid concrete pedestal permanently installed, at point of construction, where mattresses will be laying atop. To a Northerner this allows no possibility of moving the bed should you ever want to. It also predetermines the size of the bed and often disallows for the comfort of a box spring. But, it also disallows a space underneath in the dark where god knows what could hide. The Mexicans like to leave no possibilities for monsters or creepy crawlies under the bed.

Although I am fully aware that the tropics produce other creatures, in particular insects, that are larger and potentially more hostile, I have never seen any thus far, so I choose to believe what is out of sight does not exist.

While in modern Mexico it can be argued that the jungle has been pushed back significantly and the fear of any serious arthropods inside a dwelling may be a paranoid notion, it still is a reasonable concern where fast and dirty construction exists and doors and windows have large gaps that allow for a greater infiltration. And, even in the best houses, the simple truth is, you can never outright eliminate nature from coexisting and cohabitating with you.

John had trusted a sweet talking real estate agent (not Greta or Teresa) to find him this current casa on lesbian lane. It has been good enough for nature boy, but he knew he needed to have another lined up soon after my arrival. Meanwhile, I have to put up with this right angle-challenged construction that can only be described as sad. Not only are the kitchen cabinets visibly on a slant but the front door, besides being crooked, has a two inch high gap at its bottom that allows for an assortment of miniature Mexican friends to march right in and pay a visit. This makes me nervous, but at least we sleep on the second floor.

It is twilight and John has gone into town for a couple of hours to meet some people while I elect to stay home and organize things. I head into the second bedroom where we have unloaded all our extra luggage. I am about to start opening bags when I see a disturbing silhouette on the floor.

Another feature of Mexican interior design is whitewashed walls and light-colored floor tiles in order to easily spot anything that doesn't belong there, especially if it moves. This is one feature that I heartily agree with. The silhouette is a black body with eight large black legs that could comfortably cover a package of cigarettes. This is not a tarantula, though I know that they are definitely in the jungle a few minutes away, but it is almost as large and a big, big step up from a common large house spider of Northern climes.

First, let me explain to you the depth of my arachnophobia. Every roommate I have ever had, learned quickly that if Kathrin screams a blood curdling scream there is a 99% chance it means there is a spider in the room. I have never grown out of this fear. One time, I was invited to a New Year's eve party in a very nice penthouse apartment. It was a swell party and I was having a blast until someone pointed out that on a bookshelf in the living room there was a terrarium that contained a live tarantula. The boys, having pointed it out to me, were very amused at my terrified reaction and threatened to bring it out. To which I started hyperventilating simultaneous with panicked shrieks.

"No! no! no!" They found this so hilarious that they started to pretend to take the lid off of the terrarium to suggest they were going through with their threat. I ran to the bedroom and spent the rest of the party there with a pile of coats for company and became the unofficial coat check girl.

I react likewise at the sight of this enormous Mexican arachnid, running into our bedroom screaming even though there is no one around to hear me, and shutting the door behind me. Of course there is a one inch gap under the bedroom door, so I madly start stuffing any extra bedding under the door, going on the irrational assumption that the spider, having witnessed my reaction, would want to follow the crazy lady.

Having barricaded myself in, I jump onto our bed because the floor is now an evil, dangerous place. I start examining every inch of the floor and walls for similar ominous silhouettes. Any dark holes or deviations in the plaster have me in a panic. I am trying hard to relax and gain control of myself but it isn't working, so I switch on the satellite TV for distraction. Ironically, the first movie channel I flip to is showing *Spiderman*, with Spanish subtitles, and the next channel is playing *The Fly.* I muse that God is having a good laugh at me. I can hear my Zen teacher saying, "What you fear, is what you will attract." *Jeez, did it have to be spiders?*

At long last, I find something on the tube to watch that is utterly boring, completely in Spanish, but has nothing to do with insects. John returns to find his panicked princess sputtering out the details of her trauma from her carefully cordoned off area of the bed. He has lived with me long enough to know what his role will be.

Yes, John had gone native, but I now admit how much I need my wilderness warrior to come to my first world defense when it comes to creepie crawlies. The problem tonight is that no husband, partner or main squeeze can do this if they are away at the time you really need them.

I send my knight into the other room to do the dirty deed that I needed hours ago, but I refuse to watch. I suddenly remember a similar scene from the movie *Annie Hall* and wonder if I flip through the channels on the satellite TV if I might coincidentally find that movie dubbed in Spanish as well. *Did Woody Allen describe the spider in Annie Hall's bathroom as the size of a Limo, or the size of* a *Buick?* A little trivia to Google another day. I will describe that Mexican spider as the size of my fear, which is about the size of one of the expensive yachts in the 5-star marina.

John returns from the second room triumphant but admits that the spider was not only tropical-sized but as agile as Speedy Gonzáles and had presented a challenge. His squished body is dumped somewhere in the garden outside where I cannot find it, but having done this John looks at me with a sincere face.

"You know, spiders are good, they eat other insects."

This immediately starts my guilt engines, but I rationalize my irrational fear to John by giving him the facts. The chances of me falling asleep knowing that that spider is in the house is slim to none. He knows that is true. I will one day have to face my fears, but today is not it. And, little did I know there is more of the law of attraction to come, and not the good kind.

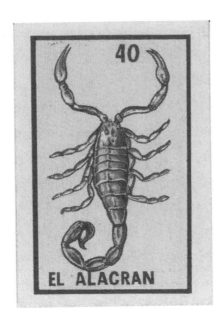

El Alacran

Tommy had once warned me while I was watering his garden to keep an eye out for scorpions. He sprayed for them, but you never knew. Inside his apartment he showed me what they looked like. He had a few dead ones preserved in alcohol in a glass jar that looked like a prop for Frankenstein's laboratory. They were small, perhaps an inch long. I asked if he had ever been stung and he said no, but one landed on his chest after falling from the roof of a palapa while he was under it. Apparently scorpions love palapas and owners are recommended to have them sprayed once a year whether they need it or not. Still, they looked small and innocuous having been neutralized in his little jar. I thought no more of it.

After my spider fright night I consoled myself that we would soon be vacating this Creepie Crawlie Casa, as I'd come to call it, for another rental, but until then I am on high alert. So when in the corner of my eye I think I see something move while reading on the bed I call John in from the other room and make him check under the nearest pieces of furniture. Nothing.

I settle into reading again. A few moments later at another part of the room I definitely see something move. Thanks to the Mexican preference for the white walls there is clearly something dark crawling across the ceiling. I'm sure John thinks I am crying wolf, and yet he comes and we both see it. On the ceiling is a sinister black scorpion three inches in length. The silhouette of a scorpion is so recognizable, like that of a spider, that it strikes a deep fear in me, less irrational because I know that the scorpion has a sting. And yet, I hate the idea of killing any living creature unnecessarily. At the same time, I do not want to find out what the sting of a scorpion feels like. Neither did I want John to find out.

John acknowledges this time that it is probably not wise to live with a scorpion in the bedroom and is ready to do the dirty deed of dispatch again. I beg him to be careful in his extermination of our foe as I don't know how toxic a scorpion sting can be.

"He's tiny, what is he going to do to me?" he says, sweeping aside my anxiety. It didn't look tiny to me, but John does everything but tut me under the chin to make me feel like I am an overreacting little woman. I dutifully leave the room, once again unable to witness the deed.

From down the stairs I hear a crash, then a *bang*!

"John!" I call out tentatively. I am answered by another crash and bang, then an anguished cry.

"Aaahhh!" I take the stairs two at a time, but halfway up it dawns on me that I am possibly being set up. Still moving forward with urgency I caution ahead.

"John, you better not be screwing with me!" I burst in the room to find him giggling on the bed. He was messing with me. But I am relieved rather than mad.

After that, I Google info about scorpions and interview people in town about how bad the local scorpion stings are. I find only one person who has been stung. In our area of Mexico they are mostly only a cut above a bee sting, but like a bee sting dangerous if you are allergic. Only a handful of deaths occur each year for those that are allergic. You can use ibuprofen with anti-histamines to help counter it, and ice and elevation of the area stung. You don't go to the hospital unless someone is having a reaction. I also find out that the bigger the scorpion the less potent the sting. It's the small ones you watch out for.

They are nocturnal creatures and like crabs at the beach, are probably hiding under rocks during the day, so I am directed to be careful when clearing in the yard. Once again, like spiders, scorpions' redeeming feature is they eat insects. But they can also eat geckos. Higher ledges on doors and windows are recommended to prevent scorpions and any creepy crawlies from getting in, but in Mexico I rarely see this in practice.

So, now that I have seen some of the other sides of tropical living in Mexico, I ask myself, *will I still brave it?* The answer comes back, *I will.* Without question. Even my phobias cannot stop me from enjoying our life in Mexico. Besides, I have my nature boy to help me, and we are leaving the Creepie Crawlie Casa in the morning for our new rental.

Se Renta (For Rent)

John picks up the keys to our new casa in the morning, and we start the process to move out of the Creepie Crawlie Casa. He has trusted the same real estate agent in their assessment of this new rental which he had only seen online which makes me wary. I have looked at the online pics too and it does look nice. It is much closer to town and only five blocks away so we foolishly decide we can roll our luggage on rock roads in the morning sun.

As we finally approach we notice a workman's battered pickup truck in the driveway. We had been told the house was ready so are wondering what maintenance is being done. Using the keys we have been given, we go in and find in the front hall a dismantled, dusty old air conditioner. Okay. On inspection of the first bedroom there are more things that should not be there, including clothes and tools. In fact, it is quite clear people are living here, and by the looks of it, a couple of working dudes. The casa is not only unready, it is occupied.

We take our bags back out on the street for a conference. John offers to hustle over to the real estate office while I wait with the luggage.

"Wait," I say as some renting-in-Mexico wisdom is now dawning on me. "Cover me."

I go back inside alone and create a list of everything that is at fault. I take a detailed inventory of what is lacking in the kitchen: missing small appliances, kitchen utensils and anything that needs cleaning. I check the bathrooms and which way the showerheads are facing. I flush the toilets. I look for papier hygenico (toilet paper) and cleaning materials. I turn lights and fans on and off.

John waits impatiently on the street looking tough in case the dudes who own the truck come back until I emerge with a list.

"Now you can go to the office."

He takes the list and my detailed verbal instructions to describe how pissed off I am. I am quite sure he will skip repeating it to the real estate agent but it makes me feel better. The office is only another four blocks away, but I am not rolling the luggage any further until I know where it is going for the night. I wait on the street in a small slice of shade.

Fortunately, John returns relatively quickly in a taxi cab.

"Que pasa?" I try out one of my fave Spanish phrases.

"We are going back," he announces. We load the bags in the cab as he explains that the real estate agent could not get a hold of the owner on the weekend to find out what was going on, but they have arranged for us to have at least a couple of free nights in what was supposed to be our former casa. I am not pleased. I realize how much I had been looking forward to leaving the Creepie Crawlie Casa and something snaps.

"We are going to Guadalajara."

"Huh?" John looks up.

"Give them three or four days to get their shit together, meanwhile we go to Guadalajara."

We had been talking about it anyways and there is still time to catch the bus. The bus station is conveniently beside the real estate office. I put a smaller bag together and John does as well. Taking all our valuables, we go to the real estate office and tell them our plans.

This time the real estate agent sees my unhappiness in person and I notice she is clutching my delivered list. Fortunate for her I am much more tempered now that I have a trip to look forward to. It is agreed, we are getting on a bus and they are going to "fix" things by the time we get back on Tuesday. I swear to John that it is the last time we will ever rent a place in Mexico without physically seeing it first.

Guadalajara - Bus Ho!

There are three kinds of buses in Mexico for travelling longer distances. Surprisingly, the first two can be described as super nice and nice, and the third is God awful, below econo. Tommy tells me that this is the way with everything in Mexico, pay a little more for top tier and it will be well worth it. Go down from middle tier and it is a long, long way down and you'll regret it.

For buses, the bottom tier is close to the little local funky buses, already described, that are rumored to be out of service buses donated by Germany. They try to hold them together and make them last a few more decades, and actually succeed in doing so. I'd say it was a triumph in recycling but the air care standards for these buses are a few decades past their best before dates so I'm not sure where that puts the funky buses on the environmental band wagon.

On the other side of the spectrum, the super nice, deluxe buses are the ETN. If I can speak fondly of travel buses, these are the ones I will speak fondly of. On the normal Greyhounds I grew up with there was always two seats on each side of the aisle. Not so, on the ETNs. There are two seats on one side for companions and one seat on the other, just for you, whoever you are. Oodles of leg room ahead and behind that I could hardly believe from a country where space can be conservatively spare. I could literally walk a full circle around that single seat. Then I found out why. They fold out and lay almost entirely flat, like your own personal lazy boy. I was in bus heaven.

It took us five hours to get to our destination. Guadalajara is terrific except for one thing, my travelling companion. Not that I don't love John to pieces, but Guadalajara Old Town area has the largest, three story, six square blocks open market space in all of Latin America, locally called, The Mercado or Mercado Libértad. Shopping! Bargain hunting. And me, without a girlfriend to appreciate it (my detachment for possessions was temporarily repressed in Guadalajara). John, like most guy guys, has the attention span of a gnat when it comes to shopping (unless it is for men's dress shirts, John loves his shirts).

The other kind of shopping that Guadalajara Old Town is known for is bridal. It is impossible not to notice the seemingly endless bridal shops with the mega displays of poofy dresses in whatever colors you can imagine. If you want fairytale princess tresses with all the gaudy accessories you can dream up, this is where you need to be. Like all other things in Mexico, they are not afraid of color and I love that. Ballroom princess dresses in bright blues, purples, oranges, reds, golds, hot pinks and hotter pinks are all acceptable. Pastels are for wimps. Cascades of tulle, lace, gathers, embroidery and embellishments are used unabashedly, subtlety be damned. I had noticed before that in Mexico clothing designs for women have an amazing ability to combine "girl next door" with "slutty tramp" in perfect balance. You can never point your finger directly at one tendency or the other in one outfit. I figure it must be the Catholic influence.

Lined up in great long rows like tempting candy are the most colorful dresses in these shops and they are not bridal. They are the quincenara dresses, or sweet fifteen dresses for the traditional coming out parties. They are like prom or graduation dresses on steroids, as if every girl gets to live out her Cinderella fantasy in Disney Technicolor, and she doesn't even have to get married to do it (if you want to see a fantastical feast for the eye go to Google Images and plug in quincenara dresses).

I am looking at the endless rows of mannequins wearing full skirt ballroom dresses thinking there must be mirrors to achieve the effect. But they are there; lined up like those terra cotta warriors in China ready to go, not to a war, but to a ball.

John ignores these shops, both as a typical guy response but I know it is also to avoid the subject of the no-ring-on-my-finger-yet conversation. A bit of a sore point for me. It has been a few years and I am not getting any younger. I've never been a bride. He hints at the idea sometimes but I wonder, *will he ever get around to popping the question?* I refuse to bring the subject up... besides I am not sure if I am ready either. I quickly put that subject out of my mind for another day.

John, instead of shopping, wants to go straight for the classical Spanish Colonial architecture to ogle, but I manage to drag him through the Mercado first. It is like being with an impatient child. We go through it at record speed and the inventory is staggering, from panchos to parrots, from leather goods to specialty foods, from sombreros to shoes. I leave it all too fast dreaming one day I might come back with a girlfriend or two in tow and find its many treasures.

Next stop, architecture. People in Guadalajara Oldtown, tourist central, are too sweet. More than once, we would stop and scratch our heads wondering where we were going and people would immediately approach us and ask, in English, if we were lost and could they help us. They are proud of their town and very gracious.

While tourist stuff can be fun, there are only so many museums, cathedrals, sculptures and art that a body can take, even if it has classical Spanish Colonial architecture surrounding it. We go back to our hotel and I am done for the night. It is so nice being in a cushy hotel bed with never a thought of creepy crawlies that I am blissed out in appreciation.

John cannot stay in. His toes and ears are itchy for the nightlife of music and dance. He had made some inquiries before we left Libé about where to go for music. Now here, he discovers exactly how late late night life is in the big G city. He is wandering around to several bars asking "musica vivo?" He keeps getting the same response. Most bars and clubs with live music and dancing do not even open their doors until 11 p.m., 10 p.m. if you are lucky. The tango dance halls typically open at 2 a.m. he is told. John is out looking at 8 p.m. Classic gringo mistake.

When he told me later what happened it sounded like a bad Mexican joke, and maybe it was, but with a happy ending...

A gringo is barhopping in Guadalajara looking for white wine and live music. The first bar he goes into is dark and smoky and has only two windows. The bartender asks what he is drinking.

"Vino blanco," he replies. The barkeep shakes his head and gives him a firm response.

"Tequila solamente." (only tequila)
The gringo orders a Tequila, drinks that, but the live music won't be for hours so he goes to the next bar.

The next bar he goes into is dark and smoky and has only one window. The bartender asks what he is drinking.

"Vino blanco," he replies. The barkeep shakes his head and gives him a firm response.

"Cerveza ou Tequila solamente." (only beer or tequila)
The Gringo orders a Corona, drinks that, but the live music won't be for hours so he and goes to the next bar where someone has told him they play his favorite music, the blues.

On his way to the next bar the gringo picks up some white wine (vino blanco) at a store and puts it in his back pack.

The third bar he goes into is dark and smoky and has no windows. The bartender asks what he is drinking.

"Vino blanco," he replies. The barkeep shakes his head and gives him a firm response.

"Vino Tinto, Cerveza ou Tequila seulemente." (only red wine, beer or tequila)

To which the gringo takes the white wine out of his pack sack and says in his broken Spanish, "You buy this wine from me and then sell it back to me."

The family who owns the bar, including the mama, the papa and the son, who is the bartender, get together and try to figure out what the crazy gringo wants. Finally they buy his white wine, pour it and charge him extra to sit and drink his vino blanco. By this time, they are at the hour for live music. A large Mexican woman singer comes out with the band and starts. She belts out the best blues the gringo has ever heard. By this time, he has had enough tequila, beer and wine that he sings along, gets up and dances up a storm and everyone is happy: the owners, the patrons, the singer, the band and the gringo.

The moral of the story is:
If you want to drink in Guadalajara you should like tequila, beer or red wine, but if you are a white w(h)iner and want to sing the blues then you have to find the win(e)-win(e) yourself.

I said it was a bad joke.

Over the next day or two we did a few more tourist things and then took the long bus ride back to Libé. There is no place like home.

***

When we report into the real estate office we are told that the working guys who were "friends" of the owners, have been evicted and the casa has been cleaned and updated. It is ready. With some trepidation we go back to it with our bags for a repeat performance that we hope has a better ending. There is no dusty pick up in the driveway. No air conditioner parts in the hall. We have a brand new microwave and blender in the kitchen and several kitchen utensils are brand new. The place is spotless and well stocked. The agent has taken care of my list. We have a new place to stay.

The Squatter Casa

Despite the upgrades our new rental house which we now call the Squatter Casa is not the best place in Libé. It has one big problem. It is too shady. I mean literally too dark. We learn that if houses here are too dark without enough windows or cross breeze it may mean that it is cool for the hot months, but it also means that in the summer and fall rainy seasons it will get mildew.

A musty scent is common in those Libé homes that are on the dark side. It looks good online, but when you move in after a rainy season you understand their flaw. They were not designed or positioned correctly for either air flow or sun. We find out pretty quickly at The Squatter Casa that we need to be on a daily dose of anti-histamines and I know I need to do something.

"What can you do?" John shrugs while I look into his red eyes.

"Exorcism," I answer.

I go to a couple of the small local grocery corner stores and clear out half a dozen large scented candles, and another half a dozen of no-scent candles. The no-scent ones are in tall glasses with the stenciled full color images of Jesus or Mary on the outside. John sees me unpack my shopping on the kitchen table and begins to think I am not kidding about exorcism. The truth is the religious candles are the only candles you can always find at any corner store in Mexico but I let John get nervous.

I put them strategically around our bedroom and light them for a few hours, closing the door but keeping the window open a crack. These are concrete houses so fire is not a fear. It generates enough heat and dryness to get rid of the mustiness. John is surprised that it works to reduce our itchy eyes, and looks on me as if I am a witchy sorceress who can cast evil demons from a house.

While my mildew exorcism works, it is not ideal. Ideally you want houses properly positioned and aired out regularly. This is our take-away for when we will build. Also a de-humidifier is a great added appliance which you can rarely find in Mexico but can be used in the rainy season to keep it nice, but you have to have property managers for that. If you have a second floor, the windows upstairs are ideally tinted so the upstairs doesn't get too hot (hot air rises). The windows need to open and be strategically placed to catch the breezes. Other ways to air out and cool the rooms are skylights, or to get air downstairs the traditional Mexican design is for an air tunnel (fully open mini courtyards) or copulas in the center of the house that are open at the roof which acts like natural air conditioning. The Squatter Casa has a small air tunnel in its centre and we enjoy eating breakfast there every morning as the only bright spot in the house.

While the Squatter Casa's downside is its darkness, its upside is that it is a little closer to town and also close to the town's football field. Location, location, location?

Two Kinds of Football (and a Marching Band)

I am dreaming that I am back in Canada and back at work, back at my old job, but nobody expects me to work—no one expects anyone to work—instead everyone is dancing. My boss and co-workers are all together cutting a rug. Then, into the room comes a marching band. I thought this was less than danceable music, but it was music, keep dancing. But it is loud, very loud, so loud that I open my eyes to my Squatter Casa bedroom, bursting the world of my dream, but the sound of a bugle blowing reveille and the taps of the marching drum don't disappear. I glance over at the clock, 8:00 a.m. My fuzzy on-vacation-and-up-late-last-night morning mind slowly calculates whether this is a weekday or a weekend. It's a weekday. I start to think whether there had been mention of yet another Mexican holiday, and can't recall. I roll over to John.

"A marching band just marched into my dream," I tell him. He is awake too.

"At first I thought it was construction," he says. "Who does a marching band at 8:00 in the morning through a suburban neighborhood on a weekday?" We both silently know the answer: Mexico.

The soccer field, or futbol field, as it is in Mexico, is only one street over from our casa but the marching band that celebrates our local futbol heroes needs practice marching on streets and has taken a trip through the neighborhood. After a half hour of regaling us with their incredibly loud renditions they move to another part of town. By then, I am up, dressed and starting on breakfast, but John stubbornly stays in bed until the other noises of Mexico hit their full fury including the gas guy, the water guy, and miscellaneous other noises, before he acknowledges defeat.

John loves soccer or what is called football in the rest of the world. When I met him, he played a pick up game that had lasted ten years, religiously every Sunday, but the group was disbanded due to bureaucratic bickering over the use of the public field. Last season, John noticed there was a pick up game of local guys in the Libé public futbol field, no gringos, just locals. So, before coming down this season he made a point to pack his cleats. Was it a coincidence that our new rental casa was close enough to the soccer field that John could keep an eye on the action? Perhaps. It wasn't long before he figured out the team's regular schedule.

The language of soccer is truly an international one. All over the world there are assembled groups of men and women who hang out at a field, choose sides and then hit the turf. All you need is a pair of shoes and you're in. In some cases you don't even need the shoes. In some cases no one even has a proper ball. That is the beauty of soccer. It's played everywhere at every level of income.

So there is John, hanging out at the futbol field in Libé when the pick up team is choosing sides. A bald, middle aged gringo wearing cleats, hovering at the sidelines with that little boy look in his eyes that says, *let me play with you.* He is a towering, pale, sore thumb standing out among the younger, shorter sun-kissed natives. But they give him a side to play on. They take him in. Because that's what they do, all over the world.

These young men grew up with soccer in a way that no Canadian or American does. We are much better versed in the other "football," the football that conversely doesn't really involve the ball next to the foot a whole lot. For futbol, these kids know how to dance with the ball at their feet. Their ball control is terrific. In comparison, John is big and unrefined, but he is relentless and fast.

Due to the multi-cultural nature of Western Canada John is used to playing with kids from every country who were brought up with the sport. At his pick-up game in Canada they called him Johnny Long Legs. Ironically, dancing guy doesn't dance with the ball, but he is respected. In Libé, he is unknown to them. That, and he can't understand what they are saying in Spanish.

Each time he passes the ball his new teammates let out a groan of disgust. *The big, stupid gringo has done it again.* John keeps passing the ball to the opposition thinking they are his teammates. It seems they all know each other and know who is on whose team without any uniforms and John can't figure it out. After so many goof ups, his new teammates quickly strip off their shirts, which they are loath to do in "winter" (a winter we would kill for at summer time in Canada but is chilly by Mexican standards). They are now playing shirts and skins so the big gringo can figure out who his teammates are.

Now the game starts to rock and roll. His teammates see that those long legs don't have fancy footwork but can still strip them of the ball and pass it down the field to the right guy. He comes home to me sweaty, dirty and with a big sloppy grin on his face. *Ah, do men ever grow up?* I don't think so.

John keeps going to the pick-up games on occasion but he also checks out the field on the weekends for any league games to watch. Today, there is a big one. The crowds are out and we decide to go. When we get to the gate they are charging 2 pesos (20 cents), when it is normally free so we know it is a big finals game.

We find some other gringos in the crowd. They let us know that this is a finals match between Libé's team and San Michele's, the town that has the crocodile sanctuary. Apparently, the two towns have a long standing rivalry and the crowds for both teams are out in their squads. These are not like Japanese organized cheering clubs, but they have their own Mexican style and charm.

Our team is in yellow and black stripes and whenever our team scores a goal, wins a call, or some other triumph, a spray of super-sized yellow and black confetti is released on the field. Each piece is about the size of the palm of your hand, made of some kind of crepe paper. Its weightlessness allows the breeze to pick it up and carry it. Imagine a black and yellow bumble bee cloud that drifts across the field gradually settling and you have the picture. Of course there are cheers and songs that go along too, but much of the time there is complete, serious focus on the game.

John and I laugh how these amateur players have the professional league diving drama down perfectly. A player is fouled, but along with the foul the injured player is rolling and writhing on the ground in a fashion that would have non-soccer people calling 9-1-1. His face is contorted in horrible pain. Yet, as soon as the ref delivers the yellow or red card or whatever the ruling, he has hopped right back up on his feet looking fit as ever and, this is the part I like, he has no remorse or cover up at how he was so obviously faking. I was told that this is so the ref will take it seriously for all the times that he misses things but it's still hilarious to me.

I have one of my writer fantasies of a drama teacher hired to teach a soccer team realistic diving dramatics. But, as soon as the drama teacher asks for them to "stay in character," to "show the pain" and transition to a gradual recovery, a coach comes in and says, "Ref calls it, get on your feet, ready to play." Coach trumps drama teacher.

Unfortunately our boys lose but the gringos have another football game to look forward to, a super one.

***

Being in Mexico in winter means we are there during the road to the Super Bowl. John knows I am not a fan. One could even say I am an anti-fan. I even asked him during our very early courtship if he watched football, trying to screen out NFL, AFL or CFL lovers. He answered that he had played a little "ball" in high school but he didn't watch it now. That was a partial lie. He wasn't watching it then because his TV was on the fritz, not because he wasn't a fanatic. Perhaps I should feel complimented that he wanted to keep seeing me enough to lie.

I remind him of this painful lie every time I see him talking to the screen with passionate delivery that I wish he would reserve only for singing the praises of our love. Okay, that is clearly asking too much. He is a jock and I did know that. But, he is a jock that reads, gets cold when I do and dances, and that's why I love him.

In the movie, *Shall We Dance*, Stanley Tucci plays a character that pretends to like football but his secret passion is dancing. When Richard Gere uncovers him and asks him incredulously, "You don't like football?" I love Tucci's answer.

"Run three yards, fall down, pile up, run three yards, fall down, pile up. After four months of that I am ready to put a gun to my head."

I feel the same as Tucci, but my dance loving husband sees no such contradiction. He loves both kinds of football and dancing too.

In Mexico, when he watches the NFL at our casa it is all in Spanish. We have fun imitating the Mexican announcers, "Incompletooo!" but he frequently turns the sound down for my benefit. And, when it gets to the big Super Bowl day we have plans to go out.

Being an expat town the public parties for Super Bowl abound at every big restaurante. We have chosen a favorite place, *Natcho's*, where there will be a big crowd. For 100 pesos (less than $10) they offer a great burger, fries, satellite TV, big screen projection, one free beer and a joyous party under an enormous palapa. The mood is celebratory and the bets are flying as I listen to my "played a little ball" husband explain the game in an expertise that has others bobbing their heads in respect that I can only guess at. There are all kinds of North American football fans: American ex-pats, Canadian ex-pats, all the tourists, Mexican fans and even the French Canadians in Mexico including John's football buddy, Lou, who I call his NFL twin.

I can't really fake that I am not a fan and the most important part about this game for me is that I will be eating a burger and fries which is a treat for me. I do like the social flow of it and just watching the crazy football fans and their passion. John teases me that I choose the side I want to root for by their uniform and logo on their helmets, which is true. I actually got a little interested in the helmets this year and let our section of watchers know about the history of the Pittsburg Steelers logo and what the three colors represent. The watchers were impressed for about three seconds before they started talking about players and offense again. I felt like Sheldon on the *The Big Bang Theory*, except Sheldon's character, being a Texan, was forced at an early age to know all about football (only a writer who appreciates character development, or a fan of the show would remember this).

As a woman, the thing I notice enough to keep me interested in the game are the players' tight little butts that those uniforms show off. As a creative type, I notice the only thing I can recognize as self-expression in the game, the touchdown dances. Other than those things I am less interested on what is going on on the screen and more interested in the action in the restaurante. First, I order my burger before any one else. I don't care who wins, I am getting fries and a burger! Second, I am not immune to a little gambling and on the way back from the washroom I pick some squares on the football pool for the score and put my pesos down. Anything to make the game a little more interesting to me.

I tell John afterward that I have put a bet on the pool for "us" thinking how nice that is for me to share. Wrong, oh wrong.

"What did you bet? What spread? Favoring who? What quarter?" The questions zoom past me and I can only answer how much money I gave the nice man. John races up and finds my name on the board. He doesn't look too happy when he gets back.

"You didn't even bet my team!" He looks exasperated, the way I look when he has returned with the wrong brand of laundry soap from the store after I have given him the name and a specific, detailed description of the bottle that he has already been using for years (I now just keep empty bottles and packages of things and hand him the whole thing to go to the store with).

"I just went with what was open," I reply, which is true as I was told by the nice man that all the favored squares were taken. The people around us are listening in and laughing. They have the right spirit. One guy, a fan of the other team, tells John he will take him on a side bet and they put 200 pesos on the outcome. The spirit of the party is there and Superbowl has started.

I am always up for watching a sporting event in a group because I like how the audience becomes a collective in its oos and aahs. Now obviously in this group not every one is rooting for the same team but there is enough who are under the same palapa roof that you get that effect. The sound of what I imagine group sex must sound like when everyone is climaxing at the same time, or at least trying to.

Well into the first quarter, my burger and fries arrive and I am the only one eating, and thoroughly enjoying it. The smell of it, and probably the silent energy waves of happiness I am giving off starts a chain reaction and everyone starts ordering their burgers. By second quarter, people are hungry but there isn't much coming out of the kitchen quickly. They are thoroughly backed up. The kitchen staff are overwhelmed. This goes right into halftime when there are 100 people very, very hungry all waiting for orders while I am chomping on a toothpick and burping. They don't like me.

They announce the first of the pool winners from first and second quarter picks and my name is announced. John looks at me baffled. I forgot I did have two squares, that nice man did suggest I might bet the quarters as well as there were better spots left. I get my prize and sit down. Now they really hate me, but I am loving this football thing for the first time.

In the second half, the burgers start getting distributed and people get happy again and the mood lightens. The oos and ahhs start to ramp up as the end of game gets closer. Before it ends I take a walk out of the palapa and into the street for a breather.

Outside, the sun is setting with a beautiful pink smear across the sky. *It is February*, I have to remind myself. I look toward the ocean and see the classic view of silhouetted palm trees. Some young Mexican kids are passing a soccer ball back and forth in the street; they are barefoot. I wonder what they think of us loco gringos. Too much money and not aware of how good we have it, or is that really true? I look at the joy on their faces. Unlike football, life is not so easy to figure out who are the winners and who are the losers.

John has lost his bet, his team didn't come through, but it is a beautiful night to walk home and console my jock who lied to me about his NFL addiction. One football season is over and the football widows breathe a sigh of relief.

The French Front

The first French European settlers in Quebec were completely dependent on the native population to learn how to survive the harsh winters. Over 200 years later with easier transportation it is not hard to see why so many Quebecois are Snowbirds. The neighbouring town to Libé, Paloma, is favoured by many French Canadians perhaps because it is less expensive, but there is a French contingent in Libé as well.

In Canada, French language classes are mandatory for three years in high school but being from the West side of Canada we rarely practice. Most French Canadians, however, speak English fluently or very well, albeit with a charming Quebecois accent. Such is true of Louis, or Lou as we call him. Lou is John's NFL football twin, and that's how John befriended him and we fell into The French Front.

Before I arrived at the Creepie Crawlie Casa, John frequently saw a round shaped older gentleman at his front porch in the casa next door. The man always had a glass of red wine and a book or a paper. This was Lou. He struck up a conversation with Lou who has a happy puppy face, thick glasses and an even thicker Quebecois French accent. They soon found out that they both had a passion for NFL football, wine and thrift. They could both speak knowledgeably about the NFL, wine was for drinking not for snootiness, and finding the best deals in town was second nature. And, when they combined these things they were both in bliss.

Lou drives all the way down to Libé from Quebec in his beat up van to get away from the same winters his ancestors could not escape. His casa is a two bedroom next to the Creepie Crawlie. He takes John into the spare bedroom and shows him a sight to behold. The room is filled with cases and cases of red wine from Spain.

"I got them for less than $3 a bottle at every Sam's Club in Mexico on my way here," he explains. "First store, I packed up four cases in my van right away."

"Why was it so cheap Lou?" John was sceptical. Lou shrugged.

"John, I don't know and I don't care."

"Are you going to be able to drink it all here?"

"Lord, love a duck! I'll be here for another five months, John." John examined the label.

"But what if you hadn't liked it Lou?"

"I would drink it anyway," he answers quickly. John laughs at the answer. Lou pours John a glass and they sit down to watch the game. John admitted the wine was not bad.

The physical contrast in the two men could not be more pronounced. As typical of men of French heritage, Lou was on the shorter side, and John, as typical of men with Dutch heritage, was on the tall side. John was sleek and athletic. While Lou might have been svelte in his younger years, he was rounding out in his retirement years. John didn't have a strand of hair on the top of his head, while Lou had a mop on top, snowy as it was. It was when I saw them watch football together that I saw it. They were NFL twins. They had the same posture. They leaned forward at the same time. They had the same gesticulations when something was good on the field, and the same when something was bad.

"Did you see that?!" One of them would cry. The other would nod emphatically, not even needing an explanation. They knew exactly when to talk and went to shut up. I ask the wrong questions at the wrong time. I find things funny that are serious and take things serious that are deemed minor. Fortunately, as an Amazon working woman, who has returned to Mexico after making some dollars in the Northlands, I am forgiven.

John finding his NFL football twin, Lou, in Mexico opens us up to a circle of French men and women in Mexico. Soon we are invited to the coveted taco Tuesdays nights in the Barrio for the hungry but thrifty. A family run restaurant called Alvaro's is the spot. John and I were the only "Anglos" in the swell of French Canadians.

Because Spanish and French are both romantic languages, many of them spoke Spanish decently, and like Lou they came here every year. We find we are straddling three languages in the conversation at the dinner table.

The Alvaro family, who own the taco restaurante, start firing up their spits and grills at about 6 p.m. and open at 7 p.m. They give you six choices on the menu:

1. Chicken Tacos
2. Beef Tacos
3. Chorizo tacos
4. Pork Tacos
5. The Volcano (super spicy meat) tacos
6. Quesadillas

First, a large disc platter of compartmentalized bowls with an array of toppings is brought in like a UFO landing at each table. Tortillas the size of a small plate, dried to a crisp are served to eat the toppings with. No knives or forks here. The toppings include the freshest salsa, three kinds of hot sauces, pickled vegetables, avocado sauce, radishes, corn, beans and an assortment of other toppings, all centered on the wheel before you.

Because The French Front have been coming here on the same night for years during the season, the Alvaro family treats them well. One of the group asks for something special and a steaming hot skillet with something in it I can't see is brought out. It is onions. They call them "cebollas frites" or fried onions, pronounced, saboyas freetas, one of those Spanish word pairings that rolls off the tongue both figuratively and literally. The onions are fried in the drippings from the meat spits. I can't get enough of them. Yum! And, I can't believe they throw them in for free. Thank you to my trilingual friends whose patronage kept up that good will.

Beers are only a dollar a bottle, and Lou and John are happy because they can bring their own wine. We joke in English, out of earshot of our hosts, that two words we never want Mexicans to learn are "corkage fee."

I am not much of a drinker of alcohol and I don't like drinking sugary pops either but it is suggested that I try one of the taco place's homemade non-alcoholic drinks. At almost every small dinette or taco restaurante there is inevitably two enormous jugs of iced liquids, one white, the other purple. I had been wondering about these for a long time before I am encouraged by my French Canadian friends to try them. The white water is rice water. I am not fond of it, but the purple is called jamaica (pronounced hamaika), a delicious and refreshing iced tea made from hibiscus flowers and sweetened lightly. It gives me something wine-looking to suck back at the table as the teetotaler among our wine loving French Canadians.

Later on, I will recognize the great big bags of dried dark red leaves in the grocery store and start making it myself. It makes the best iced drink, chock full of anti-oxidants to boost the immune system and noted to give relief from high blood pressure, high cholesterol, liver disease, as well as digestive and inflammatory problems.

Some of the other characters on The French Front were Rayann and Daniel who were a singing duo, and one of the many favorite musicians / singers who come down and pay some of their way by doing gigs for the gringos in English (and French). Then there was Alberto and Camille who we called Callie. Callie crochets up a storm when she comes down and supplies all of us with enough dish cloths to last us for the next decade. There is Frances, Lou's younger wife, who is still working like me and would often make it down later on. She is attracted to Mexican babies and cuddles, baby Romy, the latest members of the Alvaro extended family, with so much cooing and singing lullabies in French that Lou starts to get jealous.

"Lord, love a duck, why don't you fondle me that way?"

As well as crocheting, Callie is a very good cook and bakes as well. One day, while chatting she teaches me her secret for baking in Libé. She buys raw dough from bakers in town (pizza and pie) rather than try to make it from scratch with the limited supplies here.

John listening in suddenly says, "Will you teach me to make an apple pie?"

"Yeah, sure," she says, "the easy way."

Sure enough, the next day she takes my big timid baker into the kitchen and shows him how to roll dough, slice and season apples and bake a pie. I am so happy, predicting my future will be filled with John-baked pies (that never materialized).

But it is Callie who shows me that with leftover dough you take one whole apple, and assuming you have a coring tool, you core it, place it on a square of leftover dough, fill the core with sugar, cinnamon and nutmeg and wrap the apple up and bake it with the pie whole. It is so yummy that it is better than the apple pie itself.

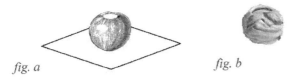

fig. a   *fig. b*

Callie is not the only French cook in the region by a long shot.

Wherever the French are, great food follows. We know the local specialties in food: tacos, chile rellenos, excellent fresh fish and seafood in a variety of sauces—this is a fishing village after all—as well as the juiciest chicken I have ever eaten (I assume it was free run since I see them running around town often enough), and excellent local steaks for half the price. But then there is the French Food department.

When John had first discovered Libé by crewing on the sailboat, one of the things that he emailed me about that inspired furious envy in me was The French Baker. Imagine, while I was freezing my fanny in the Northlands, John was waking to a sun-filled morning in the middle of a placid, paradise lagoon on a small sailing yacht. The coffee was brewing in the galley while a man steered his little ponga boat alongside. The little boat had a royal blue banner across it announcing "The French Baker" and a waft of fresh baked goodies would immediately follow.

The French Baker was Etienne who runs a café and bakery in town. Unlike our Canadian French friends Etienne is French French. He has the most popular café in town for its quaint street-side charm and its fresh baked goods with full espresso services. But, the enterprising Etienne had found a new market niche. Rather than wait for people to come to him he takes his little ponga out to each of the sailboats anchored in the lagoon, which could number anywhere from 15 to 60 boats with at least two people on each.

He takes their orders for baguettes, croissants and assorted pastries and returns the next morning with goodness fresh from his ovens. If I was up early enough, I would see him filling up his boat and taking it out to the lagoon, glad for my thighs that I wasn't on board one of those boats, but a little envious too.

We enjoy seeing our French friends and regularly share wine with Callie and Alberto who are also in the Fraccionamiento at the casa they rent every year. To get there we have to walk by our very empty corner lot—the piece of ground we own and went through so much trauma to get, but sits there hosting a tangle of weeds.

John and I get good at walking past it without looking at it any more, but inside we both wonder *what are we going to do with it?* Other people are wondering the exact same thing.

The CLC

If we thought we could put our lot out of our minds we were wrong. Greta and Teresa start to ask us if we are ever going to build a house on the beautiful corner lot they sold us. We tell them that it isn't in the cards financially this year, but we are working on it. Still, Greta insists we take a look at a freshly built white house on another corner lot two blocks away. They had sold it to a new couple in town, Hud and Ida, who quickly built a beautiful house on it.

We look at it from the outside and wow it is beautiful. It is a three story casa capped by an enormous palapa on the top floor. The house is grandly snowy white and even the walls around the house are white. This is not unheard of but rare in this color-centric country. From the outside there are small touches that are unique like the tiling outside the gate, the globe ceramic lights atop the wall and the extra deck on the second floor. Like many of the cooler houses in the neighborhood, if you peek at whatever can be seen above the perimeter wall it just makes you want to see inside all the more.

So, we decide to do our usual. We knock at their gate and demand to see their house, but in a nice way. A willowy brunette and a man who could have been a double to a younger Gary Bussey have come to the door. John uses the usual opening.

"Hi, my name's John and this is Kathrin, we know Greta and Teresa, we have a lot in the neighborhood we haven't built on yet and we would love to look at your beautiful new house."

We are in just like that. It works every time. They are giving us a full tour of the house from the kitchen-dining area to the garage that holds a collection of Hud's jet skis, to the master suite with idyllic ensuite, to the palapa bar on the roof. By the time we are done we have become friends and are planning a get-together.

"By the way," the happy-go-lucky Hud asks, "which is your lot?" John describes our corner lot. As he does, I notice Hud and Ida exchange a serious glance.

"They're the ones!" Hud declares.

Oh, oh, I think, we've already offended our new friends in some way. Perhaps it was before we cleaned up the lot when it had overgrown and someone had spilled some garbage on it, and Greta and Teresa had contacted us long distance and asked if they could get it cleaned for us for $50. *Were Hud and Ida the people that had complained before our lot was cleaned up?* John and I look at Hud's stern face in anticipation.

"You stole our lot!" he says. *Huh. What is he saying?* John and I look on dumbfounded. But I start to see a twinkle in Hud's eye. His Gary Bussey crooked grin transforms into a laugh and Greta starts to giggle. They owe us a story.

"I found photos of the corner lot you bought online and phoned from California wanting to buy it. The real estate agent we talked to here—" He then mentions the name of the large international real estate office that used to be owned by Nancy and Byron. "—said if I came down right away they could secure the lot for me. I booked a flight and was down the next day."

Hud proceeded to tell us that once they got him in their office they insisted he look at all the other real estate they had. He was polite, for awhile, but kept on insisting that he wanted to close on the corner lot he had seen online. Online pictures of Mexican real estate are consistently out of date, even more unreliable than other places. It took the new realtors at that large international real estate office two days to admit to him that the lot was no longer for sale. He walked out furious and from referrals walked into Teresa and Greta's office, who had been the original listers of the lot he wanted—a lot that John had already closed on.

Teresa had said, "You cannot buy that lot, but I have another corner lot one block away. It isn't as close to the beach but it is every bit as nice a lot." Hud was deflated but agreed to see it. When he saw it he realized it was an almost identical corner and wondered why the other office hadn't shown it to him.

"Not that I would have bought from them after they wasted my time for three days." He grunted.

We promise him our full real estate story if they come to dinner with us that night, which is exactly what happens and it cements our friendship along with a collective margarita-induced promise to improve our Spanish.

I wake up with little memory of the evening with them other than a lot of laughter. Laughter has a wonderful amnesia effect that way. But I do remember that we had all agreed to go to school, tomorrow.

The next day, the four of us meet at a Spanish language class run out of the Fraccionamiento. It has been set up by a Canadian woman we had already gotten to know a little.

In class, we are each asked our level of Spanish and why we want to learn. Hud speaks up first.

"You know those announcements they make going down the street?" He means the mobile megaphone advertising. "I just want to know if they are selling tomatoes or telling me the tsunami is coming!" The class breaks into laughter.

Ida and John quickly go to the head of the class as the teacher's pets, diligently having studied their verb tenses. Hud and I sit in the back like a couple of dolts trying to absorb whatever our English programming will allow us to. I am pretty sure Hud is also nursing a hangover, which I already know the local term for is "cruda." I teach it to Hud as a more relevant term he can use immediately and he brightens. Pretty soon he and I are giggling at the back of the class and making up new words to the sharp glances of Ida, John, the teacher and the other serious students.

Today's lesson is on fruits, vegetables and terms in the kitchen. We learn that some terms in Mexico are very much local words and not necessarily what you will find in a dictionary. We are also reminded that Js are pronounced as Hs.

Tomato is Jitomate (pronounced Heetomat)

Beans are Frijoles (pronounced Free-holays)

Garlic is Ajo (pronounced Ah-ho)

I lean over to Hud.

"So if someone calls you an ajo, don't get upset." The giggles start again. We are bad Spanish students. After class, John and Ida decide that we are not allowed to sit together again.

***

Janine of Casa Janine, Tommy's wife, has started joining Tommy in Mexico more and more. Janine is a petite little thing and like Tommy her body does not belie her age. She is ripped. They have become one of our favorite "couple" friends to yak with in their garden over some Dos Equis. But now we want to introduce our two favorite American couples to each other, over a dinner party. Hud and Ida, former Californians, and Tommy and Janine, living between Texas and Mexico, but I have one big concern. Tommy is an expert level surfer but Hud is a jet ski expert.

I don't know enough about the battle over the surf, but from what little I do know I believe surfers and jet skiers may not always be compatible. *Am I setting up two species that don't belong together?* Like the faux pas of asking a very right-wing Republican to dine with a very left-wing Democrat, but instead of political differences I may be setting up a surf turf war at the dinner table? These are things

John never considers or stresses over, so I take a page from his book and leave it alone.

The party starts with some beverages and gets lively quickly. Not only are these couples getting along, but the stories and laughs are flying. John and I are not introverts at all, yet for the first time I feel like we are polite Canadians and can barely get a word in edgewise to these gregarious Americans.

Then, my fear is realized. The subject of jet skiing comes on the table. Quiet. I look carefully at Tommy who I've known a lot longer than Hud to see if he is trying to mask any disgust. *Texans do play poker, right?*

Pretty soon it is out in the open that we have a jet skier with a surfer and they start to talk about the love of the waves that they have in common. Tommy is a business owner in Texas and Mexico, but suddenly I see a side of this man I've never heard before. I had never heard him talk surfer dude talk before, but suddenly if I had a dollar for every time he says "gnarly" and "bitchin" I would have made a tidy profit.

Hud and Tommy start to launch on their tales, tragedies and triumphs of the tides, and I am reminded of the scene in *Jaws* where they are comparing shark encounter stories (coincidentally, 75% of shark attacks are on surfers, and I am sure jet skiers aren't far behind). I bone up on all kinds of surf talk like "pointbreak" and a "barrel" and in the process learn that jet skiers often tow surfers out to their favorite surf spots. "Less paddling, dude!" The long and the short of it is, I did not need to worry about these two not getting along.

As Nora Ephron said, "Couples date each other." Well, if that is true then we seem to be having a threesome couples dating experience. For the next week, even when we are alone over at Ida & Hud's, inevitably Janine & Tommy would bang on the door and we'd all be together again. If we're over to visit Tommy & Janine, pretty soon Ida & Hud would be coming through the door, and now either of them are frequently dropping in on our rental on the way to town or market.

It is Janine who first notices that all of us own corner lots within three blocks of one another.

"Let's form The Corner Lot Club!" Janine pronounces. After a few more cerveza we shorten it to The CLC. It sounds so hoity-toity and contradictory to who any of us are as people, it makes us laugh.

The CLC agenda is to have a blast going to the coolest, cheapest or the best places to eat in Libé, Paloma and the surrounding area. We discover places that are as simple as tacos in the Barrio to the fancier sea front seafood restaurants in San Michele. Once, we go to a woman in town of Chinese heritage who is cooking Chinese food in her own home as a business. On any of our sojourns John, of course, also insists on dancing after. If we are not going out we were having dinner parties and feeding each other.

We were having so much fun that I am getting low as I know the season is counting down for us. While we are leaving, our friends are staying. I start to wonder if I could I live down here full time. One thing that I did know is I could write down here and maybe even teach writing here.

Sex Gasoline (rises again)

No more denying it, we are leaving for home once again. One final chore before heading North is to clear the fridge and give our spoilables to friends. At the back of our fridge I find the unopened and forgotten can of Sex Gasoline. *What am I to do with that?* We've already laughed about it with our CLC club so I decide to pack it and bring it home for the amusement of our Northern friends.

Today is travel day and after I pack everything in my suitcases, I pick them up and groan from exertion. John has already delivered a bag of our stuff to Tommy's for safe keeping until next season. I am worried that my luggage is overweight, yet again. I can't decide what to do. John, is packing light as usual, so with a wicked little grin I wait until he isn't around and surreptitiously sneak a few items into one of his bags just before we head to the airport.

At the smallish airport we have seen the security routines change before so we are never sure what to expect. This time it is a full inspection of all checked luggage. The inspections are done in full view so officers can question passengers if they need to. John and I are side by side with two different officers each checking our respective bags in a crowded section with numerous other passengers getting the same treatment from other officers.

Suddenly, we hear the excited and accusatory tone of John's officer. He has "the can" in his hand and is asking John what he intends by bringing a can of gasoline on an airplane! Everyone's heads lift and is looking at the scene.

"No, no, no," John says, completely panicking. He doesn't know what the officer is talking about at first since he didn't exactly pack the item in question, I did. Now I know why they ask that seemingly silly question at airports, *Did you pack your own bags?* John recognizes the can and quickly gestures for the officer to read the whole label which he does. I imagine he sees the little stylized penis logo "with erectus." Slowly, the officer starts laughing. Then, he starts really laughing.

The officer then passes the Sex Gasoline can around to the half dozen other officers. He is explaining what he found to each of them, nudging, and gesturing to the red faced, bald gringo and they all start laughing. John is sending me darts with his eyes that are enough to make a strong man under the strongest virility drug on the market, shrivel. I know I am in trouble, but, I can't help it, I am laughing too.

We started the season with sex and it seems suitable to end with it. Sex Gasoline is allowed to go to Canada with me and my nature boy. There will be a new story for me to tell along with the prop of the "can" as John and I will soon start huddling under quilts again dreaming of our return to paradise next season.

Season 3

60

EL PAYASO

My Clown

My best friend in Canada is a clown. No, I really mean a clown.
Well, a part-time clown for major public events, festivals and private
parties for kids. Most of our friends had started lining up for a visit
with us in Mexico, but Amber, my clown, had not been one of them.
I had been asking her for three years to come to Mexico with me.

"Let me show you my beautiful little town. You'll love it." But
Amber had her trepidations and perhaps she had a right to. As
much as we adore each other we are, as my British friends say, like
chalk and cheese.

She's my best friend from theater school and the one person I
can get truly goofy with, on the other hand, our organizational and
domestic styles are polar opposites. Because of this, I can be a little
bit on the bossy side, while she, in her child-like, wondrous beauty,

remains happy-go-lucky and free from constraints of right and wrong, smart and dumb, chaos and order. She is my Buddha and teaches me patience with the world.

So this season, I am thrilled that my tall clown friend has agreed to come with us to Mexico for Christmas and New Years. I had tempted her with my companion pass for a discount price so we can go down together (with John) and then just Amber and I will go back together to return us to our work commitments. I then plan to return to Libé on points and rejoin John later in the season. But to begin with, to get the discount flight from Canada, we have to be at the airport before 4 a.m. Because of this, I suggest Amber stay the night at our place where we can get the taxi together in the wee hours.

I am excited as she arrives bringing her clumsy, exploding pack sacks through our lobby that seem to come with their own debris trail.

"Amber, hon, isn't something falling out of that open zipper there?"

"Got it," she reassures me as she hastily stuffs whatever it was back inside, neglecting to close the zipper fully I notice, but say nothing.

I give her over to our second bedroom, also known as John's man cave. I am in the midst of my own organized chaos as I complete my last minute packing details. Of course I have a checklist, yet packing for a two-month period is not like average holiday packing. In short, I over think things and I definitely over pack.

John picks up my bags and says, "You're over the 50 pound mark with this one," dropping it again to let me try and re-sort and redistribute between my other bags. He has a magic sense of knowing exactly what 50 pounds is. I have tested this with the bathroom scale and he's amazingly accurate. I no longer doubt his estimates.

I have finally tucked things away and got my poundage down when I peek in on Amber to see how she is getting along. Naively, I had imagined her relaxing and ready to catch a few winks, but when I open the door I stifle a gasp. Her bags seem to be completely unpacked again and are all over the room.

"What's happening?" I ask trying to conceal my panic.

"I am trying to find the cord for my laptop. I was sure I packed it... I know it's in here."

We spend the next half an hour going through every little pouch, pocket and bag she has inside her bigger bags nesting like many organs and skin layers of a complex organism. I pull out many items completely flummoxed at what they are.

"What's this?" I ask.

"That's my balloon pump."

If I didn't know her this may require further explanation, but since my clown friend is an expert at creating balloon animals at the drop of a hat I know exactly what it is and the bag of tube balloons I will shortly come across will not be questioned, even if in my mind I wonder how in two weeks she plans to fit in a clown act along with all the other activity items she has packed. I find paint, brushes, canvasses, various crafting items, a complete set of calligraphy pens, belly dancing items and several library books due both after and before our return date.

It is almost midnight by the time we get it all stuffed back, having at last found the elusive laptop cord. We have three hours to sleep but before bed I can't resist asking, "You do have your passport, right?"

I am greatly relieved to see her rapidly produce it. I head to join John in bed confident that none of us are going to get much sleep, least of all me. I have already cast myself in the role of the overwakeful parent.

John is not particularly organized with his things either but he is manic in two respects, routines and being early, for everything. He rouses us all too early and I complain all the way to the airport that we are just going to be sitting waiting. Amber is the peacemaker between us amidst incessant yawning.

When we get to the airport we find out there has been a potential terrorist incident the night before and all airports are on high alert. They are searching every package, every piece of baggage, both carry-on and checked, and doing pat-downs of everyone. It takes hours and we barely make it on board. It turns out early was a very good idea. John is gloating. I am eating crow. Amber is still yawning.

We are late leaving so late arriving into L.A. for our connecting flight with a bare fifteen minutes to boarding time. We step off exhausted and Amber and I head to the washroom to massive line-ups. John, I know, despite there never being the line-ups that the ladies room has, has a history of taking an incredibly long amount of time in the bathroom. I can never figure out why since he doesn't even have hair, bald as a cue ball. But, being the good parent I tell him to meet us back on board the connecting flight rather than look for us.

Just before we re-board, Amber tells me she is going to buy a chocolate bar at the stand next to our gate while there is no line up and just enough time. I have warned her that some chocolate bars are harder to find in small town Mexico. I board and wait at our seat.

John boards. I'm puzzled, *where is Amber?* He never saw her. The plane is told that we are waiting for a missing passenger. I ask John to go out and find her. The parent in me is starting to panic. He tries but they will not let someone de-plane once they have planed (I will never get used to those verbs).

They are calling her name at the gate. I am now in full panic mode, begging the flight attendants to go find her, describing her exactly like a parent with a lost child. A woman in the row behind me starts getting snippy and critiquing me.

"Control yourself, you don't need to get excited," she snaps very unsympathetically. I nearly get into fisticuffs with her, John holding me back. It looks like they are going to take off without Amber, and I am nearly in tears when we spot her hustling down the narrow aisle avoiding the angry looks from passengers on a plane now extra late. I am so relieved I don't care, although I do still want to bonk the woman sitting behind us. Amber tells me she got confused and was waiting at the wrong gate ignoring the announcements. Silently, I promise to keep a closer watch on Amber.

When we land on the tarmac in Mexico, as soon as the hatch opens I embrace the sweet, soft warmth of the winter breeze after leaving our sub zero country. We have the typical line up for customs and when our turn comes I stick to Amber like glue while John goes to another open officer.

Amber has a natural talent for languages and loves people. She charms even the border guard with her first bits of Spanish. He smiles as he tucks her tourist visa card in her passport, as he does with mine, telling her in English not to lose it. I can see immediately even in English she hasn't heard a word he said.

We walk over to our baggage carousel which hasn't even started loading so I suggest we head to the bathrooms and it is my first opportunity to give my Mexican toilet paper etiquette lesson. *If it's brown, it goes down. If it's yellow, into the pail-o.* Toilet paper in a third world sewage system is a no-no.

When we get out of the "Damas" room our bags are circling and we pull them off. John is nowhere to be seen, so we pull his too.

"Where is he?" she asks.

"In the bathroom, of course," I answer. "We are in for a wait."

We sit on our stacked bags, camped outside the men's washroom like puppy dogs waiting for their master, ever hopeful every time a figure exits. Even for John it seems like an extra long time.

Twenty minutes pass. We are now pushing thirty minutes in total. Amber and I nearly jump out of skins when from behind us John asks, "What are you doing?" I am baffled. *How did he get out of the bathroom without us seeing him?*

"Where were you?" asks Amber in a much sweeter tone than I was planning.

"Didn't you see them take me away to the backroom in customs?" he asks incredulously. Apparently, everyone but us noticed.

"My God, what happened?" I have now switched my parenting focus to him.

Due to a similar last name and mistaken identity, John was hauled off to be carefully screened that he was not the "person of interest" on their list. While Amber and I were being men's room vultures, John was using his rudimentary Spanish to convince the authorities that he was not the gringo droid they were looking for. He finally succeeded.

I swear that no matter how large a group we are travelling with we will all go to any customs officer as a group from now on, but clearly I had failed as a "parent" already. I decide to lecture Amber in our cab ride into town on all possible immediate and future dangers including reminding her of the advice of the border guard to not lose that tourist card tucked in her passport. What a holiday joy I am shaping up to be.

We collapse at our casa and go directly out for food and margaritas before I start to chill and let the laid back air of Mexico soften me to the better and happier person I was meant to be. I am ready to start this season's adventures of small town Mexico with my best clown friend.

Amber is passionate about a few things, among which animals and spirituality rank highly. She's a vegetarian and literally cannot hurt a fly, so she saw our quasi-agricultural town as a big open-air petting zoo. She is delighted with the burros, the horses, the birds, the pelicans, the geckos, the iguanas and even the roosters that we curse for waking us. She is ready to adopt them all.

The next day we go for a walk in the Barrio and a small herd of goats saunter along down the main street. It's not uncommon for someone's animals to get loose and Amber's maternal instinct kicks in. She insists on following them like a paparazzi after a celebrity entourage, snapping photos and trying to get closer. We are in the middle of the Barrio and several people are out on the street. No one is thinking twice about the goats, but the crazy gringas taking photos of goats make them look twice.

Suddenly, someone's dog takes after one of the young goats who reacts to his barking by breaking away from the group. The other goats barely take notice, but this goat starts desperately running away from the dog. He tries to dash into several storefronts and homes only to be blocked by their owners. Finally he goes for the only shelter nearby, Amber.

The goat is literally trying to hide behind Amber while the dog chases it around and around her. She is shouting obscenities at the dog in English and everyone in sight is laughing. I honestly think that the canine-phobic goat is going to try to jump into Amber's arms or perhaps she will try to scoop the large animal up, but after a few rounds of ring-around-the-gringa the dog has had his fun and the goat charges after his friends and all goes back to normal in the Barrio, with us labeled the afternoon's entertainment.

On the way home from the Barrio I take Amber on a detour to show her our corner lot. It is overgrown again. It is December and the rainy season ends in early November.

"This is all yours?" asks Amber looking at the tangled field of grass and weeds. I sketch out the property lines since it has vacant lots on either side. She seems sufficiently impressed but not very excited looking at those overgrown grass and weeds until I mentioned that there is a white horse that is frequently let loose to graze and it often comes to our lot. I see her eyes light up. *No, no, no, no more livestock stalking.*

I distract her from going on the white horse hunt by suggesting we could make ice tea and have it on the roof of our rental casa. It is enough to move her off the pursuit and we head home to our rental, The Dream Casa.

The Dream Casa

pa·la·pa:
1. A traditional Mexican shelter with a thatched roofed made with palm leaves or branches.

The casa we are staying in with Amber we call The Dream Casa not because it is perfect, but because the name of the casa in Spanish has the word "dream" in it. Casas are given names in Mexico that are often displayed on a glazed ceramic plaque at the gate. 90% of the time they are named after the matriarch, ex: Casa Janine. The Dream Casa is a rare exception both in the name and that it has a feature that truly makes it a dream. While the second floor to the casa is completely unfinished (it is not uncommon for Mexicans to build as they accumulate the money and therefore leave things undone for years), you can take the stairs to the third floor roof. The roof is a finished open veranda with a cavernous palapa roof over it where we have a view of the Fraccionamiento on two sides and the ocean and distance hills on the other sides. It also has a bathroom upstairs so that you do not have to tromp down three flights to go.

The palapa truly is a dream and an ideal spot to hang the happy hammock and catch the ocean breeze and look out at the palm trees and the neighborhood. Normally, I let the master of the house have first dibs on the rainbow hammock, but we fight over the hammock now that it is under this palapa.

Even Amber, my spiritual guide of goodness, is reluctant to forfeit the hammock once she settles in it. One can believe, lightly swaying under that beautiful thatched roof and looking out at everything, that there is no wrong to be done in the world. I start to dream of our future home having a beautiful palapa.

Palapas not only keep you shaded but they have an airy magic when you are under one. There artistry in construction never gets boring to look at; on the outside they have a shaggy dog-like thatch and on the inside a neat weaving of palm stems, wood and bamboo. They usually have a very large peaked roof, or double peaked, or have dormers. They can be round or pentagonal but most are rectangular in base shape.

It is popular to have lights on the inside, often pendants of large woven basket shades or colorful globes that look either tasteful to the max, or out of the shaggadillic sixties and retro chic. Either way, they just don't go out of style. And at night, when you light up that big, rustic roof with either a few strategically placed spot lights or via the pendant lights, or both, it looks spectacular. The Dream Casa has both the baskets and the spotlights and in the evenings we invite Tommy and Janine, Hud and Ida, Jan and Dean and whoever else we can, to come and enjoy it with us.

Palapas stand up in all kinds of weather for several years—the Royal Palms for a decade or more—and are made with a renewable, environmentally friendly natural resource. The finishing shellac to seal them and the sprays for bugs and scorpions may be less environmental however.

Tommy and I were looking up at the inside of our Dream Casa palapa one day.

"You notice how some palapas have a glossy finish on the inside of the roof and some don't?" he asks me.

"Yeah, I have noticed that," I answer thinking I am about to learn something fascinating about palm leafs.

"It depends how you want to spray them for a finishing seal, with a gloss or matte finish. Which do you like better?"

"Gloss." I say without thinking.

"You are Mexican, Kath," he says with a grin. Apparently the Mexicans like it shiny, but most gringos prefer it matte. What that says about either of us or if he is trying to make a point I do not know. I am guessing the gringos like it matte because it seems more rustic, more authentic, and perhaps the Mexicans like it glossy because it looks newer. I just like shiny things. That said, gloss or matte, I still can stare at a woven palm roof from the comfort of hammock for a long, long time.

In addition to our happy hammock under the palapa, there is also a good sized, round, traditional Equipale table and matching chairs which is leather stretched over wood with a decorative cross support of bark covered wood at their bases. Strong, comfortable, attractive, definitely rustic and they last a long time. The gringos love them.

In the morning, with our coffee, while John is running or cycling, Amber and I drink our coffee under the palapa and play our new game at the table. Using our freshly caffeinated brains we test our memories using Loteria cards.

What are Loteria cards? If you go to any stores or markets in Mexico where kids games are sold you will see Loteria card game sets. They have decks of bright colored cards that are part of a lottery style game of chance. The original deck is composed of a set of 54 different images with a number assigned to each card. Each card is also titled with the name of the image, in Spanish, of course, making them neat little flash cards.

The game was brought to Mexico from Spain in 1769 and the images have been changed, adapted and Mexicanized for different decks ever since. They still have the 54 standard images like *El Gallo* (The Rooster), *La Sirena* (The Mermaid), *El Borracho* (The Drunk), etc. The images are wildly popular and now iconic of Mexican culture. People now make their own versions and create new cards with new images, like number 101, La Palapa.

Amber and I were drawn to the colorful cards when we went shopping at the markets. They reminded us of tarot cards, which Amber had taught me to read years before. We picked a couple of sets of the Loteria cards for only a few dozen pesos (less than 3 dollars each). However, since we couldn't understand the Spanish instructions that came with them, we put our two decks together and each morning play a game of Memory with them (where you take turns flipping cards over and try to find the matching card). This way we are not only exercising our memory but we are learning new Spanish words.

It was from Loteria cards that I learned the term "borracho," was delighted to find out that "pera," meant pear, that "paraguas," literally meaning "for water" is an umbrella and "soldado" is a soldier, etc. Mostly, I love the images and want to do something meaningful with them, but what? Never worry, it will come to me.

Playing with the Loteria cards and learning Spanish under the palapa at the top of The Dream Casa is a little slice of lazy heaven. Amber is far superior at the game than I and I laugh to see her competitive streak come out. I call her my Buddha, but my Buddha plays a mean game of Memory.

We are in the middle of a game as we drain our coffee and nibble our fruit when Amber turns over the *La Sirena* mermaid card.

"Oh! That reminds me, what did you dream last night?" She asks. I notice that she asks me *what* I dreamed not *if* I dreamed. That is because we have been sharing dreams for years and been members of dream groups and read everything on dream analysis either of us can find, which is a lot. We both remember our dreams every night from years of practice. While we don't share them everyday any more, we do habitually call each other when we have a good one we want to discuss.

"Oh, right," I cast my mind back as we put the game on pause, "I dreamt something about a guy at work, trying to impress me at first and then leaving me when he sees someone new. Probably one of my abandonment issue dreams. You?" I ask knowing that if she brought dreams up, she probably has a good one. She holds up the *La Sirena* mermaid card.

"She was in my dream."

"Interesting. Maybe we've been playing this too much," I quip but I am truly interested to hear. The mermaid card is one of my favorite images. She tells me the dream.

Amber is at the beach with John, me and other people. A mermaid keeps beckoning her from the ocean and she wants to go join it, but John and I are uninterested. Finally, she decides to go but hesitates, thinking to herself, "Am I a good enough swimmer?"

There is an old woman on the shore who reads her mind and says to her:

"Of course you know how to swim!" But this is the sea and she is unsure if she is a strong enough swimmer. As she hesitates the old woman looks disgusted with her and walks away so Amber runs into the ocean and dives in without thinking.

She tries to come up for air but finds she can breathe underwater. She looks for the mermaid but can't find her and is disappointed. Then she looks out and realizes that she is in an aquarium and people on the outside of the glass are looking at her. This makes her very uncomfortable. She looks down and realizes she is the mermaid. She wakes up.

"Wow, neat dream." I really mean that, and then I ask, "Do you want me to start?" She nods. We have adopted one method of dream sharing as a standard go-to, which is to tell the other person what you would think it would mean if it were your dream. This is done before they tell you what they think their own dream means so it is a fresh perspective for them and they see if any of what you thought resonates for them. Only the dreamer can say what the dream truly means.

"If it were my dream I would say that I feel I have been poised to do something extraordinary that fulfills me emotionally and artistically but don't' believe I have it in me to do. My wisdom is telling me to go for it. When I rush into it and don't let fears hold me back I find I am extraordinary but I am afraid it makes me different from everyone else and separates me."

Amber nods. "Yes, I had the same thoughts but... The old woman getting annoyed seems like a mother figure, but impatient, not nurturing, not sure if she is wisdom or pressure. I feel naked, gawked at, as if I may have made a mistake. I didn't plan to be a mermaid. Not sure I can do that or want to."

"Still hesitating on the shore?" I ask in a teasing way.

"I can't tell if it was a warning not to be seduced by emotions, you see? Not to dive in?"

"Well the Spanish for mermaid, La Sirena, references Sirens which were supposed to lure sailors to the rocks, so maybe there is a reason not to be literally, 'out of your element,'"

"Yes! I am out of my element!"

"But in the dream you can breathe in the water too, so maybe not."

"Right." She thinks about it. "I am also in my element in the water."

"Like your performances maybe? You are on stage, in your element, where you are gawked at, but it also makes you different from others. Maybe a fear of fame?"

"There is that. You know I am not into fame. I want my performances to bring joy and happiness and goodness into the world. They aren't for me." I know her well enough to know she isn't just saying this. "So what do I do with this dream?" she asks me.

We talk more about the possibilities and what is going on in her life right now and I have a thought.

"Hey, since we are going to the tianguis market today, why don't we look for a mermaid to honor your dream and you can take it home." This brightens Amber. One of our Jungian dream gurus suggests doing something in reality to honor any significant dream you had, to help with any synchronicity. The idea is, if you do some sort of ritual or something to honor it in waking life whatever wisdom the dream was telling you will manifest in reality more easily or at least you may have an aha moment. Buying something may be a tad shallow, but it's not like we are going to be able to go on a mermaid sighting tour.

Thursdays are market day in Libé. There are many stalls at the outdoor tianguis (tee-an-gay) market that are shaded under tarps. For the rich gringos there are the colorful Talavera ceramics, jewelry and irresistible crafts, but there is also everything from hardware store items to repaired small appliances to fresh fruits, juices, nuts and herbs. And clothes, lots and lots of clothes. Used and new. Amber and I are already consignment and vintage clothes shoppers and once I introduce her to the 20 pesos used clothes table, in which I often find designer labels, we are both dug in, going through mounds of bargain clothes. We can look for mermaids later.

We finally take away our used clothes finds, sated from our shopping frenzy, though the buys are a risk since there are no dressing rooms at the mobile market, but for less than $2 each we risk away. We then go by another colorful table of brand new clothes items. These I buy three or four of each year, brassieres.

I look over at Amber, I have not introduced her to this find yet. The bras on this table are cheap but so comfortable I barely know I am wearing them. They are actually not made in Mexico but in Taiwan but I can't find them in Canada anywhere. They are usually in bright colors, but have beige, black and white too. They are light weight stretch material and only 50 pesos each (under five dollars), but they are only good for women who are small and medium-sized up top.

"Why are you looking at me like that?" Amber asks.

I have received funny looks from women friends I have brought to this booth before by staring at their chests and estimating their breast size. I have since gotten better at surreptitiously sizing up their endowments, before I recommend the bra to them. I still find it can be a tricky thing to do. Fortunately, I already know Amber is a contender and I give her my pitch for trying the bra. We end up both buying a new style that is bright colored with mariposa (butterfly) motifs on it.

Now we can look in earnest at the tourist trinkets in the main jardine for La Sirena (the mermaid). We scour the dozens of colorful booths, many times distracted by the cute and original decorative arts. I love the ones made creatively from coconut shells, much better than plastic, which usually comes from China anyway. And the coconuts are better than the ceramics which are risky to carry home in luggage with high breakage while coconut shells are compared to concrete in their strength.

Last season I had seen a super cute pregnant La Sirena made out of a coconut shell and took it home successfully, which I tell Amber about, but this year they are nowhere to be found. We are a little disappointed but we decide to go into the regular shops in town to look some more. I tell Amber that I am sure we will find a mermaid somewhere there.

We don't. But we do find ice cream to console us and decide to stroll down the pretty malecón that straddles the lagoon and the open ocean. While enjoying our ice creams we watch the junior surfers hovering off shore trying to catch a good wave in.

Suddenly a small crowd of young kids encircle us playing, some sort of tag. Amber, always great with kids, whether in clown character or not, joins them running and playing with them down the malecón.

As I watch, I see my friend has the spirit, innocence and beauty of a child. Mexico seems to understand and honor the spirit and innocence of children better than other places. The catholic All Saints Day in Mexico is dedicated to children because they see children as the closest beings to living saints. When I first read this I thought it was so beautiful and insightful, as well as consistent with what John and I see in Mexico. Family is everything and children are given more freedom here.

As I watch Amber playing with the kids she abruptly stops, and is looking at something ahead of her. I follow her gaze. There, ahead of her, I see it. A bronze statue of a mermaid that I had forgotten was on the malecón. She turns to me pointing and laughing. We have found La Sirena.

Amber has her camera in her bag so I take a photo of her with the statue, a popular tourist thing to do which I don't think I have ever done before today, but now it has meaning. We laugh at the synchronicity, if you care to believe in it, and I wonder how this 'dream honoring' that we chose to do today may manifest in Amber's life.

After our shopping and tourist day in town we grab some lunch at Raul's then return home to our lazy palapa to collapse. We have started our day here under the palapa roof, but enjoy it at the end of the day too. John is in the coveted hammock now. The master is slumbering. And as the sun sets, we will soon all lie under another kind of canopy.

The Stars

After living downtown in a big city for the past 20 years, I can say I don't like big cities, but I like the suburbs less. At least in downtown there are communities in pockets, in a kind of massive way. One thing I dislike about modern cities is how much I miss seeing the stars in the sky.

Years ago I wrote a poem about the stars falling from the sky to the ground, their shining heads being stuck on poles in rows as if they had been the victims of a war-torn atrocity. If you look up from a city sky amongst rows and rows of street lights at night you will only see a few stars if any at all.

John and I were quite bowled over when we first came to Libé to see two streetlights with manual switches hanging off the poles which relied on the town's citizens to turn them off during the day and all of us frequently forgot. They eventually were removed for photosensitive ones, but more and more streetlights are put in everyday as the town loses its innocence with the rest of the world and my stars disappear.

There is something very wrong about how we have lit up the grounds and blotted out the night sky. I think we are at war with our own souls for this sin. We don't even acknowledge that it is wrong. Mother Nature is trying to tell us not to go down this path any further. Instead we now show pictures of the Earth from space all lit up by electric lights below as if we are proud of it. It may look pretty but what does it really mean? When I am in Libé, I see the stars and am happy. Seeing stars physically makes me happy. I wonder if it works better than anti-depressants.

Amber, John and I sit in loungers tonight gazing up, the sky becoming our T.V. I try to recall distant learnings from one summer when my mother stubbornly attempted to teach me and my sister the constellations at a seaside cabin upcountry. I try to tell Amber what little bit I remember and am pretty sure I have at least half of it wrong.

"The sailor's used to navigate the seas by the stars," John reminds us, "It was their GPS."

John tells us of his first night sail in Mexico when the skipper gave him the helm and went to bed with the simple warning, "Don't hit a whale." John, alone with the sea, the wind, and the stars, carrying him as fast as the elements would allow and no more. The lap of the sea against the hull as it cut the waves, the smell of the brine. A warm breeze against his face as he corrected the boat's direction to fill the sails and listen to his heart beat.

But it was the stars, he tells us, the stars made it magical, as if he could make good on that turn of phrase and reach out and touch them. They surrounded him like a glowing mysterious canopy trying to tell him of the larger peace that exists when we are at harmony with the wind, the stars and nature.

As the three of us gaze up at the stars I tell them that in the Mexican Mayan myth the male sun god gives the stars as a love gift to the female moon goddess. This gets an "Aww," from Amber. And then she adds something that makes me wince a little.

"John, is that why men give women engagement rings with a sparkly diamond?"

"I wouldn't know," he answers nonchalantly.

"Someone told me diamond jewelry is meant to be like the stars," Amber adds. *Is she hinting for me?* I know Amber to be guileless but I also know that I occasionally complain to her of John's lack of interest in marrying me after we became settled, and she may have subconsciously picked this subject. John chooses to respond with science facts.

"There are supposed to be rare diamonds that have come from the stars via meteorites, like black diamonds."

"Really?" Amber likes to hear fascinating trivia facts I've noticed. I think I am out of the woods on the engagement line of questioning, having carefully kept my mouth shut, when Amber decides to add a response that makes me half laugh, half blush.

"Is that the kind of diamond you are going to get for Kathrin?"

Oh boy. There is a small pause before he responds.

"I'm enjoying the premarital sex too much," he answers. Amber giggles and I frown. *What does that mean?*

I am about to get moody about his charming rebuff to the subject of marriage when we all see a falling star, a meteorite, and all of us exclaim simultaneously. It's as if we found a gold nugget, or a four-leaf clover in the sky that only lasts an instant but we share it together. It summons a connection to something greater than our petty concerns, or my petty concerns. The discomfort of the previous subject evaporates.

We don't say much after that, just star gazing and a few comments until we turn in. Staring into the night sky really is very calming.

"I think I am going to write a poem about stars tomorrow." Amber tells me.

"Me too," I answer. But in the morning we forget with the sun.

Three Kings and the Clown

Since we are down for Christmas, Amber has another opportunity to see animals in harmony with the community. Mary and Joseph's trip to the fateful stable in Bethlehem is recreated several times in parades called posadas. Each Christmas all the burros in town get roped into the reenactments which delight all of us, but especially Amber. Christmas lasts all night long and no one sleeps. Amber wants to experience the mass at the local church but Christmas mass is far too crowded and we can't even squeeze into the building.

By now, however, we have introduced Amber to Tommy who is happy to take her to the English speaking church he attends in the next town on the Sunday following Christmas. This church is well known for being very active in helping the poor. I, less than religious, agree to tag along when I hear there is a choir. We go and have a lovely time and learn the church is planning the famous Three Kings Day celebration for the poorest of the poor kids living way back in the mountains.

"Three King's Day, what's that?" Amber asks us.

Tommy and I explain that unlike other North American kids, Mexican kids only receive three gifts on January 6th, the day the three kings were reputed to have given their gifts to the baby Jesus. Not only is this incredibly sensible in its moderation of materialism, it is in actual keeping with the Christmas story.

And on that subject, one has to wonder what happened to that gold, frankincense and myrrh? I don't think the baby Jesus would have known what to do with them. Did Mary and Joseph start a trust account? Did adult Jesus ever see his gifts? Even if he did, no doubt would have given them to the poor. I am not sure anyone has cleared this up for me. Never mind looking for the Ark of the Covenant, what about them gifts?

In any case, the church thankfully still holds with the tradition of helping the needy and Amber, Tommy and I agree to help with the Three Kings Day celebration for the poorer kids. Traditionally, in "middle class" areas, on and around Three Kings Day you will start to see whole blocks cordoned off for kid's block parties with pinatas, decorations, fire crackers, a traditional large fruit bread cake the shape of a small race track, some modest gifts and always, always, wait for it... a clown.

The one thing you don't see much of is balloons as decorations, perhaps because of the heat, or maybe the paper and plastic cut out banners are enough and less expensive, but no balloons, let alone balloon animals. Since Amber has brought her balloons and balloon pump somewhere in the swamp of her baggage she immediately volunteers to be the clown of the day and make balloon animals.

The one big problem is that Amber and I are flying out on the late afternoon of January 6th, Three Kings Day. So Tommy agrees to get us to the party and back in plenty of time to make our plane, and we start to make our Three Kings Day game plans while we enjoy our last days in Mexico together.

The night before the event we take out those small canvases and paints found in the bowels of Amber's sacks and create signs. We paint pictures of the animals and objects she can make in balloon form, and then we look up the Spanish words and add the English too.

There is:

Chango (Monkey)
Sord (Sword)
Perro (Dog)
Corona (Crown)
Loro (Parrot)
Caballo (Horse)
Jeraf (Giraffe)

They look great. Amber doesn't have her clown costumes and make-up, and even if she did, she will be getting on a plane immediately after, so she makes herself a crazy balloon hat that I call the clown crown.

The next morning we jump into Tommy's SUV and head into the back country that neither I nor Amber have seen, though John and I did take that wrong bus once and got close, this is much further in and I am glad Tommy knows the way. You can look at the cinder block one room open houses with palm leaf or tin roofs, no windows, no running water and no electricity and see poverty or you can realize in the tropics you need open housing for breezes, and thankfully happiness and wealth are not joined together in the minds of children. Full bellies, clean water and loving care are enough happiness, and the rest is magic.

Food and beverages are being served by the other volunteers by the time we get there. To my eyes it looks like thousands of people and so many barefoot kids.

Perhaps it is the tinted windows of Tommy's dark SUV, but I start to see the whole thing like a scene for a rock star concert. Tommy parks the car in the middle of a clearing and all eyes are on the car as Amber in balloon hat emerges. It is as if they know she is "the one." Tommy and I don't even rate a glance. We are mere helpers to the bruja (sorceress) before them. We set out our signs as Amber sits on the only thing that can loosely be described as a piece of furniture and starts making her balloon magic. And it is magic to these kids and adults.

Rather than letting them crowd her Tommy organizes them in line-ups while I present them with their choices on our canvases. In no time the lineup of kids stretches for what would be blocks if they had blocks, but we are in the forest, the jungle, and I am the helper to a Goddess, a Magician, better than a clown, she is their rock star.

Amber is moving at lightening speed, producing monkeys, parrots and swords. Clearly swords and monkeys are the favorites. The kids are overjoyed with their balloons, they are not even looking at the other toys and gifts the volunteers have brought, they are not even looking at the food, everyone is watching the magic balloon woman. The line up grows and grows. I am now grateful that she brought extra bags of balloons to Mexico. We have not much time before we have to leave for the airport and I start to look at my watch nervously. Tommy picks up on this. Amber is fading, trying to get to every kid.

Finally, Tommy steps in, in his dark glasses and directs them in Spanish that the show is over. I am not sure if he is telling them she has to get to the airport as I am positive they have little idea of what that means, but just like the rock star she has become, with a few hasty thank yous, we efficiently pack up, surround her and jump back in the SUV, Amber leaning out the window waving to her fans as we pull away. I have never had an experience quite like it before.

Tommy takes us direct to the airport. We have already said our goodbyes to John, me especially, and even though I know I am returning in three weeks, I go into my usual funk. I am not returning home, I am leaving home. I once asked my American friend, Hugo, who married his local Mexican sweetheart, Julia, if he ever feared he may not get back to see his family in the U.S. He said, no, but that he has nightmares when he goes to the U.S. that they won't let him back into Mexico. I got that.

We pass the last mile of the coconut groves with hundreds of cattle grazing underneath them which looks amazing to me, as well as a surprising synthesis of agriculture. We pass the last banana groves, and finally the jalapeño crops that signal we are almost at the airport.

We give Tommy our big hugs and kisses goodbye, and after our clown/rock star experience we are more bonded. Amber leaves him some balloons to practice making animals himself. The equivalent of Adam Levine giving up a guitar pick to a roadie maybe?

We get in line early, before there are crowds and I do a passport check-in. Amber confidently produces her passport.

"And your tourist visa card?" I ask. It is conspicuously not peeking out from her passport as mine is. Amber looks befuddled.

"Amber, where is it? Remember, I told you not to lose it?"

She looks guilty and starts going through those pockets again. I swear aloud.

We step out of line and in the middle of the airport go through a similar scene we did in Vancouver looking for her laptop cord, but this time no tourist visa card.

"What will happen to me?" She looks truly frightened. The devil in me is tempted to scare her a little, but I level with her.

"You'll have to pay a fine and we may be delayed. We better get back in line now. How many pesos do you have left?" I think someone told me the fine was 500 pesos but that was ages ago, it may be more.

As we kick our luggage down a much longer line now, we scrape together our last pesos and I am also letting her know we have to accommodate our baggage charges which you have to pay in either pesos or US dollars. We think we have just enough. She knows I am a little pissed and stays solemn and silent.

We get through the baggage inspection and check-in and explain our situation. I pay for my bags, and the price has gone up cutting into our careful money rationing, but they won't let Amber's bags be checked without her tourist visa. They put hers aside and direct her to an office on the other side of the airport. I am allowed to go to the gate but I will not leave her.

I would never let her go alone. She feels she should go alone, as if it's her penance. *No way I am deserting you*, I send her my telepathic message. She looks me in the eye and we find the office together.

We sit down with a young officer at a desk. His English is there, but not fluent. We explain. He looks her up and down and then fills in some paperwork and hands it to her and tells her to be on her way. No fine.

We say numerous "graciases" and get out of there.

We are both giddy. No fine.

"Wait," I say, "they still have your bags you haven't paid for, they may charge you there when they see this paperwork."

We return, but circumvent the long line since the bags already went through inspection. We show her paperwork to the airline personnel and they click a few buttons on the computer, return her passport with a boarding pass and tell us to go to the gate, they will check her bags. No fine, and not even any baggage charges for her. *What?*

"Amber, how is it that you can lose your tourist card, not get fined, AND get out of paying $30 bucks worth of baggage charges, while I pay?" I mumble something about horseshoes in body cavities that I hope the metal detector won't pick up. She smiles mysteriously.

My grumpy mood of leaving my winter home increases, but soon we are reminiscing about this morning's scene with the kids and laughing. It was magical. But suddenly, Amber gets serious.

"Kathrin," she almost whispers. "When I realized I lost the tourist card I asked God to prove his existence to me by getting me out of the mess I made."

Me, the unreligious yet verbose one had nothing to say to that. Finally, "Oh, wow."

"Yeah, wow."

Her "wow" was how quickly and neatly her prayer for help was answered. My "wow" was a realization that once again "doing things correctly" had very little spiritual value compared to being a spiritual person and living a spiritual life. I was the one who had made her feel bad about not being the detail person that I was. But who "won" in the end? Not me. How many more times would my best friend teach me this lesson, how many more times would John, and how many times would this country teach me this lesson? I am not a fast learner.

The Circus Comes to Town

Three weeks later, after fulfilling my work obligations, I return to Libé (sans Amber this time). I settle into our new digs that John has secured but can't sleep during siesta. I hear a new megaphone being broadcast in the neighborhood. It sounds a little different from the others. It isn't recorded and I can't understand the hyper fast Spanish the man is saying, but it sounds dramatic whatever it is. I am curious, but too lazy in my "siesta head" to look outside. I miss it, but I needn't worry as we find out soon enough what it's all about.

In the large empty lot at the end of our street massive, colorful tents are being erected. The circus is in town. Another reason to love this country, small travelling circuses (I am tempted to say circi) still exist. It's as if everything good about my childhood has returned, color, bicycles, long sunny summers, and now the circus.

Before, we have only seen circuses setting up at the neighboring larger towns, not in Libé.

"We must go!" I tell John who agrees minus some of my child-like enthusiasm.

No sooner do we buy tickets for that night's performance when gringo friends warn us that there may be animals. *Duh, yeah.*

"Oh no, no!" they tell us that they may be abused animals. Oh, well no one wants to see that. But, it was a maybe, so we go as planned amid masses of Mexican families with kids of all ages in tow, ready to walk out and start a small personal protest if we see anything offensive to animal lovers.

John and I are the only gringos. We are the only ones without children. We are the only ones that look like grandparents versus parents. We tower over the families, even the adults, especially John who is six feet tall. To say we are a tad conspicuous is an understatement. Yet, we are here.

As confident as John is becoming with his Spanish, when natives speak at their normal speed, *rapido,* we don't have a prayer. The performances, of course, are all in Spanish, but it is a circus, who needs words? As it turns out, the entire show, so far, is comprised of only seven performers all playing multiple roles. The bulk of the performances seem to be acrobatics, clowning, and a bit of fire and sword swallowing thrown in.

There is one performer we keep noticing that has us the most entertained. He is a clown, then he is an acrobat, and he is wonderful as both. The performers go through numerous sparkly costume changes, albeit home spun, which is even more charming.

I see in all the kid's faces my own young, bedazzled face from long ago.

The "flying" trapeze and aerial acrobatics make me wonder if some of these young performers may wind up joining the famous Cirque de Soleil one day. Does every kid have a secret wish to run away and join the circus or is that a cliché? Yet, clearly some do. After all, my best friend is a clown and I was with her when she found out.

***

I remember teaching a course in which I unknowingly had told a lot of stories about my life, in illustration of some points or other. I had just launched into yet another tale when a student stopped me.

"You've done everything," he said.

"No, no," I quickly denied it, "I have not done everything."

"I bet you joined the circus?"

"No I did not... but I did take a 13-week clowning class," I admitted.

"I knew it," he said. "I just knew it. You've done everything."

It was there, at that 13-week introduction to clowning class, that I met my best friend, Amber, and where she discovered she was a clown and I discovered I wanted to hang around a clown. We had just done our final exams. In this case, our final clown performances in full makeup and costume where I had pretended to swallow a sword and in true clown fashion it was obvious I was faking it to everyone in the audience but me, the "clever" clown.

But it was Amber's performance that had one upped the whole class by doing the best clown dance in history, spoofing the moves and choreography of Martha Graham and Bob Fossey.

It was in the afterglow of these gem performances that she turned to me and said,

"Kathrin, I am a clown."

At first, given we were still in costume, I thought my new friend had a penchant for stating the obvious, but a quick look in her eyes and I knew she really meant it.

Perhaps going to this Mexican circus was my way of connecting not just to my childhood but to my early theatre days and especially to connect with the one goofy person I missed when I went to Mexico.

***

It is now the intermission of our Mexican circus and we get up with everyone else and exit the tent to go to the concession booths. I quickly point out to John that they are manned by the same seven people who have been entertaining us. I don't know whether to find this endearing or alarming that these artists have no support. They are like Judy Garland and Mickey Rooney putting up a show in the barn. I am moved. We buy extra popcorn.

In the second act we see our first and only animal, a beautiful white horse, clearly not abused, and I know my horses from another life where I... *maybe that student had a point*. Nevertheless, the horse is there for more acrobatics a la horseback and a nice addition, but I am waiting for the next clown act.

I don't wait long. Next, our favorite clown comes on re-dressed in a "bald" skullcap and overalls and plays a hairless, drunk janitor who wants to climb to the high trapeze despite the ringmaster trying to discourage him. He is hilarious. The crowd is roaring with laughter and even when we cannot catch the one-liners in Spanish we are thoroughly entertained as the ring master plays the straight man to the drunken clown.

This is shaping up to be the best part of the show, and the ringmaster starts to ask this crazy drunk if there is no one that will miss him if he falls to his death. The clown starts to talk about his Mama and his Papa, rubbing his "bald" head, he suddenly looks out into the audience and spies an equally conspicuous, shining, bald head and points directly at the tall gringo in the front row.

"Papa!" he cries out to John. The whole place erupts with laughter. We are in stitches for the rest of the act. A great clown improvises. My only regret is Amber isn't here to see this.

The evening ends too quickly and the ringmaster names each performer and where they are from as they take their bows. They are not Mexicans as it turns out, but from all over Central and South America. I imagine them taking their trailer all the way up crossing the equator to get to our town. They are hard-working, skilled performers and the entrance fee to see them is $50 pesos ($4 dollars).

As we head outside, thoroughly happy we came despite the gringo warnings, another surprise awaits. The performers are lined up outside the tent and shake every audience member's hands, adults and kids, and thank them for coming. It takes awhile for our turn, but when John reaches our favorite clown he recognizes him and once again cries out, "Papa!" and embraces John warmly to further laughter of onlookers.

When the circus comes to town, go.

The See Sea Casa

After The Dream Casa we shared with Amber John has secured a new casa with a few new features for us. The place consists of a casa, two rental apartment units, a dock to a canal and a terrific pool in the backyard that we have access to. The pool is large enough that I can swim lengths and deep enough that I can do flip turns which I love. The backyard has twelve foot concrete walls on each side, but the back is open to the canal way that goes to the lagoon which is sea water so we can see the fish boats come in and out. I call it the See Sea Casa... See Sea, see? Si? Couldn't resist. In any case, we get this beautiful backyard treat for a very reasonable price because we are only taking one of the small one bedroom rental apartments but enjoy all the common space knowing no one is going into the house while we are there.

When opportunity arises we are lazily interviewing many of the people who have built their own houses down here. Francine and Joe, for example, said that they mistakenly incorporated the North American tendency of filling up the lot with a big house. They later wished they had left more outdoor space since you spend a lot of time outside. We get this since with the See Sea casa the pool has a huge sitting area, bar space, and a palapa for shade under which John has hung the happy hammock. I videoed him doing this while he explained in his own charming way, "how to wallow in a hammock."

Wallow is John's term for utter relaxation and while I first contested it from a strictly dictionary definition point of view I have now adopted it happily. We posted the—alliteration alert—happy hammock hanging on YouTube and sent it out to our network. They loved it. The See Sea casa looked like it was going to be a good one. It was a deluxe outdoor space that made up for the tiny apartment.

I enjoyed that pool so much the question came up, do we create a pool with our house, when we build it, or not? To pool or not to pool? To own a pool is starting to become a hot bed issue. It takes, on average, 18,000 gallons of water to fill a small private pool. It is taking all that water times all your neighbors' pools out of the system and making it undrinkable. In California and Texas droughts, it is kind of an issue. Do you want golf courses and swimming pools, or food crops and drinking water? Then there is the issue of heating pools.

In Mexico, they don't generally heat pools, or they are "solar heated" pools—that is a joke—in other words you want a pool to be out in the open where the sun can get at it or it will be chilly. They do now have actual solar pool heaters, from solar panels, which is great, but frankly, I think unnecessary there. In Libé, I go to Cheri's weekly aquafit class where the average age is 65 and if we thin-skinned lot can all get in the unheated pool in the morning before the sun has had much of a chance to heat anything, anyone can. The trick is to keep moving. And then there are the summer hot days where you really want your pool to be nice and cool and heating would be the true waste.

The biggest deal about pools is how often they sit empty, as in no people swimming in it. As one builder told us, "people don't really get *in* the pool a whole lot, they just like sitting *around* a pool." We also found this to be true. Casas with pools can be about 25% more in price to rent, and if no one uses it, or it is used minimally, it feels kind of wasted. I do use the pool, but I am just as happy to share a pool. If we go to the local hotel in the neighborhood, Hotel Playa Azul, it has a large, terrific pool where we can buy a drink pool side, and they are happy to let us swim for free for that drink, but not all hotels do that. For Cheri's aqua fit class, the pool is private and its usage for the class is donated by a member of the community. Another example of why communities that have community-minded people in them really work.

Pools are expensive because you have to have a pool guy for maintenance. At the See Sea Casa we do have a pool guy, Jorgé.

He comes twice a week to test and clean the pool as I peer over the top of a book from the happy hammock. Although the pool was right next to one of the walls, there is a narrow walkway on that side so Jorgé can clean all the way around the pool. I see him doing this with his pool brush on an extended pole, moving it up and down in a motion that would duplicate my squats in exercise class. No, I am not lusting after the pool guy.

What I do notice is the trouble Jorgé is having maneuvering around the two spouts that stick out of the wall about a foot or so over the narrow walkway. The decorative spouts are where the water circulates on a timer at 5pm every day for a couple of hours, making a fountain in the pool. Jorgé has to be careful he doesn't back into one of these hazards while he is bobbing up and down. Who wants to hit their head, or more likely their back, on a piece of concrete?

Today, we came home to the casa to find one of the spouts broken off and laying at the side of the pool. On inspection, we discover the spouts are not concrete at all but Styrofoam, sculpted and painted to look like plaster and concrete, and very convincingly I must say.

The next day that Jorgé comes in, I ask him in my enough-to-get-by Spanish what happened to the spout. He clearly tells me that a coconut had fallen off a palm tree and knocked it off. *Uh huh.* I nod and smile. He leaves. I look up at the one palm tree anywhere near the property, belonging to our neighbor, well, well on the other side of the wall. The one that doesn't have any coconuts and never has for the past number of weeks. Even if it did have coconuts, the trajectory of one falling in order to hit that spout would be equivalent to banking a billiard's shot four times before it flies off the table and makes a successful shot on the pool table next to it. In short, impossible.

I tell John the story Jorgé gave and we chuckle that he is going to tell the absent owners it was a coconut. We are reasonably sure that he has accidentally, and quite understandably, backed into it while cleaning the pool and snapped the delicate Styrofoam off. No biggy. You build with cheap stuff and that's what happens. I had a mental note though that the cheap stuff had fooled us for weeks that it was solid concrete. *Should I use this when we build our house?*

Next week, Jorgé lets me know that he is going on holidays and there will be another guy coming in instead of him the following week. I thank him for his consideration in letting me know as you cannot just let strangers come in who say they are the pool guy. Although, that's pretty much how we got to know Jorgé, come to think of it.

Next week, sure enough, another guy is cleaning the pool sides, bobbing up and down and trying to avoid that one remaining spout. I wonder to myself if Jorgé has warned him not to back into those puppies or they will snap off as easy as you please. We have to go out, so I think no more about it. When we arrive home there is a familiar sight. The second spout is sitting by the edge of the pool snapped off. Clearly Jorgé didn't give the warning.

A few days later, as per their twice-a-week maintenance schedule, the relief pool guy is back. The little devil in me has to do it. I ask this guy what happened to the spout. His answer makes me smile. Coconut. In Mexico, it is better to blame that which cannot have a red face. It is inherent in the language. For example, I am told that when you drop and smash a glass, you would never say "I broke the glass," you would say, "the glass broke itself" or, perhaps another way to say it is, a coconut broke the glass.

We are lucky in the See Sea Casa because we had it pretty much to ourselves. The owner is not going to be in the casa for the season and the apartment next to ours, the one we share a wall with, is only occupied when friends of the family come down from Guadalajara on some weekends.

We do, however, find that the friends often get in rather late on a Friday night after driving in from the big G city. We are snuggled in, sleeping, to be woken by them struggling with their keys, entering, unpacking their stuff, all in stunning echo clarity until they finally get to sleep, and we finally get *back* to sleep.

Concrete homes are terrific for many reasons. They are fireproof, waterproof and easy to mold into anything you want with straight edges or curves they can be truly beautiful homes. But, frequently the concrete homes have a problem you don't expect.

They echo. You will not often hear people above you, or below you, but if you have people beside you and there isn't the proper extra insulation in the walls, you not only hear things, you hear them magnified. You hear them like they are right beside you, which depending on what you are up to, or they are, can be very uncomfortable, or interesting.

The other phenomenon from concrete housing is not knowing where noise is coming from. In The Dream Casa, for instance, John would be shouting from another room in the house at me, and it would echo so much I couldn't quite make out what he was saying, so I would try to find him. I would be wandering around the house trying to follow his voice. "Where are you?" I'd yell. "What?" he'd answer; neither of us hearing the other properly. The sound bounced around so much I would end up checking all the rooms before I found him. You can see how this would be very frustrating for couples who have the bad habit of shouting at each other from the other room.

At the See Sea Casa it is another Friday night and we are sound asleep after a nice night at Diego's dancing when we hear it. Rustle, rustle, keys clanging, the smack of bags hitting the floor. A couple of women have come in late. We know it is women because their high heels on the floor sound like they are strutting their stuff in our own apartment.

They do not seem to want to take their high heels off, and after a half an hour or more they do not seem to want to go to sleep either. They are walking up and down the tiled apartment, a wall away from us, producing a large echo of their every step late into the evening.

John finally looses it (it's usually one or the other of us and this time it is his turn). Late as it is, he storms next door, bare-chested with only his briefs on. I can hear him clearly. In his fury he has forgotten how to construct a sentence in Spanish.

"Zapatos! Zapatos! Zapatos!" Shoes, shoes, shoes is all he can manage to say. It seems to be effective enough. The high heels disappear.

In the morning he apologizes to them for his exuberance. No one likes to get woken up, he explains, in competent Spanish, whether you are on vacation or working. In the light of day, I can count on him to have his usual charming way with the ladies.

36

EL CAZO

The Community that Cooks Chili Together

It is now late in this season and starting to get considerably hotter. Normally the heat is no issue because we both love it and never touch air conditioners, which John is convinced make him sick anyway and we also have a cool pool to jump into. But, due to poor timing I am also hotter than usual. I have just started the female phenomenon of hot flashes that my friend used to describe as "private moments in Mexico" and I no longer find that so funny.

I tend to fall in love with four syllable Spanish words. My first year here it was "desayuno" (day-say-you-no) which not only sounds like music to my ears, it is one of my favorite things in the whole world, breakfast. This season, my new favorite four syllable word is "abanico" (aba-nee-co) which means hand fan, as opposed to "ventilador" which means an electric fan. I purchase a number of colorful abanicos for 30 pesos each and stash them around the apartment and in my bags so I will never be caught without. We have all the ceiling fans going, still refusing air conditioning, but my mantra during my hot flashes is *abanico, abanico, abanico* combined with my rapid fan flutters.

Amid all this heat you wouldn't think I would be looking forward to eating hot, spicy food, but nothing can keep me away from one of Libé's annual events, The Chili Cook Off. The cook-off is run as a fundraiser for needed projects, mostly for improvements to local schools and hospitals, but it is also one of the town social events that brings together Mexicans and gringos. The competition itself has at least 30 competitors for two coveted prizes, Best Chili for the professional restaurateurs, and one for the amateur cooks. Both are equally prized. There are also awards for the Best Salsa and the Best Decorated Booth. Each competitor gets a numbered booth where they set up their hot plate, chili, salsa, and go to town decorating it.

All of this happens in the town jardin. Jardin (pronounced hardeen) literally translates to garden, yet the jardins are really the town square. They are an open space in concrete at the centre of towns for gatherings. It sometimes has plant boxes for the garden with benches, but always has a stage and often a public toilet. It is here that the Chili Cook-off takes place.

Even on a hot day like this, the crowds come out. Awards are decided not by professional judges but by the public who sample the chilies. Tasters buy a number of "taste coupons" that come with ballots for voting. Since it is not a blind taste test which would prevent prejudice it does become a bit of a popularity contest. If your chili sucks no one but your family will vote for it, but since the ballots are anonymous even they might lie about it.

This year John and I really do have to lie through our teeth since our landlord for our current rental is entering the contest.

"Mmm, yes, we love your chili!" *And we don't want you to cut us off pool privileges because we didn't vote for you.*

This year there are 30 chilies to taste. John and I develop a rating system out of ten with notes, including if they are someone we know and whether they are an amateur or a professional. We realize that if our notes were to get into the hands of the wrong people we may alienate some good friends so we guard them with our lives.

Greta and Teresa have a chili this year. Teresa is actively and aggressively campaigning for votes. It is not uncommon to see people wandering around with shirts that say "Vote for booth #4!" along with some catchy tagline that they have come up with like, "*Vote Booth 20, Chili That Will Make You Blush.*" Thankfully Greta and Teresa's chili is excellent and we don't have to lie.

I taste my next chili and John watches me grimace. There is always one person who makes the fatal mistake of burning the bottom of the chili. Anyone who has made chili knows that if you burn the bottom, even a little bit, it will taste like someone threw cigarette butts into your precious pot. Ugh! Too bad.

The booths are under tents and the chili tent row is like a cave, out of the sun, but it is so crowded you can barely move. John and I luck out as one competitor never showed up for their booth and we nab the table and chairs and start a tag team system. One holds our great spot while the other brings in more sample cups of chili.

Most of the chili is served in Styrofoam cups but some are in more creative containers: tortilla shell cups, decorated mini clay pots and one comes with the chili on a chili dog. Yummy!

"How many is that?" John asks me. I sit with my hand over my fattened stomach and slowly review my list and make a count.

"Seventeen. A new record. I can't do another bite." John agrees. There are over 30 samples but you don't have to taste them all to vote because it's a fundraiser, and thank goodness or we would be bloated.

On stage, the prizes and announcements are made by a brother and sister team. She speaks Spanish and he translates to English or vice versa. There are some things they don't have to translate as they are the same in both languages. One moment the sister seems to have quite a lot to say in rapid fire Spanish. At the end there is a pause as we wait for the translation from her brother.

Finally he says, "Same in English."

We all laugh.

Sure this is a competition, but really it's about the community, raising money but also connecting, and of course the musica. This year it is from a great Mexican band and another gringo duo.

After an uncounted amount of margaritas, John and I dance our feet off. I have just sat down when Teresa grabs my hand and drags me back to my feet. I find myself initiating a conga line with her, and our current maid, Lola. I don't recall ever heading up a conga line before.

In no time we have dozens lining up behind us trying to reproduce our crazy moves. It is not only hysterical but a great work out too. I collapse sweating profusely as another "flash" takes me. I don't care. Everyone else is sweating too.

I smile as we walk home in the moonlight, still a little high in the head from the combo of margaritas and dancing. I am pretty convinced that the sign of a healthy community is food, music and dancing, with a few margaritas thrown in. The community that cooks together, cooks.

Writing with Earnest

In Libé, there is a Rotary club comprised mostly of American and Canadian ex-pats and some Mexicans who are fluent in English and interested in the charitable works done for the community. This season, I am asked to give a speech on writing based on my teachings about writing. It is well received and there is more interest than I had expected. Some of the expats want to join a writing group I will facilitate. That is great, and one of them approaches me and says something to me that blows me away.

"Maybe you will make this town a Mecca for writers." I instantly love that idea, and also fear it. I love reading about writing, teaching writing, collaborating with other writers and just talking about writing, but another part of me wants to be alone with the privacy to just write. While I enjoy being with my writer friends, I also notice a selfish desire to keep this town that relaxes and inspires me just for me, at least some days, other days I want everyone to know about it. *A Mecca for Writers.* I did like the sound of that though.

I started my writing career as a playwright and one of my favorite classic American playwrights, Tennessee Williams, wrote *The Night of the Iguana*, and set it in Mexico. He also wrote his masterpiece, *A Street Car Named Desire,* in Mexico. He never said why he liked to write in Mexico, but there are certain places that writers seem to polarize to. Williams also wrote in the French Quarter of New Orleans, Key West and New York, places that are unique and attract the character of a writer.

Tennessee Williams said that he wrote because he found life unsatisfactory. I don't know if I feel the same way, but I do find life humorous (a gift I got from my father), and either unbearably long or unbearably short depending on what's going on. It's a marvelous mystery and worth talking about. I can't describe it as unsatisfactory since I abandoned illusions that there was some sort of fairness that was deserved in life. It's not fair. And if it were, we would have nothing to write about and maybe that's what Tennessee was talking about. It is the things that go "wrong" that we write about. Life is not fair, but the pursuit to have human beings treat others fairly is a noble one. Meanwhile, we write about, struggle with, and even celebrate the things that keep us off balance, until we can find some temporary balance again. It's a moving target.

Feeling like a fish out of water in another country is a good way to be a little off balance just enough to bring to me, as a writer, that new perspective, that inspiration, that upside down-ness. I don't think writers thrive in mundane comfort. They thrive in a place that keeps their powers of observation awake and listening. They also thrive in a place where their ordinary life does not exist and can't catch up to them. The family, the friends, the work commitments, the routines, all those cords must be severed for their writing time.

And, perhaps Libé can be a Mecca. I already have a writer coming down to get some writing coaching from me while his wife is on holiday elsewhere doing a sport he has no interest in. This is Ernest. The thing that fascinates me about Ernest is he has been in law enforcement for many years and even in the Canadian equivalent of the FBI. I am sure he has some great stories.

Ernest had met me at a workshop of mine in Canada and started to follow me around a bit. He has a bunch of ideas for books that he wants help with. It seems timely that his wife is going away at the same time we will be in Mexico so he decides to schedule his holidays and meet me in Libé.

Ernest would not be down in time to see my Rotary talk but he could join the group later in a couple of weeks. Unlike the group, however, who were either living here permanently or seasonal regulars it would be the first time Ernest had been to Mexico.

I had sent Ernest some info about Libé including what to pack and what to wear. One of the things I said explicitly was, don't wear black. I said this because not only had Ernest worn black every time I had ever met him, but there is a tendency for everyone in Canada to wear black and gray in winter. This makes no sense to me. In the nearly snowless West Coast, at the grayest, darkest times of the year, with gray skies, gray pavement, gray concrete buildings, and short days of little sunlight, the majority of people are wearing gray and black. Are we catering to a deep survival instinct to provide camouflage? I'm never sure, but I know it always contributes to my winter malaise.

No one wears gray in Mexico. If you wear black it is in the evening and accented with pops of color, flowers and bling for the ladies, or a light or bright colored shirt for the gentlemen with black pants.

Lou has agreed to lend me his van so I can pick Ernest up at the airport. When I get there and see him walk through the Arrivals door, he is wearing black, both top and bottom. *So much for my advice.* He also carries a black rucksack bag that looks like a SWAT team gear bag. I wonder if he has packed his Kevlar too.

In the van, driving to Libé we chat with the usual small talk until we get to the Federale checkpoint. Federale, I am told, is a Spanglish word used in an informal context to denote security forces operating under a federal political system. Because the airport is technically in another state than Libé, there is a Federale stop on the highway when entering the new state where armed military guards slow the traffic and either give you a pass or can search your vehicle. Generally they are looking for drug runners we are told. John and I fondly called this station Checkpoint Charlie.

The only person I had ever heard of getting stopped at Checkpoint Charlie was Nancy. She said she had gone back and forth every day for several days and then out of the blue they stopped her. She couldn't help asking in Spanish, "Why today?" but the soldier had misunderstood and thought she was asking why they were allowed to stop her. He answered her in English grinning,

"Because we have the guns."

I had forgotten about the checkpoint until we were in the slowed line of traffic and I quickly explain it to Ernest who now looks hyper alert as I drive the van closer to the armed Federales.

If you have never been to a foreign country where soldiers openly carrying machine guns and patrol all designated government or significant areas, it is a little unnerving. It does not send a great message to new tourists. Gun estranged Canadians are particularly shocked by this. Ernest, being a Canadian but an enforcement guy, I thought would be a little cooler, but instead it takes him away from vacation mode and puts him back in hyper vigilant work mode. I can see he is wondering what I have got him into.

Though the soldier waves us through with barely a look, Ernest's sense of security is not enhanced as immediately following the checkpoint we pass through a small, chaotic town that looks shocking to first world sensibilities. We get back to the scenic agriculture route and then head toward the sea but Ernest is not relaxed. He starts to ask me all the paranoid tourist questions:

"Is there a lot of drug cartel business here?"

"Are there any gun battles?"

"Are there kidnappings?"

I answer, no, no, and no. I mean obviously they are things happening around in Mexico somewhere, but it is not evident at all in our town and hasn't been since we've been going there. It doesn't even have that history.

"It's a tourist, retirement fishing town," I tell him, but I don't see him unwinding at all. I make a mental note to take him to The

Orca as soon as he is settled. This is the hotel rooftop where Nancy introduced us to the happy hours and the view. People love it there and you can't help but feel uplifted.

We get into town and I take Ernest straight to the apartment we have arranged for him via Teresa and Greta. It is a walk up and Spartan but we chose it for the kitchenette as there are not many two week rentals that have their own. It is close to everything but it is in centro and I told him about the noise before I booked it for him and recommended he bring ear plugs. But, looking at him all in black I am not sure he got the memo, literally.

The first thing I do is show Ernest the double lock gate to get into his apartment building. I struggle with the keys, cursing myself for forgetting the quirk of these keys which in part is turning the key in the opposite direction than my first instinct. He says nothing, he is gazing at the sidewalk. When we walk to the top floor to his apartment he cheers up. The apartment is bright, clean and well stocked. I show him the walk to the rooftop where he can take in a view. I tell him I will be back in 30 minutes with John to take him to The Orca and show him the town.

Within an hour we are happily toasting drinks and looking for the green flash as we watch the sunset from atop The Orca. With the help of John's characteristic ease and the evidence that he knows everyone who walks in the place—and the happy hour mojitos—Ernest is finally grinning broadly and becoming the happy camper. We talk briefly about his writing choices, but we will leave that for mañana.

***

Having the night before extolled the many great breakfast places in his area, I meet Ernest at his apartment to take him to breakfast while John is off sweating somewhere. He looks bleary-eyed and I wonder if I have given him enough time to shake off the jet lag.

"I know what I want for breakfast," he announces.

"Oh yes," I respond cheerily.

"I want that damn rooster."

"Oh," that explains his grogginess.

"Now I know why you said to bring ear plugs," he answers. He did get the memo.

I admit it is a problem with the roosters, but he seems to be taking it with a good sense of humour and I tell him I have an extra pair of ear plugs that I will give him.

I take him to Mango's on the beach that makes a great breakfast. I love that all the restaurants are run mostly by local people and local families. Our waitress is Sissy, a charming and smart girl who has gone to school in the States, so has perfect English so Ernest doesn't feel pressure to try Spanish his first time out, although he did master, "Cerveza, por favor" last night.

We start to talk shop, my shop, writing. Ernest is struggling with three or more writing projects he wants to accomplish. A manual for work that he has been working on for years, a science fiction fantasy idea, a novel idea, and a few other ideas in the hopper. He admits he's a bit of a procrastinator. I encourage him to choose one project and learn how to take it to the end. Somewhere in there he asks Sissy for a glass of water which appears at his elbow.

We continue talking but I notice that he is staring at the glass of water.

"Is it tap water?" he asks me. He knows that we drink from the large bottled water jugs that everyone has, and that tap water is not for drinking in Mexico. Instead of answering him I call Sissy over.

"He wants to know if that is tap water," I ask Sissy for him. The horror on Sissy's face is priceless.

"I would never, ever, ever, do that to you!" Sissy starts to sputter, practically in tears at the thought of it. "Of course, it is filtered water, Señor." I reassure Sissy that we did not think any malice of her and she goes back to her usual cheerful self. Ernest looks a little sheepish.

"No one is trying to kill you here. You really can relax," I say smiling at him.

"Okay, okay I get the idea," he says.

When we walk back to his apartment he shows me some brown stains on the sidewalk in front of his apartment building. They are drips, probably from some paint years ago.

"That looks exactly like someone was stabbed here," he tells me, "I have seen this before." I look into the eyes of a city person, a crime investigator person, and remember that yesterday while I was struggling with the gate locks he had been staring at the sidewalk. Now I know what he had been thinking.

I can't help but laugh it off before I tell him the murder rate in town is very, very low and the stains likely just a spill of something else. It's not like Mexico has super street cleaning—although they actually do have a street cleaning truck, I've seen it, once.

"Okay, okay, it's just my training," he admits.

After the water and sidewalk incident, Ernest really does start to chill. He goes out at night by himself and has a blast. He meets the writing group at the See Sea Casa and learns that some of them have been coming down for 20 years. He starts to see that not only has he been overreacting but exactly how much.

The challenge of getting Ernest to unwind seems to be over. Getting him to actually write something proves to be another challenge that has just begun. Fortunately, I start off making everyone write short pieces while we are meeting, with a fun or skill focus involved, so we can share them and help each other. Ernest decides to write the work manual on ideal crime prevention, but it is coming out pretty dry, like he is giving testimony at court for a judge. I have got him relaxed socially, but how am I going to get him to relax his writing? The group is supportive and I am coaching outside the group, usually over a meal in town.

Ernest, being in the crime prevention field has some pretty enthralling stories to share. He starts to regale me with them over lunch and I encourage him to write them down, whether they fit into his project or not. Yet, after a few days, he doesn't seem to be doing any writing on his own. Nothing gets done if you let your resistance to writing dominate.

I give him the three minute rule, that he just has to write for three minutes only, and it works! For a day or two, but it still comes out pretty cold and he gives up writing completely, even when we are very encouraging. Pretty soon I am going through nearly every trick I have in my 20 year arsenal of teaching writing.

Since Ernest has now been de-stressing I discover he seems to be competing with John for the gringo man about town award. He is no longer wearing black but has bought some pretty colorful shirts, even louder than I would dare. I notice that people are greeting him in the street; the bartenders and waitresses know him, and he knows any and all upcoming local events and has snagged invites.

In short, Ernest is a social animal. He especially likes to socialize with the other writers and is looking forward to our reading night event coming up. At my rope's end as his writing coach and with Ernest's writing soul in the balance I decide that I need to get military on him. I will pull rank. I take him aside the day before the event.

"You can't come to the reading night if you are not going to write anything to read." Normally, I encourage but don't force people to read at all, ever, ever, but it is the writing part that they must do. I am firm and curt, totally the opposite of my usual supportive style. He is aghast and pissed off. He storms off and I am filled with doubts. *Did I just blow it?*

The night of our event I walk into The Blue Lagoon restaurante which I know has become Ernest's favorite. It has a very affable host we call The Dude. The Lagoon has great food—the blue cheese pineapple burger is awesome—all under a giant, cool palapa. The writers start to assemble, but no Ernest.

Just before we start to order he walks in the door and joins the group. I am happy and relieved to see him and before I can wonder he tells me that he has brought something to read.

We have a great meal, filled with jokes, laughs and stories. Ernest is taking part but a little more reserved than before. The readings start. Applause and pats on the back are plentiful. Everyone's tongues are loosened by good spirits both in liquid and ethereal forms. Finally there is only one more person to read, Ernest.

He starts slow and I immediately recognize the story he is telling. He had told me details of it at a lunch, an unsolved cold case that haunted him. I had once again encouraged him to write it down and also to include his thoughts, feelings and all the personal details—beyond his just-the-facts-ma'am style.

As I listen, I look around the room at the enthralled faces; I realize he is doing it. It is not only an engaging story but the group has never heard anything so personal from Ernest. In fact, they have heard very little from him at all. At the end, everyone is blown away and I don't have to do anything at all. They are plying him with questions and comments, clearly interested and asking for more. He has found an audience.

Later he gives me a gift of a Talavera frog and thanks me for getting "tough." He's on a journey. Can he continue without prompting? That is always the struggle with any new writer.

The day before we are seeing Ernest off on the plane home he comes over to the See Sea Casa to hang out with John. He is at the front gate while John is getting something and I am in the back.

As I am sunning myself a young Mexican man comes in and starts looking around. He is not one of our maintenance people. I ask him how he got in and he says the guy at the front let him look around for gardening. The See Sea Casa has no lawn or soil in the back. I send him on his way and ask Ernest why he let him in.

"He said he was here for gardening."

"Ernest, we don't have any gardening at this casa. I think he was casing the place."

"Really? He seemed so nice." In two weeks Ernest had gone from seeing potential stabbings in sidewalk splatters to a degree of trust that is almost naive. It is, perhaps, just the right time for him to head back home.

The Bride

It had been a whole year since our trip to Guadalajara: wedding dress central, and another year we are not officially betrothed. Though I rarely speak about it to John, as I rapidly approach 50 I get more anxious about our unwed state.

I had told John years before that I wanted to be married. Why? For me it was a combination of things. First, I had a very bad experience when I moved in with my first boyfriend at the tender age of 18. At that age, you think you know what you are doing and you do not. The word "trapped" comes to mind when I think of this relationship, and the word "depressing" is not far behind.

From this you might guess that I would never again want to move in with a man, or have a marriage-like relationship, and you would be right. After that first uncomfortable committed relationship I was unconsciously drawn to commitmentphobic men for years. Relationships that would never get off the ground, leave me broken hearted, but free.

This was exhausting and took many years of repeated mistakes and, later, counseling to understand what was going on. So, in a nut shell I was very ready for a stable, fully committed relationship when I met John in my early forties.

I had a committed relationship with him, some would call it a marriage, so why did I want to make it formal and add an expensive wedding? Especially, given the state of our finances. I had started developing a few answers.

The first was about fears. I have two competing ones. For my "abandonment" fears I want the public, traditionally recognized, sacred, bonded by vows, relationship status. I want to know that this man is not going away and will want to stay with me through all my freak outs, quirks, temper tantrums, and all the negative sides of me, as well as the positive sides of me. This is completely converse to and at odds with the woman who needs to *not* feel trapped.

For my "trapped" fears I want the trust and understanding that John will give me my independence and I won't feel like I am compromising on my life. There is that old ball and chain analogy. But, I am starting to believe maybe that ball and chain can be a good thing, like an anchor

For some creative types, it is not so much an anchor as the person at the end of the kite string not letting you fly off into the stratosphere. John is my Steady Eddy. To date, he had never held me back, ever, unless it was good for me. Maybe I need to have that string attached?

However, I am not the only one with marriage issues. John is also facing fears. He had been married before and I had not. He didn't need to have another failed marriage under his belt and I think the freedom factor in my personality scared him. I could fly off... the handle, the deep end, or just fly off. And then there is that statistic that so many like to bandy about, over 50% of marriages end in divorce.

Fortunately, I am a writer, reader and therefore a researcher. I look up the actual statistics and find a surprising fact. When people get married at 45 and older the divorce rate drops dramatically. I ponder this and it rings true for me. I was a naive, barely 18 year old when I moved in with someone I shouldn't have. At 45, I know myself. I am getting honest with myself. I don't just follow things because it's what's expected and that is probably why I dislike corporate jobs now. But, in relationships I have learned to listen to my ego less, and communicate with others more.

News flash: marriages for the over 45 have an over 90% success rate. People depend on each other and help each other as they get older and that is a good thing. I see it with my dad and my stepmother and I want to emulate it.

The second reason to have that big, potentially expensive wedding is for a true celebration of life that doesn't involve a casket. In my forties I had lost five close friends, and it started to dawn on me that this trend might start increasing with age. The downside to a funeral, or celebration of life as the new word-spin calls them, is you don't get to be there to see all those people gathering around for you at your funeral, but for your wedding, you do.

A few years ago one of my best friends who had moved hundreds of miles away passed away very unexpectedly. I felt extreme regret that before her death I had kept putting off my visit to see her (there was always time), and yet I was finally making the journey to be at her funeral. I was, ironically, allowed the time off work for that trip. Yes, maybe a true celebration of life with no dead people present might be a breath of fresh air.

The third and most important thought I have about this traditional step is the thing I am discovering in Libé that I believe many of us are missing: community. John and I are becoming more and more invested in the community of Libé in Mexico where we go to town meetings about fun topics like the sewer system, fundraisers for local police uniforms and school buildings, and we go to "fun" raising events too. We go to some of those events in Canada too but they seem splintered, separate, hard to get a hold of. But, in either country the celebrations and events together make a community. The difference in Libé, however, is that for both the practical events and the fun events we would see the same people.

We do not have a wedding but we do have one event: my 50th birthday party. John has planned an impressive bash for me that involves a lot of folks in town. It is not a surprise party but when it happens the amount of effort that goes into it is a surprise to me. So many people, so much food and they had adhered to my wish of no gifts! *Bring yourself, food and drink if you like, but please don't burden me with more things.* I am super impressed with everything.

My knight has really pulled it off well. Being unwed at 50 won't be so bad after all.

The next morning, as we bask in the afterglow of the party, John and I start to talk. First about the party, then about the future when he says something I don't expect.

"Will you marry me?" I am in shock.

"You've never said that before." Hardly a romantic response but I am thrown. *Is he teasing?*

"No," he answers, seriously. I think about it for a second. I could see he is holding his breath, unsure of what I will say. My heart, I notice is beating very fast. With one sentence this has gone from a bedroom chat to something else.

"Ask me again," I ask, a little lightheaded now.

"Will you marry me?"

"Yes." Cut to us kissing, the sun shining on the window sill... except, I had to check. *Did this really just happen?*

"Ask me again."

"Will you marry me?"

"Yes." More happy kisses with the man I decided long ago was the best kisser I could hope to find. Then, as a joke I say it for a third time.

"Ask me again."

"Will you marry me?" He dutifully asks once more with a grin and I whisper another "yes" into his shoulder, except he doesn't hear me.

"You didn't say yes this time!"

"Yes, yes I did! You just didn't hear me."

"Oh, okay."

Maybe the fears and doubts never go away. Even frightened, we knew it was totally right. I was to be a bride at 50.

***

All our friends in Libé like Tommy and Janine, Hud and Ida, Hugo and Julia, Teresa and Greta, Lou and Frances, Callie and Alberto and the rest of The French Front, as well as all the writers in my circle are all very happy for us, but we are in a dilemma, where are we getting married? For about two seconds we think about a wedding in Mexico but we do not want to put that kind of expensive burden on our families and Canadian friends. We decide on a fall wedding giving me a number of months to plan.

I am going to need a dress. I start to think about those bridal shops in Guadalajara again. I don't want to go all the way to the big G city but maybe there is something local I can look at and bring home to Canada for the big day. I ask Greta if they have any local bridal dress shops. She tells me that there is one on the main street of the nearest bigger town. Great! And I have the perfect person to shop with.

This season, fellow writer and comedienne, Lucy, has come to write her memoirs and get a little guidance from me. Lucy has a bright smile, a personality everyone loves, and a polished fashion sense that I have never been able to attain. I have always envied women who look great in short, short hair and Lucy is one of those women. She blurts things that are hysterical, but like most comedians I have known has a dark side where the humour comes from. Sheer joy coupled with continuous pet peeves and dissatisfaction is what activates the humour release valve in them. Yet, I couldn't think of anyone more fun to go shopping with.

Lucy has only been down long enough to learn the three standard get-by phrases in Spanish, gracias, por favor and cerveza (beer). Anything beyond that is lost on her. While John is diligently learning how to put sentences together correctly, I play fast and lose with grammar and syntax and instead just collect cool new Spanish words I like as if they are shiny pocket stones I pick up on the beach.

One night, I introduce Lucy to our Mexican friend, Chica, who speaks no English. I exchange a few words of Spanish with her, just enough to understand each other. Lucy is impressed, not knowing that I could easily be confused in a blink of an eye, and frequently have to glance over at my much-better-at-his-Spanish future husband to rescue me. The long and the short of this is we are going to go shopping in another small town in Mexico where few, if any, people speak English to try on what may be my wedding dress and are woefully unprepared in language skills. I wonder how this is going to go down.

We go into the town where Greta had told us, but can find only one shop with a formal dress in the window and it is a quincenara dress. Lucy and I stare at it transfixed. It is quite beautiful and a bright, jewel-tone blue. The shop itself looks way too small and doesn't advertise on the outside what I am looking for, "vestidos de novia," (wedding dresses). We continue to stare at the beautiful blue dress together behind the glass and finally I ask the question.

"Do you think I can have a blue wedding dress?"

"Why not?"

"Okay, we'll go in."

I inquire to the woman within as best I can, gesturing to the window about the "vestido aqui" (dress here). Pointing at whatever I need is one way I survive in Mexico with rudimentary Spanish. She answers in several full sentences of rapid-fire Spanish which I catch the gist of from her use of the word, "chica." Lucy, also hears the word "chica" and is suddenly elated.

"She knows Chica!" Lucy translates for me. I chuckle. Always nice to have someone around who makes your language skills look good.

"Chica," I explain to Lucy, "is also the word for girl." The likelihood this woman knows our friend Chica in Libé—who is called Chica as her permanent nickname—is highly unlikely.

"She means that the blue dress only comes in sizes for girls."

"Ohh." Lucy laughs at herself and we chuckle together as the mystified shop owner looks on. I take a breath and use my cheater Spanish to ask if they have any, by chance, "vestidos de novia."

"Para usted?" (For you?) The woman looks at me incredulously. Clearly they don't have many fifty year old brides in this country.

"Para mi," I confess to her. She breaks into a wide smile.

"Si, si!" She gestures for us to follow her into a door at the back of her very small shop and Lucy and I follow.

We enter the back room and all I can see for a few moments is a sea of white. A large warehouse of white dresses hang from floor to ceiling in the back of this shop, and they have a very high ceiling. We had indeed found the right shop. In this warehouse are two shop girls all excited to have a rare bird visit them, an aged gringa (i.e. rich) bride-to-be.

The first thing Lucy and I notice is that these are not like the dresses back home. The cuts are generally from old fashioned to less old fashioned. The fabric is light in weight and synthetic, which surprises me. Even with the bushels of undergarments to create the poof, they are feather weights.

The shop attendants are very, well, attentive, and buzzing with the excitement of it. *What about this one? What about that one?* Lucy and I are overwhelmed trying to narrow the selection down. They test all the possibilities out on me which I am discussing fluently in English with Lucy, but the women have no clue what I am saying. I have zero Spanish for such words as neckline, sleeves, waistline, etc.

We do a lot of gesturing and get by okay. I pick out four to try on. All three girls very excitedly take us back out to the front of the store which looks very full with all five of us in it. There, in the back corner of the store they gesture to a door, a change room that I hadn't noticed before. It is small. The dresses are huge.

"How am I going to do this?" I ask Lucy who looks at the phone booth sized change room before responding.

"Ask Superman for advice?"

I smile, but she doesn't know that I sometimes get claustrophobia in tight spaces. I drag the first of my dress choices over to the door and fill the change room up with its presence. Then, I push back some of the poof to make a space for me and get in closing the door. Mercifully, the change room is open at the top so I can feel air and hear Lucy's voice.

I squirm my own clothes off and find the skirt bottom to dive into head first, giving Lucy a blow by blow monologue of the tribulation. I start to sweat with the effort. It is hot in the store, though the store is much cooler than outside, it is fan cooled not air conditioned cool.

I manage to get the dress on, somewhat, when I realize I am having a hot flash. I am really sweating now. *Crap on a cracker*, as Skye, my writer friend from the South would say. I grab some Kleenex in my tiny purse I brought with me and hold a couple of pieces under each of my arm pits. They stick in place from the amount of sweat. The synthetic fabric of the dress has latexed on to me. I know I have been in the change room for a long time and I am not saying anything now.

"You okay Kat?" Lucy ventures.

"Yup," I lie. "Almost done. You are going to have to help me put it all the way on I think." I let my "flash" subside and come out, having stashed the sweat absorbed Kleenix in my purse. I am thinking to myself, *Did this seem like a fun idea this morning?*

The girls pull the dress down in the back while fawning and fussing and saying compliments only a few of which I understand. In front of the mirror, Lucy and I look at it. It's ugly. God awful ugly. Puffy princess cap sleeves from another era. My waistline looks in the wrong spot, and the poof just makes me look massive. I am clearly not a girl who can carry off a traditional ball gown. It's a quick nix to the disappointment of the shop girls.

To Lucy I tell my more pressing concern.

"I'm not going to be able to get this off by myself in that room." Lucy starts to try to peel the synthetic fabric up and over my head outside the change room and the girls all jump in quickly to help.

Three of them are peeling it off of me while trying to preserve my dignity. The strapless bra I am wearing is rolling up with the dress and Lucy and the girls are hanging onto it as they lift the whole thing off me. I am thankful no one else is shopping at siesta time and I desperately want some water but am too chicken to ask for it, unsure if they have anything other than tap water in a shop. I am exhausted and there are three more dresses that I am now pretty sure will look equally disastrous on me.

I quickly feign the next two dresses didn't fit and reject them from the change room without even trying to get them on. The last one I give a try because it seems less difficult and I am starting to cool down a little. I get it on. In the shop, we look in the mirror again. A new kind of ugly on me. Lucy is diplomatic while the shop girls fawn and coo.

"Si?" they ask. *Is this the one?*

"No."

"No?" They look skeptical and ask again. "No?"

"No, gracias. Lo siento" (I'm sorry). They don't try to hide their utter disappointment that the rich gringa is not buying a dress and keep asking and sighing loudly. I can see Lucy is part annoyed and part amused at their guilt-tripping me. If she could speak Spanish I wonder what she might say to them, but she is polite.

I buy from them some rhinestone jewelry that is on the mannequin with the blue dress in the window. I hope it is a consolation for all their efforts. We leave, thanking them profusely.

I see the blue dress in the window as we go. It still looks pretty to me. So much for that idea. Lucy pipes up.

"Something old, something new, something blue?"

"Well, I've already got the old part down. I am clearly no chica."

"Neither am I." We share a old girl's chuckle. Lucy turns to the street. "What's next, centre pieces? I can hardly wait."

Okay, maybe it is just as well I am getting married in Canada.

Season 4

LOS BOXEADORES

The Final Round

After seven years, we were married. In Canada. The wedding was a fabulously fun affair. My sister helped me find the perfect dress with a pleated, floating bottom to it like the Marilyn Monroe dress in her famous sidewalk scene (ironically the scene from the *Seven Year Itch*). I loved it. John loved it. And he looked pretty handsome too, also all in white except for a beautiful, yellow-gold satin vest and his best panama hat. One of my dearest friends had lovingly hand-crafted the flowers including the bouquets that popped on the little black dresses of my bridesmaids.

It was a community affair. Everyone played a part in one way or another. We had created numerous performances, involving music, dance, theatre and humour including a Bridesmaid's Ugliest Dress Contest. I had asked my bridesmaids to go to consignment stores and buy the ugliest bridesmaid's dresses they could find. They wore their own little black dresses for the ceremony, but later got into their finds for the contest to show them off in all their horrific glory. The guests decided who won. It was great fun.

The food buffet was yummy and included vegan choices for my Maid of Honor, Amber, and my other vegan guests. The aloo gobi and veggie moussaka was so delish, I was stealing off Amber's plate. The regular meat dishes were very standard in comparison albeit well done and made me reconsider my meat eating ways, for a few seconds.

The cake had white frosting but was chocolate and orange underneath, one of my favorite, classic combinations. For the cake cutting John and I snuck out and dressed as our older selves 30 years in the future and came back and acted like we were there for our 30th wedding anniversary. In character, we did a fun comic bit of ourselves as a hard of hearing couple nattering away to each other, before we very gently and sweetly fed each other cake and kissed.

The master of ceremonies was funny, the speeches given were an incredible hit (especially Amber's which will be forever known as The Princess speech—she let everyone know that we all deserved to be princesses), and even the impromptu speeches were terrific.

The band was out of this world good—*Brickhouse*, the same band John and I had been dancing to every Sunday for the past seven years. A number of our talented friends got up and sang, and John and I danced a rehearsed tango. Our various dance teachers put on dance demos and our tango teacher from Argentina sang while a flamenco dancer danced. People told us it was rather like being at the dinner theatre hit play, *Tony and Tina's Wedding.*

Almost everyone we knew and loved was there, friends from our multiplicity of communities, from our families, especially for me, my adored, aged papa and my stepmother. People had a great time and said it was the most fun they had ever had at a wedding. Celebration of life? Mission accomplished. Except for all the people we had left in Mexico.

I send them a video link. Greta tells me the English is too fast for her to understand in the speeches. I always thought Greta's English was excellent and for the first time I grasp that languages take a long time for anyone to fully master.

"When we build our house in Mexico," John says consoling me, "we'll have a big anniversary party there."

But I am starting to wonder if that is ever going to happen. The house that is, not the anniversary.

***

The economy, how ever artificially buoyed, is bouncing back. I am getting writing and editing work as well as teaching and other consulting. We are not making a ton of money anymore but doing okay. We are officially a team. Married. I giggle every time I call John my husband. He seems to enjoy—a little too much in my opinion—saying "my wife" but otherwise, bliss.

We arrange for a quiet four-day honeymoon on a pretty island off the West Coast of Canada just as the leaves are falling in bright colors, signally we are well into autumn.

We sit outside bundled up on Adirondack chairs reading, but it is getting nippy. I am reading *The Game of Thrones*, and I realize that, as they say in the Stark House of Winterfell, *Winter is Coming*. We will need to escape the cold for another season soon and occupy another rental casa that Teresa and Greta have already arranged for us.

Back home, I look over the details of the new rental casa which John has seen but I have not. No palapa, my heart sinks a little. No pool, ah well, I am perhaps spoiled, and we can always go to the Hotel Playa Azul two blocks away and use their pool for the price of a cheap drink served poolside. Much nicer than any private pool we have seen. The rental casa has a garden and it's in an okay location. Not the best but it will do.

I remember we will have to get all our stuff out of storage and after a few seasons we are amassing quite a collection including two bicycles that I am planning on expanding to three. Tommy has been keeping some of our stuff, Greta and Teresa some other things, and a handful of other friends have random bits and pieces that we find essential down there, like decent cookware. Rentals have notoriously poor cookware. I am suddenly feeling tired and I know why.

The thought of pulling all our Mexico stuff together again is one thing but I have just paid the annual bank trust fee on our corner lot once again. A lot we are not using, not able to camp on, and pay someone twice yearly to clear the weeds off. *What is the point? Why do we have a lot? What exactly were we thinking?* My doubts churn around my head like an annoying rattle.

We can't afford to build, because they need all-cash. We may never be able to build. The property has retained its value and even increased a little but for quite awhile we could have bought other things, except we couldn't because our all our money for a down payment is tied up in the lot.

Well, nearly all, but when we bought the lot it had been more expensive to buy a house than to build, and now it is the reverse. Building costs have been…building. Meanwhile, we knew there were some great deals on houses in Libé and nearly all these casas included furnishings, appliances and some even a car. We could also have taken advantage of the global dip in real estate prices at home to buy at a better deal in Canada. I couldn't help but lament, *Will I never get my timing right in my life?*

Maybe it wasn't too late. We could sell our Mexico property. It would mean we would not be making a dime. It would mean that we would have been paying all those years of bank trust fees for nothing. But, we could put a nice deposit on a condo in our beautiful Northern country. These are the things I am silently brooding on and about to once again share with John as part of my perpetual bitch session on our finances.

"I want to sell our lot in Mexico." Up until that moment John had been pleasantly ignoring me while I whined on a Saturday morning and he puttered around the house timing his "Uh, huhs" perfectly. He stood straight up, eyes wide, looking at me as if he had been sucker punched. But he gave a sigh. This wasn't the first time I had brought up the possibility and it was usually timed after the bank trust payment. It wasn't that it was a lot of money just an unpleasant reminder.

"Uh huh," he responded. This couldn't help but irritate me so I took my stand and reinforced my position.

"We are never going to be able to build now without financing. We have already tried to get that." This was true. Banks in Canada are not so keen to finance property in foreign lands. We had a line of credit but it wasn't enough. The Mexican and U.S. banks had some programs but you had to have a pre-approved new-build subdivision that was on their "list." Those "approved" projects were not in Libé.

"I don't understand why you need to build now. Can't you wait until I am retired? We won't be able to spend more than a couple of months there during the year until then anyway." He had jabbed this one at me before.

"You won't be retired for years, and it's wasted money. We should just sell the lot and use the money to buy up here." There was the punch again, but he blocked it resolutely.

"No."

"No? No? You can't just say no, that's not an argument."

"You still haven't explained to me why we can't wait."

"You haven't told me why I can't sell." He did not miss the "I." Ultimately, it was my name on the deed. This was a nasty little hook that defied the vows we so recently said publically.

"Fine." He said with a quick chop, "you can sell it to me." I was speechless for a second.

"Whaa... that's the most idiotic thing I've ever heard." Now I was really mad with frustration.

"There you go, calling me an idiot."

"I did not." I didn't have a chance to point out that I didn't call *him* an idiot, just his idea, before I shifted my weight and counter punched instead. "You are being hypersensitive." He made a surprising dodge to that swing.

"Sell it to me." He said again. Again this had me sputtering but I righted myself with the obvious move.

"We are married! You already have it!"

"Well I don't want to sell it."

"Clearly."

"Why can't we wait?" He asked. Here we go again.

"When you retire, your income tends to go down," I said not keeping the sarcastic edge out of my voice. "We should get the building and furnishings done little by little, while we are working and bringing in money, if we are going to build at all."

When I said 'we' are working I meant his stable money and my sporadic income. He picked up on the 'we' and threw it back at me.

"I can't do it all by myself and you are not making enough." *Oh, low blow boyo.* But it was true. I was writing, editing and coaching more but wasn't taking the corporate gigs that brought in the major cash.

"You know I can't stand being corporate any more." He had me on the ropes. John loved that when he met me I had worn suits. I don't know if he harbored the fantasy of doing it on the desk in my old office, but he did like the idea of humble yet well educated labor guy having Corporate Girl on his arm. When I changed (back) into Writing Girl he was a little mystified but very supportive. He had a diploma in journalism himself, obtained just as newspapers started to nose dive into internet oblivion and quickly turned his part time job at the post office into a full time lifer career.

We went back to our corners. Him behind a newspaper, the paper version of which he still loyally had delivered on Saturdays, and me on the couch behind a so-called Smartphone. It didn't last. I had thought of another jab.

"I don't know why you want to keep this lot so badly. You hate yard work—strike that, you hate domestic work of any kind. You have no interest in the work it would take to maintain it or make it ready for rentals when we are not there. I would be doing it all. All you want to do in Mexico is bike, drink and dance."

"Anything that makes me sweat, makes me happy," he answered. I had come out with a flurry but it was like he was holding me at arms length, until I saw the opening.

"Anything but work, that is," this was quickly followed by a jab combination, "maybe you can get your harem to do it all." John, being a dance guy, had a small group of dance partners always at the ready when I wasn't around, both in Mexico and Canada, who I affectionately called his harem. It was not cool to bring the innocent ladies into it who had never given me any reason to be anything other than grateful to them. The fight was getting ugly. Strangely, he was more offended by the work reference.

"I bust my butt for us!" It was true and that old poem needed updating. You know that one about letter carriers that says, *Neither snow nor rain nor heat nor gloom of night stays these couriers from the swift completion of their appointed rounds.* You could add, nor killer ice, nor sleep deprivation from enforced overtime, nor frothing

Rottweilers, nor impossible to finish extended routes, nor crazy drug addicts looking for welfare cheques, nor lobby vultures (it's a downtown postie thing), nor the sheer quantity and size of parcels coming from internet orders, nor mailman minefields (buckled sidewalks, hidden sprinkler heads, concealed tree roots), nor repetitive strain injuries, nor a thousand other things that kill, maim or enforce extended stress and disability leaves for our men and women of the postal services, so they really do have a hard time with any kind of completion of their rounds. It's a war zone out there.

Okay that was a blow I should not have let lose. I put my gloves down.

"I know you bust your butt. But it's because I want you to get out sooner that I think we should be thinking of the smartest thing to do."

Ding. The match was over and I could see the judges were going to have to take some time away and make a ruling.

C is for Caliente

We return to Libé with the question of what to do with the lot still in limbo, but I agree to at least meet some architects. After all, we actually don't know how much our dream home might cost. Our new rental casa, which I call Casa Blanco for its colorless exterior and interior is cheap. For a reason. It's older but it has three showers. This time we have a house and one shower all to ourselves, with an apartment and extra room for guests. And there will be some writer guests coming later.

I have to let guests who are visiting for the first time know a few things about their bathroom experiences in Mexico. First, the toilet paper etiquette, second, the geckos, and third, C is for caliente. That is, on your faucet knobs, C is for caliente, which means hot not cold. But, when I have shown people this before and let them try it, they think they must have gotten it wrong since it will often take the shower so long to get hot water coming out of it that they are certain they turned the cold on not the hot. And, that's the other thing I have to remember to tell them.

The gas heat from the gas tanks are slow to heat the water and somewhat finicky. John and I have become adept at relighting the pilot light and adjusting the controls. Or, if all else fails, flagging down the gas guys and getting them to help us. You don't want to be doing this when you are ready to have a shower. You just want a shower. Some of the gas heaters are better than others, but the Casa Blanco has an approach to showers that we have not yet tried and we are very nervous about it.

Our hot water in this older house will be solar heated from an apparatus on the roof. John is the first to get in the shower and test it.

"Yikes!" he yelps.

"Too cold?" I stick my head in.

"Too hot," he answers while adjusting the faucet.

"Already?" I am dumbfounded. No two-minute requisite wait. This is a first for us. The hottest and quickest water to the showerhead we have had to date is from this solar heated shower.

I climb a spiral staircase to the roof because I have to see it for myself. The solar hot water heating device is on the roof. It is a set of sixteen silver tubes about two meters in length. They are old; one tube is completely clogged and burned out like a spent fuse. I didn't understand the technology but I could see the thing was weather worn and likely as old as the house, and the house was one of the older ones in the Fraccionamiento. Yet, it worked like a hot damn, pardon the pun. I was seriously impressed. Who knew doing the right thing could also be the best thing?

However, it seems to work for supplying the showers and not the kitchen sinks so there was likely a consideration for the hook-up that was done at the outset that by-passed the kitchen, but we love these showers. No gas heater to play with, and no gas guy to pay.

Before the world had its financial collapse in 2008, we did talk to a builder in town. I remember I had asked if people were doing solar power here. Solar in a hot country makes so much sense. The builder had said that it was too expensive, the technology was not good enough, it won't pay for itself, etc. etc. It was clear they were trying to talk us out of solar options. The truth is people want to do what they know and what is easy, but part of me also bought it. It took our fluke rental of the Casa Blanco to realize that everyone in the neighborhood would probably rather have solar heated showers than what they have now.

"When we build our house, the whole house is going to be solar." I swear to myself, John and the planet.

"That's my girl," he says, and though it sounds corny, I am actually proud of myself. Taking advantage of my optimism to build John makes a suggestion.

"Hey, let's create a list of things we would put in our house— or avoid— from all our rental experiences." I agree, knowing we have been doing this for years just never writing it down.

Teresa and Greta have set up some appointments to meet builder/architects while we are down. But, even before we meet them I find out that the builders don't dismiss solar now, they are thumbs up, they have the contacts, they can call in "a guy." No one is really clear on how it works with the grid, but its here to stay.

We start our list and besides putting solar shower on it we put on other things about bathrooms and showers we like. John wants a seat in the shower for when we grow old together and can't stand as well. *Aww.* I want some tiling and Talavera sinks. To remind, Talavera is a beautiful style of glazed pottery with traditional and modern designs in bright colors and patterns that they make into virtually everything from lamp shades to plates to bathroom sinks and tiles.

Generally speaking, Mexican bathrooms can be terrific. One time, for a short period we stayed in a casa with a round shower. It was awesome! It was cylindrical, very sexy and big enough for a small orgy. It was on the second floor and had small vertical slit windows from which I could see the palm trees swaying outside, but no one could see me inside. But it was also awesome because of the tiling.

The Mexicans are aesthetic geniuses with tiling. The inside of that round shower had a shattered tile effect that I loved. They shatter different colored tiles and mosaic them back together with grout so that your shower becomes part art, part shower. Plus, Mexican showers rarely have any shower curtains but instead the splash zone is protected by glass block walls, or, in the case of the round shower, a sexy curved half wall. We made sure that we set up and an appointment with the architect who did that casa.

Of course, if a bathroom is built by poor construction, it doesn't matter how lovely the design, the water won't drain to the drain and it goes all over the bathroom floor. Or, almost worse, the drains may allow sewer gas to float up completely ruining any deluxe bathroom experience. We had smelt that unpleasant odor even in nicer hotels in Mexico.

Our first appointments with architects would not be until after Christmas, but in the meantime the lists of what we want (and didn't want) grows longer as if we are writing to Santa Claus.

45

EL BURRO

Navidad in Libé

"Change is good, Donkey."

For some strange reason John loves donkeys. Even before he saw the animation, *Shrek*, when he started saying the phrase, "Change is good, donkey" for every situation that it could even remotely be construed as appropriate, he told me how much he liked donkeys. So I bought him a cute little stuffed donkey that he keeps in the holiest of holy places, propped up on his cherished vintage record player that he uses for spinning the classic vinyl that he loves. His own version of an altar.

John is a city boy and I don't think he had ever seen, let alone touched, a real donkey. At least, not until Mexico. In a small town in Mexico, you are always close to either the jungle, the farms, the desert, or the sea. Libé is close to everything. That means there are always a few cows, goats, some scrawny looking horses and some lovely burros (small donkeys) in barb-wired fields around the corner. And, the other thing it means, is that they escape their fences every once in awhile. Even in the ritzy Pueblo Blanco neighbourhood you will see the cows, goats and horses trotting down the road, stirring up a little dust as if it were their regular route to the pasture as they pass the sumptuous, fully decked out, stylish houses.

One day we met a renegade horse and donkey walking down the street. John was finally eye to eye with the animal he adored. I wondered what would happen. I grew up being a horse nut so was comfortable with bigger domestic beasts, but for others, especially city boys, being around such creatures is an awe-inspiring novelty. I could see that the burro was friendly by the way he kept his ears up and I encouraged John to reach out to him. But, I guess it was a little like the enthusiastic fan who finally meets the star they have idolized only to be tongue twisted, miss their chance, and remain admiring them from afar. The donkey and his side-kick, trotted off to nibble some grass in an empty lot. He missed it, but Christmas (Navidad) was coming when the burros are pressed into service.

***

We had been looking forward to another Christmas in Libé. It didn't disappoint. On Christmas Eve we find ourselves walking through town late at night after a great meal with The French Front in which we once again straddle three languages. Peeking into the open doorways the families are all up having their parties. All night long, fireworks and fire crackers; Mariachi and dancing. Party, party,

party. Everyone. All ages. Up until the wee hours of the morning when people start to crash.

In contrast to my memory of Christmas mornings as a kid in Canada, with everyone up early and rushing down to open presents, Christmas morning in Libé is quiet since everyone is sleeping in. At least, it is until we hear something we can't identify.

We wake up to what sounds like a very strange horn blaring. *Maybe a drunken Mariachi player on his way home?* But not even that could sound this off-pitch. John pokes his head out the window and then back in again.

"Take a look at this, you won't believe it." I did, and if I hadn't seen it myself I might not have.

A burro is galloping down the middle of the street braying at the top of his lungs. I had never heard an animal, relatively small, make such a big sound. It is like a call to Christmas morning. Perhaps, this burro had something to celebrate. In the weeks leading up to Christmas there are several posada parades, the re-creations of the trip to Bethlehem, with a live burro always carrying an "immaculately conceived, pregnant Madonna" and a young man playing Joseph knocking on all the doors looking for lodging. This burro might have been yelling his freedom from all this Christmas stuff at the top of his lungs. Everyone poking their heads out their windows is laughing, including us. I guess it is time to get up. For once, I couldn't blame the roosters or the megaphones.

Since we were up, we decide to go to brunch at my favorite breakfast place, La Casa de Mi Madre that stays open for Christmas and all other holiday hangovers. I ride my little vintage folding bike that makes me feel like I am twelve again while John walks. The restaurante is packed. Good food and service always attract. There is always an array of 10 different kinds of fruits on their fruit plate and I have to have the pancakes.

By accident, John and I discovered a new taste sensation. Since the Mexicans put lime on everything, one day I tried it on my pancakes with the Canadian favorite, maple syrup. Damn if that wasn't the best taste combo discovery I have made in my life. The sour lime and the sweet maple syrup compliment each other perfectly, and with Mi Madre's fluffy pancakes, it is *to die for*. I could go on about their spiced potatoes and their excellent complimentary condiments like granola, yogurt, marmalade and cookies with your coffee, but I think you get the idea.

When we return home to our block, we encounter the runaway burro across the street from our rental casa eating garbage in an empty lot. I told John I am worried for the burro. They will eat anything. We decide right then to hatch a rapid rescue plan. John is very excited about this.

"What are we going to do?" He looks to me as the child horsy nut. And, in fact, I did know exactly what was irresistible to four legged hoofed domestic beasts.

"Get that big plastic bowl and dry it out."

"Check."

"Get my granola and dump half of it in."

"Check."

"Follow me."

We had already tried to approach the burro and he was clearly very wary, so this time armed with the perfect lure, I smugly tell my city boy to shake the plastic bowl so that the burro can hear the sound of the granola in the plastic bowl. He does. Immediately the burro's ears prick up. I take the bowl a little closer. It is much easier to rope in an animal that comes to you willingly. The little burro moves in to enjoy my Mexican granola that had been audibly masquerading as oats in a bucket.

Okay, we have a burro, and he is friendly, now what? John looks at me. I tell him to fill up a small bucket with water so he can give the burro a drink. John, tentatively moves closer offering the burro the bucket at my encouragement. The burro happily plunges his nose into the bucket and drinks heartily. For the first time, John reaches out his hand and strokes his head as he has seen me doing. He has finally touched a donkey, and it is good.

"Time to find out who he belongs to," I say.

Trouble is, I only know one place. An expat who keeps burros on the outside edge of the Pueblo Blanco. Why do people keep burros, you may ask? Usually because they own goats, cows or sheep. The burros are terrific watch dogs to other field animals and will chase off dogs and predators, and yes you can load them up with cargo and young girls dressed up as the Madonna with child as well.

We lead our Christmas burro to Sandy's casa. By now we have given him a name, Nav. Nav is immediately drawn to Sandy's burros behind the barbed wire fence. Sandy comes out and tells us Nav is not her burro. We ask if she can take him in until we find out who he belongs to.

"Oh no," she say, "I can't do that. I have girls and this is a little boy. I am not ready to have more burros." We laugh at that. Immaculate Conception is not for burros.

We take our little Nav to two more places, tempting his good behavior with all of my granola. Nav is a sweet little burro and I am already fond of him, but our casa is no place for a burro. So, after all our rescue plans, we let him go, hoping he will find his own way back home.

Over the next few days we spot Nav time and again grazing in the vacant lots for grass, no garbage this time. He can find plenty of grass to eat in the Pueblo Blanco, shade to rest under, but clean water is not so easily found, so either John or I go out with a bucket of water and reconnect with our four-legged friend. We are starting to worry about our lost little burro, so we get online to the local gringo bulletin boards and ask if anyone knows someone missing a burro. Some offer to take him, but the consensus is that since it is the holidays the owners are probably away and if he doesn't get picked up by January 2nd, someone with the capacity (and no girl burros), will take him in.

Sure enough January 2nd arrives and we have no more watering visits with Nav. He has disappeared, and we are both a little sad. John's stuffed toy would never suffice; he had had the real thing.

The Garden

Our first appointment with a builder/architect is next week. In Mexico, for building houses, if you are hiring the architect you are hiring their crew of people to build it, which presents an interesting thought. You could have potentially a great design and not a great crew, or a flawed design but good crew of builders. The craftsmanship of the builders ranges from excellent to slip-shod, but more often than not they are very good because if they aren't they won't get more work, and there is plenty of competition.

Sometimes there can be decent building crews who are not properly supervised. You have to trust that your builder/architect is: on top of everything, understands your wishes, has standards, has integrity, will get the job done, and will set right anything that is not okay.

When we talk to people who we think have a reasonable idea about some of the better builders and architects in town. We ask and look at their designs and also look at the execution. We get tons of advice from people. The ones who have built in Libé and own houses are mostly loyal to their builders with one or two caveats. We have narrowed our appointments to two architects, one of whom has no English and we will need a translator.

Greta is our translator to Samuel, an architect with no English, but who she and Teresa recommend. He also happens to be the builder of Tommy's house, Casa Janine (which Tommy bought already built). Before we go into our meeting with him we cobble together our notes, prepared to throw everything and the kitchen sink at him, so to speak, that has been accumulating on our casa wish list including a pool.

The translation is going along well until we get to the pool. I have it in my head that I don't want a giant pool that takes up nearly the entire footprint of the courtyard. John agrees imagining a band and dancers there, not just a pool. My boy, dancer, not swimmer. I also don't want a deep pool. I want to be able to put my feet on the bottom, but still be able to do laps and flip turns. For some reason these pool details prove to be the most difficult to translate. In any case, he goes away promising us drawings and a quote soon. We have no doubts he is a good builder but I wonder about the translation aspect.

All in all I get a sense from Samuel that he is fairly conventional but solid. We have some days before our next appointment and I have been really enjoying one aspect of our new rental casa, the garden.

Mother Nature is a wonderful gal but we don't give her enough compliments, credit or consideration; we don't even make her breakfast in bed on Mother's day. Science is now telling us wonderful health benefits from being in nature (maybe it should seem obvious but science likes proof beyond the obvious). Studies say that hospital patients who have a courtyard garden to gaze at or visit, heal much, much quicker. This is because being in nature seems to boost the strength of our immune system. It goes up and even stays up after we take some time in nature. Likewise, when in nature, anxiety, blood pressure and even glucose levels go down, and your pulse will slow.

I am out in our garden laying on my back doing my yoga when I hear a whirring sound. A hummingbird, wings a blur, methodically approaches each of the colorful trumpets of flowers blooming from vines climbing up the garden wall—I have to remind myself that this is January.

In the garden we see the geckos, lizards or sometimes even an iguana scurry. We listen to a variety of birds chattering in the trees and the bees buzzing. The swallows swoop in, out and around with the background of the deep blue Mexican sky above. An occasional lazy cloud will paint a drifting design as a perpetually changing work of art. If it is cool enough at night, the lightning flies can be seen lighting up the grass like static electricity. I didn't really need Science to tell me all this was good for me, but nice to know for sure.

One of our gardeners is 80 if he is a day. I tiny man shuffling along. John and I watch him each time he comes, half protectively and half for amusement. We want to see if the large lawnmower is ever going to get the best of him. It never does, but every time he bends over we wonder if he is going to keep going.

Maybe he could keep doing his work because of all that healthy interaction with nature. There is no "retirement" for the ordinary people here, and I wonder if it is healthier to not worry about pension plans but instead just cut the grass, water the plants, cut the dead leaves, weed the garden, harvest the fruit. Just do what needs to be done in front of you. Nature puts things into perspective. It doesn't judge you, it just is and let's you be you.

I love to have our group writing sessions in the garden. Science has also proved that after being in nature your brain will be more alert and focused and you will do better on tests or exams. I just know I enjoy writing in the garden and watching others write there. And even if it can't be proved absolutely that it will improve our writing, everyone in the group agrees that's where they want to write.

I don't understand why people settle for just grass and a palm tree in a country where you throw just about anything in the ground and it grows like a weed, even when it is a fruit tree or a flowering bush. Bougainvilleas come in white, purples, pinks and reds and flower all year long, overflowing like a living rainbow over the garden walls. Yes they leave a mess with the shedding flowers, but you are in a country that has great gardeners and they need your money to make a living for their families. This is part of being in the community. Employing each other.

***

Every year, before we rent John says to Greta and Teresa the same thing.

"It must have at least one of three things, pool, palapa or garden." After the Squatter Casa, we have always managed to have one of those three things, but to get it all three is difficult and expensive. *Could we ever own it all?*

Before our next architect/builder meeting John and I try to get a little better organized with the architectural details on our wish list of things.

- Palapa on top
- Garden / Courtyard
- Pool
- Decent Kitchen
- Solar hot water and power
- Lots of light and windows (but tinted as needed)
- 3 bedrooms at least with each their own full bathrooms
- Modern design with a few traditional elements (John is mad for arches)
- Outdoor covered dining area off the kitchen
- Have a balance of sun and shade and cross breezes
- Look out area

In the North, our condo wish lists have always included that we must be in a quiet, nice neighborhood. But our lot in Libé is already in the quietest and nicest neighborhood in town. And when I say quiet, I mean Mexican quiet. Roosters, we avoided, megaphones we know, marching bands and celebrations, we know, but you never know for certain about your neighbors and especially dogs that bark all night.

Mexicans like their dogs to bark at night or when anyone passes, for security reasons, but the amount the dogs bark would be considered egregious in most neighborhoods in Canada. Most of these Mexican dog owners will listen politely to any complaints and comply graciously by taking their dog inside at night…for awhile, but usually they will forget at some point. So, if you are coming and looking for accommodation at a casa in small town Mexico, you are taking a risk that someone noisy won't move in next door either temporarily or permanently, and the best you can do is invest in some ear plugs and be prepared to repeat your request politely.

Everyone says they would love to be on the beach but only the best and most expensive hotels and condos have that space and there are restrictions to buying for foreigners—it is possible, but has other problems. Nearer the sea means nearer salt water and the corrosion factor for any fixtures goes up ten fold. Beaches are public property in Mexico so there are also some security issues, plus the very real danger of encroaching storm waves. Also, we have stayed in hotels right on the beach for a few nights and unlike those soothing audio tapes the crashing of the waves kept me awake. John and I decide that we really don't need to live right next to the water when we are only two blocks away.

In fact, we know another Canadian couple, Pete and Cheyenne, who want to build inland to have a bigger space than their beach front bungalow they built years before. They want to build another house. Cheyenne asks me, familiar with our corner lot, if we are ever going to build on it.

"We are just looking into that now. We may, we may not." I add on a whim, "Do you have any regrets building here?"

"None at all. We wouldn't be wanting to build another if we did."

Later I get a follow up email message from Cheyenne. If we are considering selling the lot, they will be happy to make us an offer. I tell John and he shrugs. Cheyenne's offer has made the pinnacle decision more real. Yet, we have agreed that the conversation of what we will do will be tabled until we get quotes from the architects.

Our next architect appointment was with Juan Diego, who compared to Samuel was very unconventional, creative and the one known for his curved rooms and surfaces. His English was great and I very much enjoyed talking to him. His houses were beautiful but not always practical. Try to fit rectangular furniture into a round room or against a curved wall.

We had also heard mixed reviews about his crews. Building the house was perhaps not his favorite part. I was smitten with many of the house designs I'd seen, but was trying to think practical too.

Whomever we chose we knew it was going to be considerably more expensive to build than when we had bought the lot years ago now. Building costs had gone through the roof (pun intended), which was the opposite when we started.

We were just going to have to wait on the drawings and the cost numbers of. Meanwhile, there was writing, writers, friends and a busy town in the full swing of tourist season to constantly distract us.

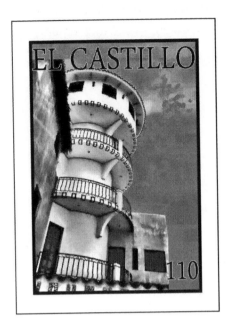

The Castle

At the Casa Blanco we seem to have more guests than ever and a new place to take them for dinner. Our dear friends, Hugo and Julia, opened a part-time outdoor restaurante in centro. John first met Hugo on his first season of crewing. Hugo was crewing on another sailing vessel and neither of them had ever been to Libé.

They would meet at The French Baker café where Julia was working as a waitress and perfecting her English. Little did John or Hugo know that this town would end up being a big part of their lives. After John left back to the cold of Canada, Hugo stayed and he and Julia became friendlier and friendlier, and over croissants and coffee they fell in love.

Libé, they say, is for lovers, and it didn't take long for a Mexican wedding to happen. Like John, Hugo and Julia were on their second marriages. But, how to make a living in Mexico? Hugo was a sailor, an artist, and had worked in restaurants a lot. Julia also had restaurant experience and is a fabulous cook, the answer seemed easy.

The first two seasons they had no location to set up a restaurant, and John had no idea his old sailor buddy was even in town, let alone that he was a newly married permanent resident. But one day, we met them on the main street where they were trying to set up a little art shop.

Hugo was so happy to see him and even more tickled to know we came back every year and had a lot. *Oh, oh, more pressure to build.* They became our new best friends in Libé. It was wonderful having Julia as a friend whose family had grown up in town for generations. She tests me on my Spanish which I am still a little red faced about.

This season however, they have their restaurante thanks to Julia's abuela (grandmother), who left Julia her casa. Julia was raised by her grandmother. Mexican women have explained to me that sometimes your sister, brother, mother, aunt, grandparent or uncle would take a shine to one of your children and ask to raise them. This informal adoption was welcomed and normal.

Julia's grandmother had adopted Julia and showed her how to garden and how to cook. Now, in that very same casa she was raised, Hugo and Julia were creating an open air, magical restaurante in the middle of the garden courtyard. People were drawn to its friendliness and warmth. John and I would take all our guests there, or, if alone, we would go there for drinks after dinner and sit and laugh with our friends long after the regular diners had gone home. John drinks the wine and I drink my pretend jamaica "wine."

We decide to pop in on them tonight and end up around the fire pit with just the four of us talking. To my curious enquiries Hugo explains to us how they started their renovations of Abuela's casa to their artistic restaurante.

"I had a vision of what we could do and we just started at it in the off season." They had decided that they would only open the restaurante two days a week so it wouldn't stress any one out, especially Julia.

"While we were building it I was reading a biography of Steve Jobs, so I was really inspired to create a vision. I kept telling Julia about Steve and what I learned in the book and how we could create something big here."

Julia was listening to Hugo tell this story wearing her Frida Kahlo smile. Hugo is clearly the enthusiastic entrepreneur in this duo.

"I was always saying, 'what Steve Jobs would have done is...' or 'if we were more like Steve Jobs, we would....' Finally, Julia got sick of me trying to create a Steve Jobs empire and the next time I mentioned Steve Jobs she just looked at me and said, 'Steve Jobs is dead.'"

We all laughed. I could just hear Julia saying this. She was the calming, realistic influence to Hugo's driving American entrepreneurism.

"I realized that I was trying to put on this place something that doesn't fit," Hugo continued. "We just needed to do things little bit by little bit and have all our friends and community come here and support us." He was starting to realize that more wasn't better.

The restaurante has an email list that is rapidly expanding that Hugo sends out every week, telling what unique but classic Mexican dishes Julia is creating, like her famous Chili Rellenos. This is her abuela's recipe and takes her nearly all day to make. Of course, they serve many other seafood favorites and meat. They had constructed not only dining tables in the garden but a lounge in back. And, after dinner, the favorite fire pit area that Hugo calls his playa. They also added a private room and a gallery where Hugo's artwork is displayed and another dining room where others in the community may have their artwork.

Hugo was now very proud of what they accomplished and Julia's kids all worked in the restaurante. Hugo tells us that he still had a niggling feeling he should be doing more, until one of his guests pointed out something.

"I had a wealthy stockbroker on holiday come here and he said to me, 'You've got it figured out here. You work part of the year at the pace you want' So, I realized what a great life we have and I let go of the empire building thing."

Hugo looked John and I in the eye.

"Not too big, not too fast, just part-time, the important thing is we started."

John and I looked at each other. We admired how little by little Hugo and Julia have worked together and improved their place. For John and I if something isn't done quickly then it is endless analysis paralysis, and some old fashioned head butting. But now, sitting in the cool of the garden, enjoying our wine with our friends it is blissful and simple. The dedicated diners are gone and the clean up from the staff has been done. Julia has put her feet up, and her little dog, Baguette, is curled up at her feet.

I know that John and I were thinking the same thing, we should just start. We told Hugo and Julia that we had been talking to architects.

"You should talk to one more," Hugo suggested, "Julio. He's a good guy and he just finished Michael and Amy's place." John was impressed because he knew Michael was a contractor in Canada and knew about building and construction and we were about as green as they come.

So the next day we called to set up a meeting. Julio barely spoke any English but had a sweet manner and little boy face that made you trust him. It didn't matter about his English because he always had his smooth talking, sidekick and translator, Rico, beside him. It was Rico who told us that Julio was famous for building "The Castle."

I knew exactly what he was talking about. Everyone did. You could see the cylindrical tower from the highway and I had often wondered about it. A brightly colored castle tower with look outs at the middle and top. It was located in the next town, but not in the nicest neighborhood, like an opera house built on the wrong side of the tracks. It was a home that Julio had meant to rent out but never had the time. I would have rented it too if it was somewhere else, but as they say it always comes down to location, location, location.

Unlike the other architects Julio and Rico insisted that they take us on a tour of all of Julio's recently built houses in the neighborhood tomorrow, including Michael and Amy's house which we had yet to see. We heartily agreed.

I love, love, love going on real estate tours and so I am really looking forward to the tour of Julio's houses. Rico picks us up and we meet Julio at the first casa. It is small but lovely with neat designs and a dipping pool. You can see there is attention to detail. The dipping pool has an Aztec design over it and a water feature pouring into it. There is a large tiled shower with cubby holes for shampoos. There is a small garage and small decks and a place on the roof to hang out. The owner is very happy with it.

The second is also small but really cool ideas for shelving and staircases. The shelving is open in at the top of the kitchen where the beauty of their colorful glass and table ware can be seen. The lower cabinets are a beautiful wood, described as Parota, a Mexican hardwood that the aggressive Mexican termites can't eat. The staircase is a floating design that captures the eye as soon as you enter. By the time we get to Michael and Amy's I am getting excited, my mind full of possibilities.

Michael and Amy's house is much grander and on primo real estate with views of the canals and the lagoon. It is brand new. They have just moved in and are finishing the landscaping as we arrive. The pool in the back near the waterway is heavenly and there is a little palapa with a hammock under it for chilling and a huge outdoor dinning area right off the kitchen where they have a large, colorful table and chairs.

Michael and Amy are happy to show us around and talk up their house and answer our questions. I do most of the asking and, as per usual, much snapping of pictures.

Really, Julio and Rico didn't have to do a thing. They just let the chatty gringos talk. Julio did suggest we go to the roof and so up the staircase we go where the insets of color glass blocks with light peering through made the stairwell delightful. On the roof, we appreciate the terrific view but also see something familiar. There are sixteen shiny new tubes for their solar hot water heater. It is the exact same one as the one on the roof of the Casa Blanco but brand new. There is another small palapa and hammock up here too and Michael explains that on the now vacant part of the roof they will be installing solar panels. A man after my own heart.

The best thing that Michael tells us is what a great job Julio and his crew have done. Michael, being a contractor in Canada, had watched them carefully with skilled eyes and could see they were doing things right. They are thrilled with their house and tell us that they were happy to advise us on our building project. We go away happy.

I think our building tour is over when Rico mentions that Julio would be happy to let us stay in his house for free, The Castle, while he is building our house. He has done this for other clients before. In fact, they insist that we take an extra trip to the next town so we could see it. Bonus!

A short trip down the highway and we are there. Rico gets out of the SUV and opens up the enormous contemporary Meso-American style gates into the driveway of The Castle. John has a big smile on his face. John is impressed with anything grand, but my eyes are popping out too. Looking at the cylindrical tower I am excited that I am finally going to find out what it is like to be inside, looking out.

We start at the patio and swimming pool area first. It has a lovely, large kidney-shaped pool bordered by the huge walls that are a combination of contemporary sleekness and nods to Aztec roots. On the patio, looking up, you see the Spanish colonial influence in the next floor up with its columns and arches. The pool area is so large you can easily envision a grand party or event happening there.

That impression isn't hurt when you go inside and see the cool circular bar that is at the base of the spiral steps up the tower. This level has an impressive circular room to match the circular bar with edge seating all around that could easily hold dozens of people. There is an additional lounge space with more seating by the bar and windows that flows into a large, modern kitchen and dining area. It is enormous. The only words were, "Wow."

Of course the first thing one wants to do in a castle, if you have any child left in you at all, is to climb those stairs up the tower. The staircase is right behind the bar and I notice that the railings are unique posts of rare wood and the steps are inlaid with colorful tiles in a geometric design. The posts are sunk into the concrete stairs so close together that there is no need for a rail. A line of polished smooth wood knobs guides us to the next flight.

Julio bids us to lead the way and we scramble up like a couple of excited kids. On the next level is the master bedroom in front with another circular room and circular bed to match with a curved inset bathtub. The bed has a huge concrete sea shell for a headboard. This headboard design is a Mexican favorite but we find it a little on the tacky side. Nevertheless, it matches the grandness of the house and suite. *And we can stay here while our house is being built?* Hmm, I can hear the wheels turning in my own head.

We looked at the other bedrooms down the hall, all with modern, large showers with the glass frosted in an Aztec motif. There is also the veranda outside with those arches from where you can look out at the entire town to the ocean, on one side, and the jungle on the other.

The neighborhood is on the other side of the freeway, or the wrong side of the tracks as we say. I have no doubt that Julio bought the property for a song. The Castle stands out like a sore thumb there, but inside we have two more floors to discover above us.

As we go up the circular staircase, round and round, we peek out the windows able to see more and more of the surrounding area, including Libé in the distance. The next level, does not come out at an inside floor but an enormous outdoor deck with two huge thatched palapa-topped round bungalows. We go in the first bungalow and it is an entire self contained circular apartment complete with kitchen, bedroom, bathroom and small seating area. The back windows looked out on the lush, refreshing jungle. Across the huge deck, where you had better have an umbrella to protect you from the sun if you want to lounge, is an identical bungalow. Identical from the outside but inside it has unique paint colors and tiling. Both have the fabulous palapa roofs you can gaze up in from bed. I notice they are finished with a shiny finish, bearing up Tommy's observation.

The last level up is a single look-out room at the top of the tower for gazing. If you allow yourself to gloss over the dilapidated, messy neighborhood surrounding it, you can see in the distance both the mountains on one side and the ocean on the other. I imagine taking a laptop there and writing the great Mexican-Canadian novel.

I am already dreaming of living there for a season until we take the SUV out those magnificent gates and into the street level of the 'hood. It is dirty, dusty and if not sketchy, definitely a let down after the grandness of Julio's castle. This did not bother me as much, but I knew it might bother guests. I also knew that it is several blocks to the beach with the highway in between and no easy way to cross it for those who are not so quick. In short, it just wasn't Libé.

All of this just made me want to return to Libé and think about our own castle. So, that's what we do. We sit down with Julio and Rico and sketch out what we think we want built on our own humble lot. We are getting a little more practiced at this. Julio has other projects on the go, but said he would send to us the drawings and a detailed quote in a few weeks. We hug both of them goodbye and I thank them for the best real estate tour I have ever had. Maybe we are going to own a Mexican castle even when we owned no property of our own in Canada. I ask myself again, *is this insane?* The answer comes back, of course it is, but Libé is starting to feel more like home than our other home even when we spend less than one sixth of our time there, *how did that work exactly?*

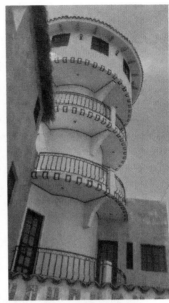

Writers in Mexico

One of the reasons living in Libé was working for me was I had now assembled some pretty interesting writers who were either already in Libé and the surrounding area, or had come to meet me south of the border.

When north, I would often talk glowingly about the warmth in winter which gets most Northerners excited, writers or not, but not everyone likes the heat or writing in the heat. My Southern friend, Skye, originally from Atlanta, Georgia, who now lives in Canada to get out of the heat, comes to Mexico not for the weather but to work with me. She is writing a vampire novel, but she is a teacher of communications including conflict resolution which means she is nice. I had pointed out more than once in her novel that everyone seemed so nice and civilized and all the characters got along. In short, not enough conflict.

"We can't learn anything if everyone is so nice, and it's also boring," I point out as diplomatically as possible. She promises me that conflict is coming up—after all this is a vampire novel—but even after we move ahead I still find too much niceness. She "fixes" any parts I point out to deliver to me next time, but this is not the way to fix a whole story. In fiction, a story comes out of the characters (even in non-fiction), and you will find a wholeness in the stories by understanding the characters deeply, their frailties, fears, their secret desires and the world they are in. Great characters should not be fashioned to be *like* people, not facsimiles, they should *be* people, as close to you as your good friends.

Vampires live in a dark world, literally. I start to suspect that Skye is not in touch with her own dark side. If that is true, it's understandable why it is hard for her to see her own characters as flawed, selfish, frightened, and having the potential for deep, deep trouble. Ego will do that. It will protect us from our shadows.

"Vampires go under the horror genre," I remind her. "Violent murders are being committed by them. This isn't just about how sexy vampires can be."

Skye is pretty good at the sexy parts already. There are many great erotica writers now, and ones that dabble on the dark side. *50 Shades of Grey* is the tip of the iceberg. People would laugh at what these authors are really like in person. I've met many erotica authors who are far from their young, beautiful, avatar-like protagonists and who are more likely to remind you of your favorite auntie or uncle than a person you would imagine is thinking up wild sex scenes all the time. Skye herself is petite but a little north of middle age, gray hair and glasses—albeit fashionable frames, but after her readings I have had other people lean over and tell (while they are fanning themselves), boy I can't believe *she* writes such hot stuff.

You never know what is hiding beneath a person's public exterior and that is the point I want to make to Skye. Instead of her trying to fix the "too nice" places that are not working, or the parts that are not her strength, I ask her to stop writing about her fictitious characters completely.

"Write me a story about your past, when something very, very bad happened to you. Something not pretty. Something that made you feel vulnerable. Something that could be described as dark."

Why was I so sure that sweet little Skye who always told John and I or anyone she knew that she loved us whenever she parted from us, had such an incident in her past? First, she is a human being who has been on the planet long enough, and all human beings have something dark that has happened to them, and often more than one thing, it just depends on how much they have pushed it down. Second, a person does not choose a horror genre for no reason. It is not just the sexiness of vampires that Skye is attracted to. I knew that, but she didn't, not really.

There is also an old saying, 'Don't be quick to destroy the devil in yourself, you may be destroying the best part of you.' I think this saying works well for writers.

Because Skye is amazing and always says yes to coaching, she writes the story. It is dark. It is not pretty. It describes the horror that human beings really endure on this planet. It is about her childhood abuse and trauma and some of the best writing I had seen from her thus far. People have these things that happen to them and yet they survive and move on to grow and learn and come to terms with those past events, or not. Whichever it is, coming to terms or not, their writing about it gets them in touch with that place in themselves where their ego and their identity barely survived... but it did. This is a powerful place to write from.

I like to think that Skye coming to the heat of Mexico reminds her of her Southern roots, her upbringing and some of those less than warm memories in Atlanta. Or, perhaps she just needs to get away and leave her norms behind, like the rest of the writers that come here. Or she comes because she knows this is where we do some deep writing work. In any case, after she comes in touch with the roots of her darkness again, it helps. She stops being so nice and her characters acquire more depth. Perhaps it isn't writing in Mexico that gives this to her, but for me, writing away from home, writing here in Mexico, connecting with writers here, seems to work.

Unlike Skye, Lois spends more time here than we do, but in the next town of Paloma. She is a dedicated travel blogger. After Mexico, she will go home for a bit and then she and her husband will find another place on the globe to discover or rediscover and write about it. Lois is a disciplined blogger, but like many writers wants to learn how to write a long-form piece, a book, a novel, mysteries maybe, she tells me.

That's what she tells me but instead she chooses a story about women in Mexico. This is a story about women's liberation and the initiative of women to organize and run coffee plantations. It's a story about community. We start to use some fiction techniques and it morphs into one of those "based on a true story" pieces that movies are often made from. In the process, I discover that Lois has a strength. While Skye is good at erotica, Lois is good at dialogue.

Lois's characters can dish out a lot of sass when they want to. Together we explore giving each character qualities that produce different voices. Being a fiction writer is a little like suffering from multiple personality disorder, but in a good way.

Lois reads me her latest pages of dialogue and I hear them clearly, the bossy woman, the voice-of-reason character, the scaredy-cat, the naive and innocent one, etc. I am happy to tell her that she's got it. Her dialogue is working well. I know she loves to hear this and starts to believe me that she may have some ability, but like a lot of writers doesn't fully believe in herself.

If I had a dollar for every time a writer asked me, "Is it good? Do I have talent?" I'd have enough dollars to take care of my café addiction at least. At first, I didn't know how to respond to these questions. My first impulse is to reassure writers, build them up, focus on their strengths and give some solutions for their deficits, but over time I have developed another tack. By the time I hear the "Do I have talent?" question from Lois I know what to say.

"What if I said no?" I respond.

"Huh?" They are never expecting that.

"If I say you don't have talent, will you give up?" Lois laughs nervously. We go on to explore whether it is ever helpful to question your abilities, or frame a question that way. You can create talent through work. We decide it is better to ask, "Do you think there is much more to do on this piece?" Focus on the work at hand.

I tell her something else, "A writer needs to be their own biggest fan." This is about a writer's self esteem which can be fragile. The title of writer has been deemed lofty and intimidating and people add such pressure on themselves that we have developed a term called writer's block for those not dealing with it very well.

The self esteem component to being a writer can be a biggy. I wrote *Writing with Cold Feet* from my experiences with all my students dealing with this when I long ago learned in my classes to start including self esteem exercises and to focus on their strengths as writers. It doesn't mean you don't shore up the things you are not good at, or learn new techniques, but you don't want to let the insidious seeds of doubt sift in when you see that there is more to do. It doesn't mean there isn't talent, just learning, and your process isn't complete. Or as I tell them, it is all "process," and extremely little of your life is "product." We aren't finished, we just move on.

Some writers, bestsellers, just focus on their strengths, get more efficient and get better simply by repeating, and by having great editors. That's valid. One or two I know could stand to be challenged again, but there are others like Lois who just need to keep going despite their pinches of doubt. They have to nurture their inner fan.

Harris, by contrast, isn't worried about his self esteem as a writer. He's not a writer. But he has some stories in him. True stories. The group starts to nickname him Indiana Jones. He literally has been on quests all over South and North America, treasure hunting. Since he is a pilot he also has the ability to get to the remote places too and meet the natives who actually are natives. He tells us about following myths and hints of treasure with varying degrees of success, and all kinds of dangers and adventures. Who can resist those tales?

My classes on story structure are helping Harris make his already good stories great. He suddenly appreciates the difference between telling a good yarn and writing one.

"This is a lot of work," he tells me. I nod, knowing I might be losing him. In fact, in a couple of weeks he goes north (far north) and starts working on a gold mine he has a stake in. He writes me an email telling me the gold mine isn't producing and bleeding him of money. Harris has gold fever bad. Gold mining is "a lot of work" he tells me. Hmm.

"I think there is gold in your stories," I respond.

"Yes," he says, telling me he may get back to that, but I suspect he will be on to the next treasure hunt soon.

An amazing amount of people wait until retirement to get back to writing. Isn't that great! What other professions could you start at 60 and older? On the other hand, they have to play some catch up. Bobbi put away her writing for decades. She used to like it. Teachers, not me, but other teachers a long time ago, told her she had talent. But, life gets in the way, doesn't it always. No regrets. She has had a full life, career, married, children and then grand children. Surviving her husband she started to join friends in a little town in Mexico to get winter out of her bones.

Then one day in México, Bobbi was inspired by watching a gecko in the shower jump out, scramble up the porcelain toilet and disappear. A lizard in the potty! Now she'd seen everything, so when she got back to Canada she told her grandson about it making it into a very quick bedtime story. He laughed and laughed and every night asked granny to tell him about it again. So, when Bobbi heard from Lois that she was having great fun and learning a lot in my writing group in Mexico Bobbi came too and the birth of her children's book began.

Yes, she had gotten rusty in writing, and she didn't have a teacher who was telling her how talented she was any more. She just has me, building her self esteem and showing her the elements that make a good story from fully fleshed out—or in her case, scaled out—characters.

***

I hate the term wanna-be authors. I prefer to reframe it will-be authors, or they *are* writers because they write. I surround myself with writers and authors both in my life in Canada and now in Mexico. Some of my author friends up north are quite accomplished and are my inspiration. They work hard. Super hard. I admire them and if I am honest, I envy many of them. Yet, as they see me steal away to Mexico with John every year to get some writing done, books written, and writing coaching done, they start to say, *Hey you've got something of your own going on there.*

"Yes," I tell them "I am starting a Mecca." I don't know for sure, and part of me wants to keep Libé to myself still, but that might be what is happening.

I reflect that being able to write here is one thing, but being able to "be" here is what I really feel. I don't try to prove anything in Mexico. There is no pressure to be anything other than what I am. And what am I? A writer, a teacher, married, who loves the sun and warmth, who loves being a part of a community that is tied to the earth and the sea and its creatures, and a person who tries, just tries to do the right thing.

When I am in my northern city, I have to have a job, an identity, enough money, places to go to, things to own, communications to make, and I feel a little bit swallowed up, as my time is also swallowed up. In Mexico, my time doesn't disappear in the same way, it wallows, it doesn't try to keep pace with anything in particular. And, I think others here would understand. We are at the same pace here, and we are not trying to outrun each other.

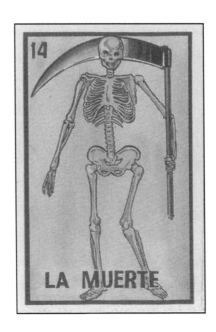

La Muerte

When people become full-time or part-time residents of Mexico many take Mexican first names. John became Heimie (Jamie) and I became Katrina. Olga, our neighbor who is a long-time Mexican resident was mortified when I tell her my Mexican name.

"Perhaps you would prefer Catalina," she suggests. Olga's sweet round face beams at me. Her husband Darin tries to hush her as if he were trying to keep her from saying something shocking, which simply piques my curiosity further.

"Why is that?" I ask as Darin rolls his eyes knowing his wife now has free rein.

"La Catrina is the female figure of death famous in Mexico. You have likely seen her as the female skeleton with the large hat, jewelry and gown that is recreated all over Mexico?"

"Oh yes!" I say happily. Everyone has seen the humorous skeleton figures, and the female figure in the hat is the most prevalent.

"La Catrina is always dressed elegantly, but she is moody," Olga tells me.

"Perfect." I say. Her husband giggles. Olga seems nonplussed.

And so I am Katrina with a K in Mexico and become fascinated with the La Catrina figure, the Grande Dame of Death, and her husband, El Catrin; they harken back to the Goddess and God of the underworld that the Aztecs worshipped. Many may be surprised to know that she, La Catrina, came before El Catrin, and in their current form, neither are that old. Artist José Guadelpe Posada created La Catrina in 1910 at the birth of the Mexican revolution to mock the rich, elite supporters of the Diaz dictatorship and also to remind us that even the rich cannot escape death.

Many artists have added to her since, including creating her mate, El Catrin. Now, both La Catrina and El Catrin are dressed to make people laugh and mock our silly selves that think the image we want to project in our dress, manners and status makes us important. Death makes us equals in the end.

The first joke I make in Spanish in Mexico is to introduce myself.

"Yo soy Katrina pero no *La* Catrina." (I am Katrina but not *The* Catrina). I am delighted to make a small group of Mexicans laugh at this. But they are always quick to laugh in any case, much more so than stuffy white bread North Americans and Europeans.

For a long time I have been fascinated by how other cultures celebrate or honor death. La Catrina has been incorporated very easily into the Mexican *Day of the Dead* celebrations. Similar to our Halloween, the Mexican *Day of the Dead* celebrations are on November 1 and 2 of each year, coinciding with the Catholic holidays *All Saints' Day* and *All Souls' Day*, but *Day of the Dead* also harkens back to the ancient Aztec traditions to honor the God and Goddess of the underworld. After death, travelers to the underworld go through nine levels of gruesome obstacles. Things like: rivers of blood, pus and scorpions, attacks by spinning obsidian knives and arrows, fearsome jaguars, high mountains that move and crash into each other, and even the sacrifice of one's own heart. In short, you really had to work for that afterlife.

In modern Mexico, the *Day of the Dead* celebrations include colorful parades, costumed skeleton characters and community visits to the cemetery where the graveyards are covered in marigold flowers. There is art, music, dancers, poetry (small humorous poems called calvaritas), and food (especially skull candy). In the ancient mythology the food and other objects could help the dead stay hardy to get through all the obstacles to the underworld.

Mexicans always add to these celebrations a terrific sense of humor and lightness. Death is something embraced rather than feared, like in many Indian religions, it is a cycle not an end and this is perhaps what attracts me.

When I was about three years old my mother told me about death. Because my mother was a daughter of science, not religion, and because, in retrospect, we suspect that she might have had a degree of Asperger's (an autism where people may be very intelligent, as my mother was, but they can't really grasp social niceties), when I asked what happened after death she basically described the equivalent of worm food. No one knew what happened to "you" or your consciousness after death she told me. I was in shock.

At three, I already loved life so much *and it ended? What was the point in that?* Even so young, I thought it was a cruel joke and I cried for three days. My mother tried to comfort me saying it was a long, long way away and you will be old and ready to go by then. This did not comfort me.

From that day forward I have always filtered nearly everything with a knowledge of the specter of death, standing in the background. Some may say that this is why I have a good sense of humour. Comic genius Woody Allen, was recently asked if after exploring death for six decades in his films he still felt the same way about it?

"Yes," he answered, "I'm against it."

So, without a religion to guide me, I began my own unorthodox spiritual quest in the form of reading books, non-fiction and fiction. My research lead me to the following choices you can believe on the subject of life after death:

1. No afterlife: worm food
2. Afterlife
3. Reincarnation (a kind of recycling for souls)
4. Some other kind of transformation that we are unaware of

I had rejected the idea of worm food from a state of innocence, but I was less repulsed by the idea now. Now, it seems fair to me that I have been eating creatures and plant life my whole life that keep me alive, so it has to be my turn at some point. The destroyer becomes the destroyed. I think of it as returning to the same nature that created me and will be transforming my Katrina energy into some other energy, for some other purpose. As the Buddhist's say, *what was your name before you were born?*

As to an afterlife, I can't help but see the politics of religion. Let's face it, the threat of hell or promise of heaven has been a proven way to keep sinners (normal people) in line. Then again, maybe it's true that there is a heaven, hell or purgatory? There are all those near-death, or return-from-death accounts that describe the tunnel, the white light and a heavenly place or feeling. Science has tried to explain that as your creative brain flooding you with endorphins which keep you calm. If that is true, how compassionate it is of nature to provide this comfort. You can only say about an actual afterlife, no one knows for sure, it is truly an act of faith to believe. And, if there is one, as my father and stepmother say... "Bonus!"

Reincarnation. I have a couple of people in my life who firmly believe this. For myself it falls into all those other afterlives that leave a few critical questions unanswered about how it works, for which religions will give you answers without any scientific proof. The one idea I do like about reincarnation is, if you truly think you may be coming back to the Earth, there is a much better chance you will take care of the Earth and your relationships while you are here.

In contrast, there are those who believe they are going to

heaven and not returning. Some of these take care of their religious duties like punching a time clock, but have no great consciousness towards nature or humanity. As long as they are told weekly that themselves and theirs are the "chosen ones" who are going to heaven, they are good. These people scare the bejesus out of me, so to speak.

And what about some other kind of transformation that we are unaware of? I am still running after this one, trying to balance science and spiritualism because part of me does believe *there are more things in heaven and earth, Horatio, than are dreamt of in any philosophy.*

It is this thought that brings me to my own eerie, personal La Catrina story in Mexico.

***

Once a week on market day, sellers set up a massive chain of tarps to create the open-air market known as a tianguis (tee-an-gay), so buyers are shielded from the morning and afternoon heat. They start at 8 or 9 a.m. and pack up around 3 p.m. past the beginning of siesta time.

Gina, a lovely expat from California, sells me my locally grown and roasted coffee and home baked goodies on market day. We chit chat and catch up and if I want to know where something in particular is, she will tell me where to go and who to talk to in any of the multiple colorful stalls that line the five blocks of street and into the jardin (town square).

This market day morning, I try to get there early to have a cup of Gina's coffee and stroll the market cup in hand. Along with tourist trinkets, jewelry and everything and the Talavera sink, there are the less than legal things at the market, such as pirated movies and music that go along with these mobile market places all over Mexico. I have been told they are sanctioned, not just by the city officials, but by cartels, no one I know really knows for sure.

I ask Gina about this and she doesn't know either. This morning, we start talking about my chosen Mexican name and the Catrina figures of which there are many at the market. I am on the hunt for a Catrina figure I can take back home. She tells me where I might find some beautiful Catrinas in the next town, but they are bigger and I need something smaller for the suitcase. I bid her a temporary adiós as I go on my market shopping. I will speak to her again on my way back.

After I get my necessities including some zazamoras (blackberries) I look through the vendors selling colorful items for the touristas including figurines. I spot a small Catrina clutching a guitar with more of a sombrero that her usual elegant hat, but it is clearly La Catrina. I bargain with the vendor in Spanish careful to let him know I am not a naive tourist and get a good price.

I show Gina on the way out and ride my little vintage bike home. It won't be long until we have to pack up the bicycles again finding homes for them with friends in town until next season. An inconvenience, but I now see it as life is good to have such good friends and neighbors.

I show John my market finds including The Catrina and then start putting away my goods. While handling The Catrina figure I have a butterfingers moment. She slips through my fingers and as she hits the tile floor her head separates from her body. I see this in slow motion yelling out what I think is an inner, "Noooo!" But, I am not saying it to myself, I am exclaiming it loudly.

John comes rushing. I am on the verge of tears, my throat constricts and I am very, very upset. I am still shouting between hyper-ventilations. John is trying to calm me down. He's never seen me like this. The Catrina is inexpensive and we know that ceramic figurines are fragile from past experiences of trying to take things home, but that's not why I'm upset.

John can't fathom why I am so upset. Finally I get it out.

"Something bad is going to happen!"

"Nothing bad is going to happen, it just broke." He rejects my investment in a bad omen.

"No, I have a bad feeling about this." I say, still visibly upset, my heart is racing. He tries to shrug off his irrational woman's proclamations of dread. I am sure someone, maybe me, maybe John, maybe someone else is going to be hurt. I am sure someone's head is going to be lopped off. It is crazy but the feeling of dread stays.

Suddenly, I wonder if it's not too late.

"Do we have any glue?" I ask. John tells me that he has none. Not the kind of thing we use in our seasonal sojourns. But I still have a desperate feeling that this is important.

"Maybe I can fix it. Maybe the bad thing won't happen if I glue it back together."

John is looking at me like I am crazy. I am crazy. He doesn't understand what I am feeling. Maybe if I fix the figurine I can avoid this horrible prophecy. In my own heart I doubt it.

Nevertheless, I jump back on my bike and go back to the market place and start scouring the hardware and notions stalls for glue. I don't know Spanish for glue, but just as I am feeling defeated and have had a few vendors shake their heads I spot Gina. I explain to her quickly what happened and also explain my feeling of dread that someone is going to get a serious injury, perhaps fatal, to their head. She reassures me that that is unlikely but tells me exactly which vendor has super glues that I will need to mend it and tells me how to ask for it since she knows it will not be found out front. I find the vendor and get the glue and am somewhat relieved. Mostly because Gina also thinks I am overreacting in this premonition.

I cycle home and get right to mending my Catrina, all the while feeling a sense of futility. What's done is done, a feeling inside me pulses. Yet, it was a clean break and I am able to put the head back together with not even a crack visible. I look around for somewhere to keep her while the glue sets I spot a currently unused eye glass case. As soon as I gently lay her in it I cannot help but notice that she looks exactly as if she is laying in a coffin. My optical case is the perfect size for her body and the soft velvety material of my eye glass shammy underneath resembles the shiny, polished lining of a coffin and the hinged case lid like a casket lid. A chill comes back to me, but rational thoughts push it away. I push it away.

In another two days, I have forgotten about the Catrina and am back to normal. It is then that I get a call from a friend of Lucy's family. Her family has been looking for her. Lucy, who helped me with my Mexican bridal dress experience, is down here again along with my other writers working on her humorous, but dark memoir. Lucy's bungalow has no phone but Lucy gave her 20 year old daughter our phone number. Her daughter was the only one who knew this number, but her daughter was unable to call it so a friend tracked us down.

Back in Canada, walking down the street, her daughter has been struck by a car that had just hit another car and careened onto the sidewalk. Her daughter has been thrown several feet and dies almost instantly from head trauma. Lucy's sister is already on a plane to come and collect Lucy in person. She will arrive in a matter of hours to break the news while it is our job to try to surround Lucy with love and support. We can barely fathom the news. To tell a woman, a friend, that her child is dead? I am selfishly thankful her sister will be the one to do it. A black cloud has descended on the day.

I am so distracted with this horrible happening that it takes me awhile to connect it with the Catrina premonition. We have just left Lucy, our hearts heavy, and it literally hits me as I am walking down the street. Wham! Something strikes me in the head, hard. I am crying in pain and anguish as John who has been walking in front of me rushes to my aid.

"What happened?"

"The Catrina." I manage to get out barely, grasping my head with both hands where I was struck but not bleeding. I don't care about my injury but I am baffled by it. "What hit me?"

"I think you walked into that tree branch," he speculates. It appears to be a branch from a tree I have walked into, but somehow tall John walking in front of me missed it.

"That? But the Catrina… remember how I was so upset, remember I thought something bad had happened. This was it. It was Lucy's daughter."

John, a very rationale person tries to talk me out of this idea as we go home after an emotionally exhausting day.

I wake and my head has a bump on it now, a further reminder. I find out about the head trauma part of Lucy's daughter's fatal injury and calculate the tragedy as happening almost simultaneously to my Catrina premonition. John is still shaking his head suggesting it as a coincidence. I say it is synchronicity. I ask him point blank.

"In ten years of knowing me, have you ever seen me act like that? Telling you something bad is going to happen?" He admits that he has never seen me act that way before though I sometimes get other feelings that turn out to be true, like in a large public crowd, in an unlikely place, I know that someone we know is nearby, but that is always thought of as pure coincidence.

I tell Gina the whole story on the next Market day and she treats me to a cup of coffee. She is my Horatio and I have just experienced something outside both of our philosophies.

Despite all that has happened I take the repaired Catrina figurine back to Canada and one day decide that I will put her up on the wall along with a Mexican Milagro—an icon decorated with small nickel objects, symbols for healing and luck that I had custom made in the shape of an angel—and, my pregnant Mermaid (La Sirena), made with a coconut shell who represents the opposite of Catrina, life and fertility. It will be my small display of Mexican mythologies I think.

I go to my closet to get my picture hanging tools and in the dark reach for the pull chain light switch which is usually easy to find thanks to a Halloween decoration attached to the end of it. In the dark, looking for the light string I bump my head, reminding me of another bumped head, simultaneously I find the string and pull it to illuminate the Halloween decoration staring me in the face with a ghostly smile. The decoration is a skeleton. Catrina is laughing at me, again.

***

I don't know if death is the theme behind all writing, but I do know that death is a factor in more than just my writing. Several of the writers I have worked with, including the ones who have come to Mexico, are often writing from a place of personal loss of a loved one or ones. Skye's vampire novel came with the beginning of her widowship to her soul mate husband. Josie lost her fiancé and her mother within six months of each other. And Lucy's memoirs are populated by losses, the last now being the most horrible.

This year there is Ria, who also lost both her parents, long since divorced, within six months of each other, leaving a bitter dispute about the estate settlement amongst her family.

It's the first time Ria has been down to Mexico to work with me, but not the first time to Mexico and not the first time anywhere. She is a habitual globetrotter from a family with means. A fiery redhead with a quick wit and perfect Spanish that she speaks so rapidly that the Mexicans think she is Cuban, if she didn't look decidedly white. She has brought down with her, her mother's ashes... well some of them. They were divided between her sisters and she thought that she should return her portion where she remembers her mother being happy. Her family lived in Mexico for two years not far from Libé before the family moved on to live in several other South American and Spanish language countries - hence her perfect Spanish. Ria is here not just to let go of the ashes, she also wants my help to work on a screenplay.

It was her Dad that has more recently passed and since he was a notable artist it is the ownership of his artworks that there is now some dispute, to put it mildly. I try to encourage Ria to put her frustration, anger and grief into her creativity but sometimes we just end up talking about things.

I admit that I am worried as my own father is now seriously unwell while we are down for the season. I talk to him on the phone as much as I can. And, as I listen to Ria's family stories I can see my own family fracturing as certain events pass. Things said, letters written, things done, have cast a pall over the family in the past year with my father's declining health. I feel guilty for being in Mexico but I will see him when I get home since there is only a little time left before we have tickets back.

Ria tells me about her parents and I tell her about mine. I tell her I got my sense of humour from my father. I tell her that one day when I was still in my twenties he called me up.

"Kat, will you be the executor to my estate?" Pause. And then without thinking I blurt.

"Sure. Anyone you want me to pie in the face for you?" He and I laugh like crazy together at this. It feels great.

Later, I will decline the offer to be executor, saying that I don't want to have that responsibility while I grieve. I am also cautioned that it is not good to be the executor and a beneficiary both. I remember that I feel wise that I sidestepped the executor role while listening to Ria's tribulations. She decides to fashion a few characters in her screenplay after some members of her familial soap opera. That's the ticket. Use the anger. But it is also so fresh I know that the writing might just be for healing and not for sharing.

When Ria goes to her room to write I take a chance that my own Dad may be up and call him. I know he is sleeping whenever he can sleep. My stepmother informs me that I am in luck, but he may not want a long call.

"Hola Papa." I greet him in Spanish but I have been calling him Papa as a term of endearment for decades. "How are you?" I ask, a little afraid to hear the answer.

"Not good. Managing." I am not used to *not* hearing the bubbly, contagious enthusiasm of the man who loves life and laughs at all of it given half a chance. His tone makes me know all is not well. I babble on for a bit, nervous, finally I realize I am babbling and sum it up.

"I like it here."

"Yeah, I know you do."

"But, I'll be home soon to see you and then we can talk." He doesn't respond to this. "Dad, do you remember how you used to sail?" He grunts in response the way he does. This is more normal.

"I always wanted to buy you a sailboat one day, but I realized that would have been silly. That, and I never became rich and famous." I hear a hee-hah breath that tells me he is half laughing and I might have made him smile.

"Did my sailing. Enjoyed it," he says with a brevity that he has adopted lately.

"John likes it too."

"I have some more sailing books here for him."

"Okay, you know he'll enjoy them." There is a pause. I get nervous again. I am thinking of asking him, *do you think we should build our house in Mexico?* But I don't. He is unwell, he doesn't need my dilemmas. I am remembering my stepmother saying he may not be able to do a long call. We say a few bits of chit chat and it feels like he has reached his limit.

"Well, we'll be home next week and then we can really talk." Again, he doesn't respond. "I love you Dad." It's our little game. I say it and he doesn't. It just wasn't the way when he grew up, but we've worked this one all out years before. It's okay that I say "I love you" and he doesn't because it's understood.

"Okay," he says acknowledging the end of the call is coming.

"Bye," I say softly.

"Bye Kath," he says softly.

I tell John that my Dad doesn't sound good so I am glad we will be back next week. I have already had a false alarm or two but he always springs back, so I will be glad to see him.

Meanwhile, Carnival starts tomorrow and there will be a parade today and a midway has been set up with rides for the kids and booths are all over the jardin and centro. We will go out for dinner and dancing and walk through the midway.

I spot our real estate friend Teresa and she tells me all the things that will be happening for carnival over the next few days, being on the town board for the event this year. I ask her a question knowing her to be a good Mexican Catholic.

"If carnival signals the end of Lent, does that mean you have given up something?"

"Nunca, we don't give up anything." She smiles her big party-girl, flashy smile. *How Mexican*, I think, *don't' dare give up anything fun.* She elaborates.

"When we party, we do it all night long, go home, have a shower, eat something light and go back out and party some more."

We have a lovely night out dancing. The French Front, Ria, John and I and a few others walk home from the festivities. On the way home Ria and I start talking movies and I tell her I have a DVD she must see and we can play it on my laptop. John peels off for a nightcap with Callie and Alberto who have the house right next door to our Casa Blanco (another reason we like it, in addition to the great solar showers).

As I crank up my laptop there is a phone message forwarded to my email from the area code of home. I play it. It is my brother. My father has passed away three hours before, after an emergency run to the hospital. I am floored. How can the half-expected be so unexpected for me? It wasn't supposed to happen this way.

Ria is there steadying me as I process what has happened.

"I'll go get John," she says. We can hear him, Alberto and

Callie talking in their courtyard next door, so she leans out our window and calls to them.

"John, pronto! El padre de Katrina es muerto." I am immediately thankful she has said this in Spanish as I can't bear to hear it in English right at this moment. John rushes over and Ria lets him take over my fragile, breaking heart.

I speak to my brother and there is no reason to change our tickets or rush home. My other sister, also away, hasn't been found yet. We get off the call after getting all the details.

"He knew," I tell John. "I told him we would be home next week and he didn't say anything. He knew."

La Muerte has struck at my core. It has entered my life as never before. I thought I was grounded and realistic until now, but I could never truly fathom that my Papa would ever be gone from my life.

Over the next days we are packing up the house and I am in touch with the family frequently by email and phone as plans are made. Ria will also be leaving at about the same time.

A day before we are to leave she shows me a box. It contains her mother's ashes.

"Why don't we go to the beach together? We'll take some wine and toast our parents. I will let go of my Mom's ashes to the sea, and you can let go of some flowers for your father?"

I love the idea, remembering my father's love of the sea. It will be just the two of us. Just the grievers. We go down just before sunset, me laden with a bowl of flowers and some glasses, and her with the vino and her mother's ashes.

It's another beautiful Mexican end of day. We sit in the sand together like a couple of kids and talk about my father and her mother. We realize that her mother and my father would have gotten along very well together. We toast them and then decide we are ready. We both move toward the edge of the surf and she wades into her knees. She says her last words to her mother and let's the withdrawing surf take the ashes out and I take some photos for her. She withdraws and it's my turn.

As soon as I go into the water the tears are flowing down my cheeks. I taste the brine of them as they fall into the seawater; the sea, where I am letting my father go, if symbolically. It doesn't seem symbolic. The sea where I know he would approve of being. I let the bright blossoms float out into the water and say my last words to him. Ria, now behind me on the beach, exclaims but I can't hear what she is saying over the surf. I walk back to her.

"I saw a whale come up in the distance, and blow, just after you let your flowers go!" She tells me. It feels magical, even if she made it up, I appreciate it. I feel lighter. I feel my father's deep throated chuckle. I can go home now.

Post-Mortem

We return to Canada with heavy hearts. My family grieves and struggles. It is so apparent now that Dad has been the glue that kept my family together.

I keep working, helping writers all over North America now achieve their dreams of writing books and triumphing over their blocks. Normally, I love this work, but inside I am questioning everything. Every time I close off with a client I feel relief and never replace them with another. I take less and less teaching contracts. Less and less money is coming in.

I had written a number of books and should be promoting them but I am listless. I also have a screenplay that receives some interest and one option that doesn't pan out. I should be promoting that too, but I am distracted by family and settling things. I am again thankful that I had declined being the executor, but that doesn't mean I am distant from all the fall outs either.

During this time I receive an email from Julio in Spanish but I don't have the patience or heart to translate it, so I flag it to review later. John is having trouble at work as well and I feel myself falling into a funk. I miss Mexico. I want to hide there, but now it represents the place I was when I heard my father died and I feel guilty I was there when it happened.

With a misplaced sense of responsibility I try to repair my family, but it is just dragging me further down. I leave things undone and I start seeing a counselor.

The counselor helps and John and I decide to take a course on life fulfillment. I am going for my grief, the family fall out and this depression I am in. John is wanting a new perspective on things. My low-risk, steady Eddy man wants more courage to achieve the things he wants, to take risks that he normally feels uneasy about.

I feel dependant, depressed and very cash poor and try to find the working attitude for all of this. The course helps for a bit, but grief is still affecting me. The crisis has revealed so many flaws in my relationships, especially with my family. My friends only know so much. I have been the pillar for too long, it feels unnatural to be the one in crisis, but I start to rely on them more.

Things start to get better. I gradually attend to things and in that process I start to realize that my ongoing plans are what I insisted I should do, but not what I really want. I want to simplify. I want to live what I have learned in Mexico in my heart, both in Canada and in Mexico.

Looking through all the emails I have been ignoring for months, I find the email from Julio again and translate it. I had missed that there are attachments before or I am sure I would have opened them right away. It is the quote for his version of our casa and also drawings, 3-D renderings. I open it.

"John!" I yell from my office, a bad habit of mine.

"What? What is it now? Why are you yelling?" He is cranky and wants to be left alone after a hard day at work.

"Look!" I shout as he reluctantly comes into my home office.

There on the screen is our first 3D vision our potential house to be. We are silent and then in a flurry of activity. We look at all the plan drawings and the 3D renderings, and at the quotes. It was more than we thought, but it is also beautiful. I look at the numbers again converting it to dollars for us. It seems impossible. But, I look at John and he looks at me. We both know it is going to happen, somehow. Hugo's words come back to me. *You just have to start.*

The Future

It was in the late 1980s when I had my first trip to Mexico and loved it. I went with my big sister who was freaked out at the more primitive elements, but I didn't mind them. I loved the big town we were in (which is now a large resort city north of Libé). There was something about it. I almost felt like I had lived there before. It felt like home. Yet, I don't believe in reincarnation and there was nothing about it that was like my northern home.

On that visit, we had travelled rather late in the season to get the "deal" so there weren't as many tourists around. Consequently, the travelling vendors along the beach and malecón were aggressively selling to us every time we encountered them. When we decided to stop for lunch at a restaurant along the malecón, I told my sister we needed to have a table way back from the malecón where they couldn't get to us. So we wound our way past at least twenty tables to find a place back near the restaurant itself.

We were waiting for our food and looking out at the sun on the water and the pelicans diving, when a vendor walked by on the malecón. He was quite a distance from us and would never have seen us, but he held aloft something in his hand that grabbed the rays of the sun and exploded the light. I gasped an audible gasp.

As far away as that vendor was from us, he heard my gasp, changed his direction to the restaurant and wound his way through twenty tables to find me. What he had held aloft was a crystal ball, a real crystal ball, with a brass stand. I loved it. The negotiations began and I took it home with me.

It was over twenty years later that I returned to Mexico with John for our first time in Libé together. As much as I have wanted to detach myself from objects, you can't help but have a fondness for some and I like to think that the crystal ball was foretelling my future in Mexico. I show the crystal ball to John which I have had long before I met him.

"When we build our house, I will bring that crystal ball back to Mexico, back to where it came from and it can shine in the sun again," I tell him.

"No ifs?" He asks, "It's a when?"

"Uh-huh," I answer with a smile. I don't know how but I know we are going to build our house. I will not be taking any offers on the lot. While no one knows the future for certain—there is both anxiety and relief in that—I predict the hammock will be hanging again in

Mexico. There will be more chapters to our story and next time there may even be a crystal ball in a casa.

IF YOU ENJOYED THIS BOOK PLEASE REVIEW ON AMAZON.COM

and…

Look for the sequel to this book. Get invited to the sequel book launches—both in Vancouver and in Mexico—by getting on the author's list where you can also get invited to retreats and readings.

The Happy Hammock Builds a House

Simply email info@buddhapress.com with subject "On Author List" or go to **kathrinlake.com** or **vancouverschoolofwriting.com** and sign up to their lists.

About the Author

When Kathrin Lake was eight, she made up stories, cast the other kids in parts, raided her mother's closet and then started rehearsals immediately. Much later she studied theatre and film at Simon Fraser University in Vancouver, Canada. Although she developed a passion for non-fiction by writing for newspapers and other publications, it was being in Theatre that reignited her storytelling days as a child. She collaborated with award-winning Canadian playwrights Marc Diamond and Guillermo Verdecchia, and even formed a brief writing partnership with the late, great comedy writer, Irwin Barker, who would go on to write for Rick Mercer (in Canada that is equivalent to writing for David Letterman). She even won some awards and prizes herself in playwriting. Later, Kathrin founded *The Vancouver School of Writing* and is a full time writer, story coach and professional speaker. Her first non-fiction book was *From Survival to Thrival,* but she also published her successful book, *Writing with Cold Feet,* as well as other books on writing. She frequently holds workshops and retreats about writing and publishing in Canada, the U.S. and Mexico.

http://www.kathrinlake.com
http://www.vancouverschoolofwriting.com

Printed in Poland
by Amazon Fulfillment
Poland Sp. z o.o., Wrocław